THIRTEEN TERRIFYING TALES

THIRTEEN TERRIFYING TALES

Foreword by Kirsty Logan

BODLEIAN
LIBRARY
PUBLISHING

The stories in this book were first published in the nineteenth and early twentieth centuries. They reflect the views and attitudes of the period.

First published in 2026 by Bodleian Library Publishing
Broad Street, Oxford OX1 3BG
www.bodleianshop.co.uk

Adapted from *Terror At Night*, edited by Herbert Williams, Avon Book Company, 1947. Part of the Florence & Samuel Davenport Russell Collection in the Bodleian Library, Oxford.

ISBN 978 1 85124 681 6

PUBLISHER: Samuel Fanous
MANAGING EDITOR: Susie Foster
EDITOR: Janet Phillips
PICTURE EDITOR: Leanda Shrimpton
COVER DESIGN by Dot Little at the Bodleian Library
DESIGNED & TYPESET by Lucy Morton of illuminati in 11 on 15 Caslon
PRINTED & BOUND in China by C&C Offset Printing Co., Ltd
on 115 gsm Chinese Yulong Pure paper

MIX
Paper | Supporting responsible forestry
FSC
www.fsc.org
FSC® C008047

EU GPSR Authorised Representative Logos Europe,
9 rue Nicolas Poussin, 17000, La Rochelle, France Contact@logoseurope.eu

British Library Catalogue in Publishing Data
A CIP record of this publication is available from the British Library

CONTENTS

FOREWORD

Kirsty Logan

We like to imagine that our experience of fear is modern. Pandemics and political turmoil, collapsing climates and the sinister security of our phones as a personal home fire, keeping us company in the wee hours. But turn the pages back a century, two centuries, and the shadows look remarkably familiar. Our recent ancestors were unnerved by many of the same things that haunt us now.

The thirteen stories you hold here were written in the late nineteenth and early twentieth centuries, roughly between 1880 and 1937. That half-century was a time of huge upheaval: gas lamps overtaken by electricity, horse-drawn carriages overtaken by motor cars, telegrams overtaken by telephones. It was a time of relentless forward motion, when—stop me if this sounds familiar—progress was irresistible and the line of profit had to continually rise. Factories consumed the countryside; machines were fed with low-waged workers' bodies. Medical and scientific advancements saved lives; X-rays revealed the skeletons moving inside our living flesh. Women fought and died for the right to vote, entered universities and medical schools, threatened the very foundations of patriarchal control (now these gains, so hard-won, are beginning to feel shakier than I'd like). Empires stretched greedily across continents, siphoning wealth and labour from colonized lands.

Is it any wonder that the stories being written and read at the time were so steeped in dread? Even as we move from the Victorian and Edwardian eras, and onwards to the 1920s and 1930s, the mindset lingers: many of these later writers still look back, haunted; reflecting on their recent pasts to make sense of the contemporary moment.

Bram Stoker, best known for *Dracula*, gives us "The Judge's House," where superstition and scholarship collide in a crumbling building rotten with vermin. Stoker's learned man (the scientist, the rationalist) was meant to banish old wives' tales—but his protagonist finds that reason is nothing against the weight of history.

In "The Haunter of the Dark," H.P. Lovecraft brings a different sort of terror: a universe so vast and indifferent that human concerns shrivel into meaninglessness. Written in 1935, after one world war and on the brink of another, Lovecraft's horror is not of a ghost in an attic or a shadow on the wall, but of humanity itself being insignificant dust on a spinning rock. He takes the motifs of a dawning scientific age—the telescope, the microscope, the unravelling atom—and shadows them in older Victorian anxieties with the image of the "three-lobed burning eye."

Between Stoker and Lovecraft we find 1925's "The Interruption," a story of everyday domesticity unravelled by an unexpected horror by W.W. Jacobs (best known for his cautionary tale "The Monkey's Paw").

Thomas Burke often wrote of London's East End, its Chinatown, its immigrant communities—fittingly, "The Black Courtyard" reflects the (unfortunately) timeless British unease of the "other," distorted through prejudice and fantasy. To read it now is to glimpse how Empire wrote itself into fiction, both in fascination and in dread.

We might know E. Nesbit for her children's stories of the Psammead, but her ghost stories are having a well-deserved resurgence. At a time when women were expected to be angels of the house, Nesbit wrote about women cursed, haunted, and—sometimes fatally—resisting.

Algernon Blackwood's "The Second Generation" asks: is what we pass on beyond our control? At a time when heredity and eugenics were hotly debated (again—the more things change, the more they stay the same), Blackwood took the language of genetics and made it monstrous.

Edith Wharton knew well the gilded parlours of the privileged, but writes them full of unease: of women and men who cannot shake off the sense that they are being followed, that their beautiful homes are not fortresses but traps. Here, the ghost is not a wailing ghoul but the haunting inevitability of a debt unpaid.

For Arthur Machen, horror lay in what lurks beneath. "Change," with its exploration of the changeling myth, exposes a culture hungry for spiritual meaning yet terrified of what might be revealed.

Mary Wilkins Freeman's 1902 story "Luella Miller," published when women were fighting for legal and social autonomy, gives us a new take on the vampire: a female figure who feeds not with teeth but with her need, draining the life from those around her. It's domestic horror at its most biting.

Ambrose Bierce's "A Watcher by the Dead" comes from an America in the shadow of civil war. Bierce himself vanished mysteriously in Mexico in 1914, and in this story the simple act of watching a corpse becomes a gauntlet of terror.

With "The Two Bottles of Relish," Lord Dunsany brings us a puzzle-box tale, a curious merging of crime and supernatural. Dunsany, known for lush, dreamlike fantasy, here offers a lean, unsettling little riddle.

M.R. James's ghosts are rarely vague; they are embodied, clawing, grasping things. His folklore-inspired "Lost Hearts" draws on the unease of orphaned children in the care of men who may not mean them well.

We travel, finally, to Italy in E.F. Benson's "Caterpillars," to the decadent and decaying Grand Hotel. Benson, like James, reveals the uncanny menace beneath the thin skin of the respectable middle-class world.

I'm not the first person to suggest that we're living in Victorian times. Our libraries and museums, our sewers, our railways, our bridges and tunnels, our very homes: we literally walk in the footsteps of the Victorians. We've inherited not only their architecture, but their fears. Those dreaming, writing and reading in the immediate post-Victorian decades show how long a shadow these times cast—and how they continue to haunt us now.

Industrialization has shifted into automation; colonial expansion into globalization; the motor car into the electric car.

The Victorians worried about telegrams disrupting sleep and fraying nerves; now we doomscroll until dawn.

They feared smog and contagion; we fear pollution and pandemics.

They fretted about women riding bicycles; we still police women's bodies and movements.

The same vast expansions and rapid progress that thrilled them also terrified them—just as our technologies do now. Which means that when we read their ghost stories we are also reading our own reflections: distorted by gaslight perhaps, but still recognizable.

These stories remind us: while the old fears may shift shape and change costume, they never die.

So turn the page. The doors are open. The judges are waiting. The rats are gathering behind the walls.

Let the terror begin.

THE JUDGE'S HOUSE

Bram Stoker

When the time for his examination drew near Malcolm Malcolmson made up his mind to go somewhere to read by himself. He feared the attractions of the seaside, and also he feared completely rural isolation, for of old he knew its charms, and so he determined to find some unpretentious little town where there would be nothing to distract him. He refrained from asking suggestions from any of his friends, for he argued that each would recommend some place of which he had knowledge, and where he had already acquaintances. As Malcolmson wished to avoid friends he had no wish to encumber himself with the attention of friends' friends, and so he determined to look out for a place for himself. He packed a portmanteau with some clothes and all the books he required, and then took ticket for the first name on the local timetable which he did not know.

When at the end of three hours' journey he alighted at Benchurch, he felt satisfied that he had so far obliterated his tracks as to be sure of having a peaceful opportunity of pursuing his studies. He went straight to the one inn which the sleepy little place contained, and put up for the night. Benchurch was a market town, and once in three weeks was crowded to excess, but for the remainder of the twenty-one days it was as attractive as a desert. Malcolmson looked around the day after his arrival to try to find quarters more isolated than even so quiet an inn as "The Good Traveller" afforded. There was only one place which took his fancy, and it certainly satisfied his wildest ideas regarding quiet; in fact, quiet was not the proper word to apply to it—desolation was the only term conveying any suitable idea of its isolation. It was an old rambling, heavy-built house of the Jacobean style, with heavy gables and windows, unusually small, and set higher than was customary in such houses, and was surrounded with a high brick wall massively built. Indeed, on examination, it looked more like a fortified house than an ordinary dwelling. But all these things pleased Malcolmson.

"Here," he thought, "is the very spot I have been looking for, and if I can only get opportunity of using it I shall be happy." His joy was increased when he realised beyond doubt that it was not at present inhabited. From the post-office he got the name of the agent, who was rarely surprised at the application to rent a part of the old house. Mr Carnford, the local lawyer and agent, was a genial old gentleman, and frankly confessed his delight at anyone being willing to live in the house.

"To tell you the truth," said he, "I should be only too happy, on behalf of the owners, to let anyone have the house rent free for a term of years if only to accustom the people here to see it inhabited. It has been so long empty that some kind of absurd prejudice has grown up about it, and this can be best put down by its occupation—if only," he added with a sly glance at Malcomson, "by a scholar like yourself, who wants its quiet for a time."

Malcolmson thought it needless to ask the agent about the "absurd prejudice"; he knew he would get more information, if he should require it, on that subject from other quarters. He paid his three months' rent, got a receipt, and the name of an old woman who would probably undertake to "do" for him, and came away with the keys in his pocket. He then went to the landlady of the inn, who was a cheerful and most kindly person, and asked her advice as to such stores and provisions as he would be likely to require. She threw up her hands in amazement when he told her where he was going to settle himself.

"Not in the Judge's House!" she said, and grew pale as she spoke. He explained the locality of the house, saying that he did not know its name. When he had finished she answered: "Aye, sure enough—sure enough the very place! It is the Judge's House sure enough." He asked her to tell him about the place, why so called, and what there was against it. She told him that it was so called locally because it had been many years before—how long she could not say, as she was herself from another part of the country, but she thought it must have been a hundred years or more—the abode of a judge who was held in great terror on account of his harsh sentences and his hostility to prisoners at Assizes. As to what there was against the house itself she could not tell. She had often asked, but no one could inform her; but there was a general feeling that there was something, and for her own part she would not take all the money in Drinkwater's Bank and stay in the house an hour by herself. Then she apologised to Malcolmson for her disturbing talk.

"It is too bad of me, sir, and you—and a young gentleman, too, if you will pardon me saying it—going to live there all alone. If you were my boy—and you'll excuse me for saying it—you wouldn't sleep there a night, not if I had to go there myself and pull the big alarm bell that's on the roof!" The good creature was so manifestly in earnest, and was so kindly in her intentions, that Malcolmson, although amused, was touched. He told her kindly how much he appreciated her interest in him, and added:

"But, my dear Mrs Witham, indeed you need not be concerned about me! A man who is reading for the Mathematical Tripos has too much to think of to be disturbed by any of these mysterious 'somethings,' and his work is of too exact and prosaic a kind to allow of his having any corner in his mind for mysteries of any kind. Harmonical

Progression, Permutations and Combinations, and Elliptic Functions have sufficient mysteries for me!" Mrs Witham kindly undertook to see after his commissions, and he went himself to look for the old woman who had been recommended to him. When he returned to the Judge's House with her, after an interval of a couple of hours, he found Mrs Witham herself waiting with several men and boys carrying parcels, and an upholsterer's man with a bed in a cart, for she said, though tables and chairs might be all very well, a bed that hadn't been aired for mayhap fifty years was not proper for young bones to lie on. She was evidently curious to see the inside of the house; and though manifestly so afraid of the 'somethings' that at the slightest sound she clutched on to Malcolmson, whom she never left for a moment, went over the whole place.

After his examination of the house, Malcolmson decided to take up his abode in the great dining room, which was big enough to serve for all his requirements; and Mrs Witham, with the aid of the charwoman, Mrs Dempster, proceeded to arrange matters. When the hampers were brought in and unpacked, Malcolmson saw that with much kind forethought she had sent from her own kitchen sufficient provisions to last for a few days. Before going she expressed all sorts of kind wishes; and at the door turned and said:

"And perhaps, sir, as the room is big and draughty it might be well to have one of those big screens put round your bed at night—though, truth to tell, I would die myself if I were to be so shut in with all kinds of 'things,' that put their heads round the sides, or over the top, and look on me!" The image which she had called up was too much for her nerves, and she fled incontinently. Mrs Dempster sniffed in a superior manner as the landlady disappeared, and remarked that for her own part she wasn't afraid of all the bogies in the kingdom.

"I'll tell you what it is, sir," she said; "bogies is all kinds and sorts of things—except bogies! Rats and mice, and beetles; and creaky doors, and loose slates, and broken panes, and stiff drawer handles, that stay out when you pull them and then fall down in the middle of the night. Look at the wainscot of the room! It is old—hundreds of years old! Do you think there's no rats and beetles there! And do you imagine, sir, that you won't see none of them! Rats is bogies, I tell you, and bogies is rats; and don't you get to think anything else!"

"Mrs Dempster," said Malcolmson gravely, making her a polite bow, "you know more than a Senior Wrangler! And let me say that, as a mark of esteem for your indubitable soundness of head and heart, I shall, when I go, give you possession of this house, and let you stay here by yourself for the last two months of my tenancy, for four weeks will serve my purpose."

"Thank you kindly, sir!" she answered, "but I couldn't sleep away from home a night. I am in Greenhow's Charity, and if I slept a night away from my rooms I should lose all

I have got to live on. The rules is very strict; and there's too many watching for a vacancy for me to run any risks in the matter. Only for that, sir, I'd gladly come here and attend on you altogether during your stay."

"My good woman," said Malcolmson hastily, "I have come here on purpose to obtain solitude; and believe me that I am grateful to the late Greenhow for having so organised his admirable charity—whatever it is—that I am perforce denied the opportunity of suffering from such a form of temptation! Saint Anthony himself could not be more rigid on the point!"

The old woman laughed harshly. "Ah, you young gentlemen," she said, "you don't fear for naught; and belike you'll get all the solitude you want here." She set to work with her cleaning; and by nightfall, when Malcolmson returned from his walk—he always had one of his books to study as he walked—he found the room swept and tidied, a fire burning in the old hearth, the lamp lit, and the table spread for supper with Mrs Witham's excellent fare. "This is comfort, indeed," he said, as he rubbed his hands.

When he had finished his supper, and lifted the tray to the other end of the great oak dining-table, he got out his books again, put fresh wood on the fire, trimmed his lamp, and set himself down to a spell of real hard work. He went on without pause till about eleven o'clock, when he knocked off for a bit to fix his fire and lamp, and to make himself a cup of tea. He had always been a tea-drinker, and during his college life had sat late at work and had taken tea late. The rest was a great luxury to him, and he enjoyed it with a sense of delicious, voluptuous ease. The renewed fire leaped and sparkled, and threw quaint shadows through the great old room; and as he sipped his hot tea he revelled in the sense of isolation from his kind. Then it was that he began to notice for the first time what a noise the rats were making.

"Surely," he thought, "they cannot have been at it all the time I was reading. Had they been, I must have noticed it!" Presently, when the noise increased, he satisfied himself that it was really new. It was evident that at first the rats had been frightened at the presence of a stranger, and the light of fire and lamp; but that as the time went on they had grown bolder and were now disporting themselves as was their wont.

How busy they were! and hark to the strange noises! Up and down behind the old wainscot, over the ceiling and under the floor they raced, and gnawed, and scratched! Malcolmson smiled to himself as he recalled to mind the saying of Mrs Dempster, "Bogies is rats, and rats is bogies!" The tea began to have its effect of intellectual and nervous stimulus, he saw with joy another long spell of work to be done before the night was past, and in the sense of security which it gave him, he allowed himself the luxury of a good look round the room. He took his lamp in one hand, and went all around, wondering that so quaint and beautiful an old house had been so long neglected. The carving of the oak on the panels of the wainscot was fine, and on and round the doors and windows it was beautiful and of rare merit. There were some old pictures on the walls, but they were coated so thick with dust and dirt that he could not distinguish any detail of them, though he held his lamp as high as he could over his head. Here and there as he went round he saw some crack or hole blocked for a moment by the face of a rat with its bright eyes glittering in the light, but in an instant it was gone, and a squeak and a scamper followed.

The thing that most struck him, however, was the rope of the great alarm bell on the roof, which hung down in a corner of the room on the right-hand side of the fireplace. He pulled up close to the hearth a great high-backed carved oak chair, and sat down to his last cup of tea. When this was done he made up the fire, and went back to his work, sitting at the corner of the table, having the fire to his left. For a little while the rats disturbed him somewhat with their perpetual scampering, but he got accustomed to the noise as one does to the ticking of a clock or to the roar of moving water; and he became so immersed in his work that everything in the world, except the problem which he was trying to solve, passed away from him.

He suddenly looked up, his problem was still unsolved, and there was in the air that sense of the hour before the dawn, which is so dread to doubtful life. The noise of the rats had ceased. Indeed it seemed to him that it must have ceased but lately and that it was the sudden cessation which had disturbed him. The fire had fallen low, but still it threw out a deep red glow. As he looked he started in spite of his *sang froid*.

There on the great high-backed carved oak chair by the right side of the fireplace sat an enormous rat, steadily glaring at him with baleful eyes. He made a motion to it as though to hunt it away, but it did not stir. Then he made the motion of throwing something. Still it did not stir, but showed its great white teeth angrily, and its cruel eyes shone in the lamplight with an added vindictiveness. Malcolmson felt amazed, and seizing the poker from the hearth ran at it to kill it. Before, however, he could strike it, the rat, with a squeak that sounded like the concentration of hate, jumped upon the floor, and, running up the rope of the alarm bell, disappeared in the darkness beyond the range of the green-shaded lamp. Instantly, strange to say, the noisy scampering of the rats in the wainscot began again.

By this time Malcolmson's mind was quite off the problem; and as a shrill cock-crow outside told him of the approach of morning, he went to bed and to sleep.

He slept so sound that he was not even waked by Mrs Dempster coming in to make up his room. It was only when she had tidied up the place and got his breakfast ready and tapped on the screen which closed in his bed that he woke. He was a little tired still after his night's hard work, but a strong cup of tea soon freshened him up, and, taking his book, he went out for his morning walk, bringing with him a few sandwiches lest he should not care to return till dinner time. He found a quiet walk between high elms some way outside the town, and here he spent the greater part of the day studying his Laplace. On his return he looked in to see Mrs Witham and to thank her for her kindness. When she saw him coming through the diamond-paned bay-window of her sanctum she came out to meet him and asked him in. She looked at him searchingly and shook her head as she said:

"You must not overdo it, sir. You are paler this morning than you should be. Too late hours and too hard work on the brain isn't good for any man! But tell me, sir, how did you pass the night? Well, I hope? But, my heart! sir, I was glad when Mrs Dempster told me this morning that you were all right and sleeping sound when she went in."

"Oh, I was all right," he answered, smiling, "the 'somethings' didn't worry me, as yet. Only the rats; and they had a circus, I tell you, all over the place. There was one wicked looking old devil that sat up on my own chair by the fire, and wouldn't go till I took the poker to him, and then he ran up the rope of the alarm bell and got to somewhere up the wall or the ceiling—I couldn't see where, it was so dark."

"Mercy on us," said Mrs Witham, "an old devil, and sitting on a chair by the fireside! Take care, sir! take care! There's many a true word spoken in jest."

"How do you mean? 'Pon my word I don't understand."

"An old devil! The old devil, perhaps. There! sir, you needn't laugh," for Malcolmson had broken into a hearty peal. "You young folks thinks it easy to laugh at things that makes older ones shudder. Never mind, sir! never mind! Please God, you'll laugh all the time. It's what I wish you myself!" and the good lady beamed all over in sympathy with his enjoyment, her fears gone for a moment.

"Oh, forgive me!" said Malcolmson presently. "Don't think me rude; but the idea was too much for me—that the old devil himself was on the chair last night!" And at the thought he laughed again. Then he went home to dinner.

This evening the scampering of the rats began earlier; indeed it had been going on before his arrival, and only ceased whilst his presence by its freshness disturbed them. After dinner he sat by the fire for a while and had a smoke; and then, having cleared his table, began to work as before. Tonight the rats disturbed him more than they had done on the previous night. How they scampered up and down and under and over! How they squeaked, and scratched, and gnawed! How they, getting bolder by degrees, came to the mouths of their holes and to the chinks and cracks and crannies in the wainscoting till their eyes shone like tiny lamps as the firelight rose and fell. But to him, now doubtless accustomed to them, their eyes were not wicked; only their playfulness touched him. Sometimes the boldest of them made sallies out on the floor or along the mouldings of the wainscot.

Now and again as they disturbed him Malcolmson made a sound to frighten them, smiting the table with his hand or giving a fierce "Hsh, hsh," so that they fled straightway to their holes.

And so the early part of the night wore on; and despite the noise Malcolmson got more and more immersed in his work. All at once he stopped, as on the previous night, being overcome by a sudden sense of silence. There was not the faintest sound of gnaw, or scratch, or squeak. The silence was as of the grave. He remembered the odd occurrence of the previous night, and instinctively he looked at the chair standing close by the fireside. And then a very odd sensation thrilled through him.

There, on the great old high-backed carved oak chair beside the fireplace sat the same enormous rat, steadily glaring at him with baleful eyes. Instinctively he took the nearest thing to his hand, a book of logarithms, and flung it at it. The book was badly aimed and the rat did not stir, so again the poker performance of the previous night was repeated; and again the rat, being closely pursued, fled up the rope of the alarm bell. Strangely too, the departure of this rat was instantly followed by the renewal of the noise made by the general rat community. On this occasion, as on the previous one, Malcolmson could not see at what part of the room the rat disappeared, for the green shade of his lamp left the upper part of the room in darkness, and the fire had burned low.

On looking at his watch he found it was close on midnight; and, not sorry for the *divertissement*, he made up his fire and made himself his nightly pot of tea. He had got through a good spell of work, and thought himself entitled to a cigarette; and so he sat on the great carved oak chair before the fire and enjoyed it. Whilst smoking he began to think that he would like to know where the rat disappeared to, for he had certain ideas for the morrow not entirely disconnected with a rat-trap. Accordingly he lit another lamp and placed it so that it would shine well into the right-hand corner of the wall by the fireplace. Then he got all the books he had with him, and placed them handy to throw at the vermin. Finally he lifted the rope of the alarm bell and placed the end of it on the table, fixing the extreme end under the lamp. As he handled it he could not help noticing how pliable it was, especially for so strong a rope, and one not in use.

"You could hang a man with it," he thought to himself. When his preparations were made he looked around, and said complacently: "There now, my friend, I think we shall learn something of you this time!" He began his work again, and though as before somewhat disturbed at first by the noise of the rats, soon lost himself in his propositions and problems.

Again he was called to his immediate surroundings suddenly. This time it might not have been the sudden silence only which took his attention; there was a slight movement of the rope, and the lamp moved. Without stirring, he looked to see if his pile of books was within range, and then cast his eye along the rope. As he looked he saw the great rat drop from the rope on the oak armchair and sit there glaring at him. He raised a book in his right hand, and taking careful aim flung it at the rat. The latter, with a quick movement, sprang aside and dodged the missile. He then took another book, and a third, and flung them one after another at the rat, but each time unsuccessfully. At last, as he stood with a book poised in his hand to throw, the rat squeaked and seemed afraid. This made Malcolmson more than ever eager to strike, and the book flew and struck the rat a resounding blow. It gave a terrified squeak, and turning on its pursuer a look of terrible malevolence, ran up the chair-back and made a great jump to the rope of the alarm bell and ran up it like lightning. The lamp rocked under the sudden strain, but it was a heavy one and did not topple over. Malcolmson kept his eyes on the rat, and saw it by the light of the second lamp leap to a moulding of the wainscot and disappear through a hole in one of the great pictures which hung on the wall, obscured and invisible through its coating of dirt and dust.

"I shall look up my friend's habitation in the morning," said the student, as he went over to collect his books. "The third picture from the fireplace; I shall not forget." He picked up the books one by one, commenting on them as he lifted them. "*Conic Sections* he does not mind, nor

Cycloidal Oscillations, nor the *Principia*, nor *Quaternions*, nor *Thermodynamics*. Now for the book that fetched him!"

Malcolmson took it up and looked at it. As he did so he started, and a sudden pallor overspread his face. He looked round uneasily and shivered slightly, as he murmured to himself: "The Bible my mother gave me! What an odd coincidence." He sat down to work again, and the rats in the wainscot renewed their gambols. They did not disturb him, however; somehow their presence gave him a sense of companionship. But he could not attend to his work, and after striving to master the subject on which he was engaged gave it up in despair, and went to bed as the first streak of dawn stole in through the eastern window.

He slept heavily but uneasily, and dreamed much; and when Mrs Dempster woke him late in the morning he seemed ill at ease, and for a few minutes did not seem to realise exactly where he was. His first request rather surprised the servant.

"Mrs Dempster, when I am out today I wish you would get the steps and dust or wash those pictures—specially that one the third from the fireplace—I want to see what they are." Late in the afternoon Malcolmson worked at his books in the shaded walk, and the cheerfulness of the previous day came back to him as the day wore on, and he found that his reading was progressing well. He had worked out to a satisfactory conclusion all the problems which had as yet baffled him, and it was in a state of jubilation that he paid a visit to Mrs Witham at "The Good Traveller." He found a stranger in the cosy sitting room with the landlady, who was introduced to him as Dr. Thornhill. She was not quite at ease, and this, combined with the Doctor's plunging at once into a series of questions, made Malcolmson come to the conclusion that his presence was not an accident, so without preliminary he said: "Dr Thornhill, I shall with pleasure answer you any question you may choose to ask me if you will answer me one question first."

The Doctor seemed surprised, but he smiled and answered at once.

"Done! What is it?"

"Did Mrs Witham ask you to come here and see me and advise me?"

Dr Thornhill for a moment was taken aback, and Mrs Witham got fiery red and turned away; but the doctor was a frank and ready man, and he answered at once and openly:

"She did: but she didn't intend you to know it. I suppose it was my clumsy haste that made you suspect. She told me that she did not like the idea of your being in that house all by yourself, and that she thought you took too much strong tea. In fact, she wants me to advise you if possible to give up the tea and the very late hours. I was a keen student in my time, so I suppose I may take the liberty of a college man, and without offence, advise you not quite as a stranger."

Malcolmson with a bright smile held out his hand. "Shake! as they say in America," he said. "I must thank you for your kindness and Mrs Witham too, and your kindness deserves a return on my part. I promise to take no more strong tea—no tea at all till you let me—and I shall go to bed tonight at one o'clock at latest. Will that do?"

"Capital," said the Doctor. "Now tell us all that you noticed in the old house," and so Malcolmson then and there told in minute detail all that had happened in the last two nights. He was interrupted every now and then by some exclamation from Mrs Witham, till finally when he told of the episode of the Bible the landlady's pent-up emotions found vent in a shriek; and it was not till a stiff glass of brandy and water had been administered that she grew composed again. Dr Thornhill listened with a face of growing gravity, and when the narrative was complete and Mrs Witham had been restored he asked:

"The rat always went up the rope of the alarm bell?"

"Always."

"I suppose you know," said the Doctor after a pause, "what the rope is?"

"No!"

"It is," said the Doctor slowly, "the very rope which the hangman used for all the victims of the Judge's judicial rancour!" Here he was interrupted by another scream from Mrs Witham, and steps had to be taken for her recovery. Malcolmson having looked at his watch, and found that it was close to his dinner hour, had gone home before her complete recovery.

When Mrs Witham was herself again she almost assailed the Doctor with angry questions as to what he meant by putting such horrible ideas into the poor young man's mind.

"He has quite enough there already to upset him," she added. Dr Thornhill replied:

"My dear madam, I had a distinct purpose in it! I wanted to draw his attention to the bell rope, and to fix it there. It may be that he is in a highly overwrought state, and has been studying too much, although I am bound to say that he seems as sound and healthy a young man, mentally and bodily, as ever I saw—but then the rats—and that suggestion of the devil."

The Doctor shook his head and went on.

"I would have offered to go and stay the first night with him but that I felt sure it would have been a cause of offence. He may get in the night some strange fright or hallucination; and if he does I want him to pull that rope. All alone as he is it will give us warning, and we may reach him in time to be of service. I shall be sitting up pretty late tonight and shall keep my ears open. Do not be alarmed if Benchurch gets a surprise before morning."

"Oh, Doctor, what do you mean? What do you mean?"

"I mean this; that possibly—nay, more probably—we shall hear the great alarm bell from the Judge's House tonight," and the Doctor made about as effective an exit as could be thought of.

When Malcolmson arrived home he found that it was a little after his usual time, and Mrs Dempster had gone away—the rules of Greenhow's Charity were not to be neglected. He was glad to see that the place was bright and tidy with a cheerful fire and a well-trimmed lamp. The evening was colder than might have been expected in April, and a heavy wind was blowing with such rapidly increasing strength that there was every promise of a storm during the night. For a few minutes after his entrance the noise of the rats ceased; but so soon as they became accustomed to his presence they began again. He was glad to hear them, for he felt once more the feeling of companionship in their noise, and his mind ran back to the strange fact that they only ceased to manifest themselves when that other—the great rat with the baleful eyes—came upon the scene. The reading-lamp only was lit and its green shade kept the ceiling and the upper part of the room in darkness, so that the cheerful light from the hearth spreading over the floor and shining on the white cloth laid over the end of the table was warm and cheery. Malcolmson sat down to his dinner with a good appetite and a buoyant spirit. After his dinner and a cigarette he sat steadily down to work, determined not to let anything disturb him, for he remembered his promise to the Doctor, and made up his mind to make the best of the time at his disposal.

For an hour or so he worked all right, and then his thoughts began to wander from his books. The actual circumstances around him, the calls on his physical attention, and his nervous susceptibility were not to be denied. By this time the wind had become a gale, and the gale a storm. The old house, solid though it was, seemed to shake to its foundations, and the storm roared and raged through its many chimneys and its queer old gables, producing strange, unearthly sounds in the empty rooms and corridors. Even the great alarm bell on the roof must have felt the force of the wind, for the rope rose and fell slightly, as though the bell were moved a little from time to time, and the limber rope fell on the oak floor with a hard and hollow sound.

As Malcolmson listened to it he bethought himself of the Doctor's words, "It is the rope which the hangman used for the victims of the Judge's judicial rancour," and he went over to the corner of the fireplace and took it in his hand to look at it. There seemed a sort of deadly interest in it, and as he stood there he lost himself for a moment in speculation as to who these victims were, and the grim wish of the Judge to have such a ghastly relic ever under his eyes. As he stood there the swaying of the bell on the roof still lifted the rope now and again; but presently there came a new sensation—a sort of tremor in the rope, as though something was moving along it.

Looking up instinctively Malcolmson saw the great rat coming slowly down towards him, glaring at him steadily. He dropped the rope and started back with a muttered curse, and the rat turning ran up the rope again and disappeared, and at the same instant Malcolmson became conscious that the noise of the rats, which had ceased for a while, began again.

All this set him thinking, and it occurred to him that he had not investigated the lair of the rat or looked at the pictures, as he had intended. He lit the other lamp without the shade, and, holding it up, went and stood opposite the third picture from the fireplace on the right-hand side where he had seen the rat disappear on the previous night.

At the first glance he started back so suddenly that he almost dropped the lamp, and a deadly pallor overspread his face. His knees shook, and heavy drops of sweat came on his forehead, and he trembled like an aspen. But he was young and plucky, and pulled himself together, and after the pause of a few seconds stepped forward again, raised the lamp, and examined the picture which had been dusted and washed, and now stood out clearly.

It was of a judge dressed in his robes of scarlet and ermine. His face was strong and merciless, evil, crafty, and vindictive, with a sensual mouth, hooked nose of ruddy colour, and shaped like the beak of a bird of prey. The rest of the face was of a cadaverous colour. The eyes were of peculiar brilliance and with a terribly malignant expression. As he looked at them, Malcolmson grew cold, for he saw there the very counterpart of the eyes of the great rat. The lamp almost fell from his hand, he saw the rat with its baleful eyes peering out through the hole in the corner of the picture, and noted the sudden cessation of the noise of the other rats. However, he pulled himself together, and went on with his examination of the picture. The Judge was seated in a great high-backed carved oak chair, on the right-hand side of a great stone fireplace where, in the corner, a rope hung down from the ceiling, its end lying coiled on the floor. With a feeling of something like horror, Malcolmson recognised the scene of the room as it stood, and gazed around him in an awe-struck manner as though he expected to find some strange presence behind him. Then he looked over to the corner of the fireplace—and with a loud cry he let the lamp fall from his hand.

There, in the Judge's armchair, with the rope hanging behind, sat the rat with the Judge's baleful eyes, now intensified and with a fiendish leer. Save for the howling of the storm without there was silence.

The fallen lamp recalled Malcolmson to himself. Fortunately it was of metal, and so the oil was not spilt. However, the practical need of attending to it settled at once his nervous apprehensions. When he had turned it out, he wiped his brow and thought for a moment.

"This will not do," he said to himself. "If I go on like this I shall become a crazy fool. This must stop! I promised the Doctor I would not take tea. Faith, he was pretty right! My nerves must have been getting into a queer state. Funny I did not notice it. I never felt better in my life. However, it is all right now, and I shall not be such a fool again."

Then he mixed himself a good stiff glass of brandy and water and resolutely sat down to his work. It was nearly an hour when he looked up from his book, disturbed by the sudden stillness. Without, the wind howled and roared louder than ever, and the rain drove in sheets against the windows, beating like hail on the glass; but within there was no sound whatever save the echo of the wind as it roared in the great chimney, and now and then a hiss as a few raindrops found their way down the chimney in a lull of the storm. The fire had fallen low and had ceased to flame, though it threw out a red glow. Malcolmson listened attentively, and presently heard a thin, squeaking noise, very faint. It came from the corner of the room where the rope hung down, and he thought it was the creaking of the rope on the floor as the swaying of the bell raised and lowered it. Looking up, however, he saw in the dim light the great rat clinging to the rope and gnawing it. The rope was already nearly gnawed through—he could see the lighter colour where the strands were laid bare. As he looked the job was completed, and the severed end of the rope fell clattering on the oaken floor, whilst for an instant the great rat remained like a knob or tassel at the end of the rope, which now began to sway to and fro. Malcolmson felt for a moment another pang of terror as he thought that now the possibility of calling the outer world to his assistance was cut off, but an intense anger took its place, and seizing the book he was reading he hurled it at the rat. The blow was well aimed, but before the missile could reach it the rat dropped off and struck the floor with a soft thud. Malcolmson instantly rushed over towards it, but it darted away and disappeared in the darkness of the shadows of the room. Malcolmson felt that his work was over for the night, and determined then and there to vary the monotony of the proceedings by a hunt for the rat, and took off the green shade of the lamp so as to insure a wider spreading light. As he did so the gloom of the upper part of the room was relieved, and in the new flood of light, great by comparison with the previous darkness, the pictures on the wall stood out boldly. From where he stood, Malcolmson saw right opposite to him the third picture on the wall from the right of the fireplace. He rubbed his eyes in surprise, and then a great fear began to come upon him.

In the centre of the picture was a great irregular patch of brown canvas, as fresh as when it was stretched on the frame. The background was as before, with chair and chimney-corner and rope, but the figure of the Judge had disappeared.

Malcolmson, almost in a chill of horror, turned slowly round, and then he began to shake and tremble like a man in a palsy. His strength seemed to have left him, and he was incapable of action or movement, hardly even of thought. He could only see and hear. There, on the great high-backed carved oak chair sat the Judge in his robes of scarlet and ermine, with his baleful eyes glaring vindictively, and a smile of triumph on the resolute, cruel mouth, as he lifted with his hands a black cap. Malcolmson felt as if the blood was running from his heart, as one does in moments of prolonged suspense. There was a singing in his ears. Without, he could hear the roar and howl of the tempest, and through it, swept on the storm, came the striking of midnight by the great chimes in the marketplace. He stood for a space of time that seemed to him endless, still as a statue and with wide-open, horror-struck eyes, breathless. As the clock struck, so the smile of triumph on the Judge's face intensified, and at the last stroke of midnight he placed the black cap on his head.

Slowly and deliberately the Judge rose from his chair and picked up the piece of the rope of the alarm bell which lay on the floor, drew it through his hands as if he enjoyed its touch, and then deliberately began to knot one end of it, fashioning it into a noose. This he tightened and tested with his foot, pulling hard at it till he was satisfied and then making a running noose of it, which he held in his hand. Then he began to move along the table on the opposite side to Malcolmson, keeping his eyes on him until he had passed him, when with a quick movement he stood in front of the door. Malcolmson then began to feel that he was trapped, and tried to think of what he should do. There was some fascination in the Judge's eyes, which he never took off him, and he had, perforce, to look. He saw the Judge approach—still keeping between him and the door—and raise the noose and throw it towards him as if to entangle him. With a great effort he made a quick movement to one side, and saw the rope fall beside him, and heard it strike the oaken floor. Again the Judge raised the noose and tried to ensnare him, ever keeping his baleful eyes fixed on him, and each time by a mighty effort the student just managed to evade it. So this went on for many times, the Judge seeming never discouraged nor discomposed at failure, but playing as a cat does with a mouse. At last in despair, which had reached its climax, Malcolmson cast a quick glance round him. The lamp seemed to have blazed up, and there was a fairly good light in the room. At the many rat-holes and in the chinks and crannies of the wainscot he saw the rats' eyes; and this aspect, that was purely physical, gave him a gleam of comfort. He looked around and saw that the rope of the great alarm bell was laden with rats. Every inch of it was covered with them, and more and more were pouring through the small circular hole in the ceiling whence it emerged, so that with their weight the bell was beginning to sway.

Hark! it had swayed till the clapper had touched the bell. The sound was but a tiny one, but the bell was only beginning to sway, and it would increase.

At the sound the Judge, who had been keeping his eyes fixed on Malcolmson, looked up, and a scowl of diabolical anger overspread his face. His eyes fairly glowed like hot coals, and he stamped his foot with a sound that seemed to make the house shake. A dreadful peal of thunder broke overhead as he raised the rope again, whilst the rats kept running up and down the rope as though working against time. This time, instead of throwing it, he drew close to his victim, and held open the noose as he approached. As he came closer there seemed something paralysing in his very presence, and Malcolmson stood rigid as a corpse. He felt the Judge's icy fingers touch his throat as he adjusted the rope. The noose tightened—tightened. Then the Judge, taking the rigid form of the student in his arms, carried him over and placed him standing in the oak chair, and stepping up beside him, put his hand up and caught the end of the swaying rope of the alarm bell. As he raised his hand the rats fled squeaking, and disappeared through the hole in the ceiling. Taking the end of the noose which was round Malcolmson's neck he tied it to the hanging bell-rope, and then descending pulled away the chair.

❦

When the alarm bell of the Judge's House began to sound a crowd soon assembled. Lights and torches of various kinds appeared, and soon a silent crowd was hurrying to the spot. They knocked loudly at the door, but there was no reply. Then they burst in the door, and poured into the great dining room, the Doctor at the head.

There at the end of the rope of the great alarm bell hung the body of the student, and on the face of the Judge in the picture was a malignant smile.

THE HAUNTER OF THE DARK

H.P. Lovecraft

> I have seen the dark universe yawning
> Where the black planets roll without aim—
> Where they roll in their horror unheeded,
> Without knowledge or lustre or name.
>
> —*Nemesis*.

Cautious investigators will hesitate to challenge the common belief that Robert Blake was killed by lightning, or by some profound nervous shock derived from an electrical discharge. It is true that the window he faced was unbroken, but Nature has shown herself capable of many freakish performances. The expression on his face may easily have arisen from some obscure muscular source unrelated to anything he saw, while the entries in his diary are clearly the result of a fantastic imagination aroused by certain local superstitions and by certain old matters he had uncovered. As for the anomalous conditions at the deserted church of Federal Hill—the shrewd analyst is not slow in attributing them to some charlatanry, conscious or unconscious, with at least some of which Blake was secretly connected.

For, after all, the victim was a writer and painter wholly devoted to the field of myth, dream, terror, and superstition, and avid in his quest for scenes and effects of a bizarre, spectral sort. His earlier stay in the city—a visit to a strange old man as deeply given to occult and forbidden lore as he—had ended amidst death and flame, and it must have been some morbid instinct which drew him back from his home in Milwaukee. He may have known of the old stories despite his statements to the contrary in the diary, and his death may have nipped in the bud some stupendous hoax destined to have a literary reflection.

Among those, however, who have examined and correlated all this evidence, there remain several who cling to less rational and commonplace theories. They are inclined to take much of Blake's diary at its face value, and point significantly to certain facts such as the undoubted genuineness of the old church record, the verified existence of the disliked and unorthodox Starry Wisdom sect prior to 1877, the recorded disappearance of an inquisitive reporter named Edwin M. Lillibridge in 1893, and—above all—the look of monstrous, transfiguring fear on the face of the young writer when he died. It was one of these believers who, moved to fanatical extremes, threw into the bay the curiously angled stone and its strangely adorned metal box found in the old church steeple—the black windowless steeple, and not the tower where Blake's diary said those things originally were. Though widely censured both officially and unofficially, this man—a reputable physician with a taste for odd folklore—averred that he had rid the earth of something too dangerous to rest upon it.

Between these two schools of opinion the reader must judge for himself. The papers have given the tangible details from a sceptical angle, leaving for others the drawing of the picture as Robert Blake saw it—or thought he saw it—or pretended to see it. Now, studying the diary closely, dispassionately, and at leisure, let us summarise the dark chain of events from the expressed point of view of their chief actor.

❦

Young Blake returned to Providence in the winter of 1934–5, taking the upper floor of a venerable dwelling in a grassy court off College Street—on the crest of the great eastward hill near the Brown University campus and behind the marble John Hay Library. It was a cosy and fascinating place, in a little garden oasis of village-like antiquity where huge, friendly cats sunned themselves atop a convenient shed. The square Georgian house had a monitor roof, classic doorway with fan carving, small-paned windows, and all the other earmarks of early nineteenth-century workmanship. Inside were six-panelled doors, wide floorboards, a curving colonial staircase, white Adam-period mantels, and a rear set of rooms three steps below the general level.

Blake's study, a large southwest chamber, overlooked the front garden on one side, while its west windows—before one of which he had his desk—faced off from the brow of the hill and commanded a splendid view of the lower town's outspread roofs and of the mystical sunsets that flamed behind them. On the far horizon were the open countryside's purple slopes. Against these, some two miles away, rose the spectral hump of Federal Hill, bristling with huddled roofs and steeples whose remote outlines wavered mysteriously, taking fantastic forms as the smoke of the city swirled up and enmeshed them. Blake had a curious sense that he was looking upon some unknown, ethereal world which might or might not vanish in dream if ever he tried to seek it out and enter it in person.

Having sent home for most of his books, Blake bought some antique furniture suitable to his quarters and settled down to write and paint—living alone, and attending to the simple housework himself. His studio was in a north attic room, where the panes of the monitor roof furnished admirable lighting. During that first winter he produced five of his best-known short stories—"The Burrower Beneath," "The Stairs in the Crypt," "Shaggai," "In the Vale of Pnath," and "The Feaster from the Stars"—and painted seven canvases; studies of nameless, unhuman monsters, and profoundly alien, non-terrestrial landscapes.

At sunset he would often sit at his desk and gaze dreamily off at the outspread west—the dark towers of Memorial Hall just below, the Georgian courthouse belfry, the lofty pinnacles of the downtown section, and that shimmering, spire-crowned mound in the distance whose unknown streets and labyrinthine gables so potently provoked his fancy. From his few local acquaintances he learned that the far-off slope was a vast Italian quarter, though most of the houses were remnants of older Yankee and Irish days. Now and then he would train his field-glasses on that spectral, unreachable world beyond the curling smoke; picking out individual roofs and chimneys and steeples, and speculating upon the bizarre and curious mysteries they might house. Even with optical aid Federal Hill seemed somehow alien, half fabulous, and linked to the unreal, intangible marvels of Blake's own tales and pictures. The feeling would persist long after the hill had faded into the violet, lamp-starred twilight, and the courthouse floodlights and the red Industrial Trust beacon had blazed up to make the night grotesque.

Of all the distant objects on Federal Hill, a certain huge, dark church most fascinated Blake. It stood out with especial distinctness at certain hours of the day, and at sunset the great tower and tapering steeple loomed blackly against the flaming sky. It seemed to rest on especially high ground; for the grimy façade, and the obliquely seen north side with sloping roof and the tops of great pointed windows, rose boldly above the tangle of surrounding ridgepoles and chimneypots. Peculiarly grim and austere, it appeared to be built of stone, stained and weathered with the smoke and storms of a century and more. The style, so far as the glass could show, was that earliest experimental form of Gothic revival which preceded the stately Upjohn period and held over some of the outlines and proportions of the Georgian age. Perhaps it was reared around 1810 or 1815.

As months passed, Blake watched the far-off, forbidding structure with an oddly mounting interest. Since the vast windows were never lighted, he knew that it must be vacant. The longer he watched, the more his imagination worked, till at length he began to fancy curious things. He believed that a vague, singular aura of desolation hovered over the place, so that even the pigeons and swallows shunned its smoky eaves. Around other towers and belfries his glass would reveal great flocks of birds, but here they never rested. At least, that is what he thought and set down in his diary. He pointed the place out to several friends, but none of them had even been on Federal Hill or possessed the faintest notion of what the church was or had been.

In the spring a deep restlessness gripped Blake. He had begun his long-planned novel—based on a supposed survival of the witch-cult in Maine—but was strangely unable to make progress with it. More and more he would sit at his westward window and gaze at the distant hill and the black, frowning steeple shunned by the birds. When the delicate leaves came out on the garden boughs the world was filled with a new beauty, but Blake's restlessness was merely increased. It was then that he first thought of crossing the city and climbing bodily up that fabulous slope into the smoke-wreathed world of dream.

Late in April, just before the aeon-shadowed Walpurgis time, Blake made his first trip into the unknown. Plodding through the endless downtown streets and the bleak, decayed squares beyond, he came finally upon the ascending avenue of century-worn steps, sagging Doric porches, and blear-paned cupolas which he felt must lead up to the long-known, unreachable world beyond the mists. There were dingy blue-and-white street signs which meant nothing to him, and presently he noted the strange, dark faces of the drifting crowds, and the foreign signs over curious shops in brown, decade-weathered buildings. Nowhere could he find any of the objects he had seen from afar; so that once more he half fancied that the Federal Hill of that distant view was a dream-world never to be trod by living human feet.

Now and then a battered church façade or crumbling spire came in sight, but never the blackened pile that he sought. When he asked a shopkeeper about a great stone church the man smiled and shook his head, though he spoke English freely. As Blake climbed higher, the region seemed stranger and stranger, with bewildering mazes of brooding brown alleys leading eternally off to the south. He crossed two or three broad avenues, and once thought he glimpsed a familiar tower. Again he asked a merchant about the massive church of stone, and this time he could have sworn that the plea of ignorance was feigned. The dark man's face had a look of fear which he tried to hide, and Blake saw him make a curious sign with his right hand.

Then suddenly a black spire stood out against the cloudy sky on his left, above the tiers of brown roofs lining the tangled southerly alleys. Blake knew at once what it was, and plunged toward it through the squalid, unpaved lanes that climbed from the avenue. Twice he lost his way, but he somehow dared not ask any of the patriarchs or housewives who sat on their doorsteps, or any of the children who shouted and played in the mud of the shadowy lanes.

At last he saw the tower plain against the south-west, and a huge stone bulk rose darkly at the end of an alley. Presently he stood in a windswept open square, quaintly cobblestoned, with a high bank wall on the farther side. This was the end of his quest; for upon the wide, iron-railed, weed-grown plateau which the wall supported—a separate, lesser world raised fully six feet above the surrounding streets—there stood a grim, titan bulk whose identity, despite Blake's new perspective, was beyond dispute.

The vacant church was in a state of great decrepitude. Some of the high stone buttresses had fallen, and several delicate finials lay half lost among the brown, neglected weeds and grasses. The sooty Gothic windows were largely unbroken, though many of the stone mullions were missing.

Blake wondered how the obscurely painted panes could have survived so well, in view of the known habits of small boys the world over. The massive doors were intact and tightly closed. Around the top of the bank wall, fully enclosing the grounds, was a rusty iron fence whose gate—at the head of a flight of steps from the square—was visibly padlocked. The path from the gate to the building was completely overgrown. Desolation and decay hung like a pall above the place, and in the birdless eaves and black, ivyless walls Blake felt a touch of the dimly sinister beyond his power to define.

There were very few people in the square, but Blake saw a policeman at the northerly end and approached him with questions about the church. He was a great wholesome Irishman, and it seemed odd that he would do little more than make the sign of the cross and mutter that people never spoke of that building. When Blake pressed him he said very hurriedly that the Italian priests warned everybody against it, vowing that a monstrous evil had once dwelt there and left its mark. He himself had heard dark whispers of it from his father, who recalled certain sounds and rumours from his boyhood.

There had been a bad sect there in the old days—an outlaw sect that called up awful things from some unknown gulf of night. It had taken a good priest to exorcise what had come, though there did be those who said that merely the light could do it. If Father O'Malley were alive there would be many the thing he could tell. But now there was nothing to do but let it alone. It hurt nobody now, and those that owned it were dead or far away. They had run away like rats after the threatening talk in '77, when people began to mind the way folks vanished now and then in the neighbourhood. Some day the city would step in and take the property for lack of heirs, but little good would come of anybody's touching it. Better it be left alone for the years to topple, lest things be stirred that ought to rest forever in their black abyss.

After the policeman had gone Blake stood staring at the sullen steepled pile. It excited him to find that the structure seemed as sinister to others as to him, and he wondered what grain of truth might lie behind the old tales the bluecoat had repeated. Probably they were mere legends evoked by the evil look of the place, but even so, they were like a strange coming to life of one of his own stories.

The afternoon sun came out from behind dispersing clouds, but seemed unable to light up the stained, sooty walls of the old temple that towered on its high plateau. It was odd that the green of spring had not touched the brown, withered growths in the raised, iron-fenced yard. Blake found himself edging nearer the raised area and examining the bank wall and rusted fence for possible avenues of ingress. There was a terrible lure about the blackened fane which was not to be resisted. The fence had no opening near the steps, but around on the north side were some missing bars. He could go up the steps and walk around on the narrow coping outside the fence till he came to the gap. If the people feared the place so wildly, he would encounter no interference.

He was on the embankment and almost inside the fence before anyone noticed him. Then, looking down, he saw the few people in the square edging away and making the same sign with their right hands that the shopkeeper in the avenue had made. Several windows were slammed down, and a fat woman darted into the street and pulled some small children inside a rickety, unpainted house. The gap in the fence was very easy to pass through, and before long Blake found himself wading amidst the rotting, tangled growths of the deserted yard. Here and there the worn stump of a headstone told him that there had once been burials in this field; but that, he saw, must have been very long ago. The sheer bulk of the church was oppressive now that he was close to it, but he conquered his mood and approached to try the three great doors in the façade. All were securely locked, so he began a circuit of the Cyclopean building in quest of some minor and more penetrable opening. Even then he could not be sure that he wished to enter that haunt of desertion and shadow, yet the pull of its strangeness dragged him on automatically.

A yawning and unprotected cellar window in the rear furnished the needed aperture. Peering in, Blake saw a subterranean gulf of cobwebs and dust faintly lit by the western sun's filtered rays. Debris, old barrels, and ruined boxes and furniture of numerous sorts met his eye, though over everything lay a shroud of dust which softened all sharp outlines. The rusted remains of a hot-air furnace showed that the building had been used and kept in shape as late as mid-Victorian times.

Acting almost without conscious initiative, Blake crawled through the window and let himself down to the dust-carpeted and debris-strewn concrete floor. The vaulted cellar was a vast one, without partitions; and in a corner far to the right, amid dense shadows, he saw a black archway evidently leading upstairs. He felt a peculiar sense of oppression at being actually within the great spectral building, but kept it in check as he cautiously scouted about—finding a still-intact barrel amid the dust, and rolling it over to the open window to provide for his exit. Then, bracing himself, he crossed the wide, cobweb-festooned space toward the arch. Half-choked with the omnipresent dust, and covered with ghostly gossamer fibres, he reached and began to climb the worn stone steps which rose into the darkness. He had no light, but groped carefully with his hands. After a sharp turn he felt a closed door ahead, and a little fumbling revealed its ancient latch. It opened inward, and beyond it he saw a dimly illumined corridor lined with worm-eaten panelling.

Once on the ground floor, Blake began exploring in a rapid fashion. All the inner doors were unlocked, so that he freely passed from room to room. The colossal nave was an almost eldritch place with its drifts and mountains of dust over box pews, altar, hourglass pulpit, and sounding-board, and its titanic ropes of cobweb stretching among the pointed arches of the gallery and entwining the clustered Gothic columns. Over all this hushed desolation played a hideous leaden light as the declining afternoon sun sent its rays through the strange, half-blackened panes of the great apsidal windows.

The paintings on those windows were so obscured by soot that Blake could scarcely decipher what they had represented, but from the little he could make out he did not like them. The designs were largely conventional, and his knowledge of obscure symbolism told him much concerning some of the ancient patterns. The few saints depicted bore expressions distinctly open to criticism, while one of the windows seemed to show merely a dark space with spirals of curious luminosity scattered about in it. Turning away from the windows, Blake noticed that the cobwebbed cross above the altar was not of the ordinary kind, but resembled the primordial ankh or crux ansata of shadowy Egypt.

In a rear vestry room beside the apse Blake found a rotting desk and ceiling-high shelves of mildewed, disintegrating books. Here for the first time he received a positive shock of objective horror, for the titles of those books told him much. They were the black, forbidden things which most sane people have never even heard of, or have heard of only in furtive, timorous whispers; the banned and dreaded repositories of equivocal secrets and immemorial formulae which have trickled down the stream of time from the days of man's youth, and the dim, fabulous days before man was. He had himself read many of them—a Latin version of the abhorred *Necronomicon*, the sinister *Liber Ivonis*, the infamous *Cultes des Goules* of Comte d'Erlette, the *Unaussprechlichen Kulten* of von Junzt, and old Ludvig Prinn's hellish *De Vermis Mysteriis*. But there were others he had known merely by reputation or not at all—the *Pnakotic Manuscripts*, the *Book of Dzyan*, and a crumbling volume in wholly unidentifiable characters yet with certain symbols and diagrams shudderingly recognisable to the occult student. Clearly, the lingering local rumours had not lied. This place had once been the seat of an evil older than mankind and wider than the known universe.

In the ruined desk was a small leather-bound record-book filled with entries in some odd cryptographic medium. The manuscript writing consisted of the common traditional symbols used today in astronomy and anciently in alchemy, astrology, and other dubious arts—the devices of the sun, moon, planets, aspects, and zodiacal signs—here massed in solid pages of text, with divisions and paragraphings suggesting that each symbol answered to some alphabetical letter.

In the hope of later solving the cryptogram, Blake bore off this volume in his coat pocket. Many of the great tomes on the shelves fascinated him unutterably, and he felt tempted to borrow them at some later time. He wondered how they could have remained undisturbed so long. Was he the first to conquer the clutching, pervasive fear which had for nearly sixty years protected this deserted place from visitors?

Having now thoroughly explored the ground floor, Blake ploughed again through the dust of the spectral nave to the front vestibule, where he had seen a door and staircase presumably leading up to the blackened tower and steeple—objects so long familiar to him at a distance. The ascent was a choking experience, for dust lay thick, while the spiders had done their worst in this constricted place. The staircase was a spiral with high, narrow wooden treads, and now and then Blake passed a clouded window looking dizzily out over the city. Though he had seen no ropes below, he expected to find a bell or peal of bells in the tower whose narrow, louvre-boarded lancet windows his field-glass had studied so often. Here he was doomed to disappointment; for when he attained the top of the stairs he found the tower chamber vacant of chimes, and clearly devoted to vastly different purposes.

The room, about fifteen feet square, was faintly lighted by four lancet windows, one on each side, which were glazed within their screening of decayed louvre-boards. These had been further fitted with tight, opaque screens, but the latter were now largely rotted away. In the centre of the dust-laden floor rose a curiously angled stone pillar some four feet in height and two in average diameter, covered on each side with bizarre, crudely incised, and wholly unrecognisable hieroglyphs. On this pillar rested a metal box of peculiarly asymmetrical form; its hinged lid thrown back, and its interior holding what looked beneath the decade-deep dust to be an egg-shaped or irregularly spherical object some four inches through. Around the pillar in a rough circle were seven high-backed Gothic chairs still largely intact, while behind them, ranging along the dark-panelled walls, were seven colossal images of crumbling, black-painted plaster, resembling more than anything else the cryptic carven megaliths of mysterious Easter Island. In one corner of the cobwebbed chamber a ladder was built into the wall, leading up to the closed trapdoor of the windowless steeple above.

As Blake grew accustomed to the feeble light he noticed odd bas-reliefs on the strange open box of yellowish metal. Approaching, he tried to clear the dust away with his hands and handkerchief, and saw that the figurings were of a monstrous and utterly alien kind; depicting entities which, though seemingly alive, resembled no known life-form ever evolved on this planet. The four-inch seeming sphere turned out to be a nearly black, red-striated polyhedron with many irregular flat surfaces; either a very remarkable crystal of some sort, or an artificial object of carved and highly polished mineral matter. It did not touch the bottom of the box, but was held suspended by means of a metal band around its centre, with seven queerly designed supports extending horizontally to angles of the box's inner wall near the top. This stone, once exposed, exerted upon Blake an almost alarming fascination. He could scarcely tear his eyes from it, and as he looked at its glistening surfaces he almost fancied it was transparent, with half-formed worlds of wonder within. Into his mind floated pictures of alien orbs with great stone towers, and other orbs with titan mountains and no mark of life, and still remoter spaces where only a stirring in vague blacknesses told of the presence of consciousness and will.

When he did look away, it was to notice a somewhat singular mound of dust in the far corner near the ladder to the steeple. Just why it took his attention he could not tell, but something in its contours carried a message to his unconscious mind. Ploughing toward it, and brushing aside the hanging cobwebs as he went, he began to discern something grim about it. Hand and handkerchief soon revealed the truth, and Blake gasped with a baffling mixture of emotions. It was a human skeleton, and it must have been there for a very long time. The clothing was in shreds, but some buttons and fragments of cloth bespoke a man's grey suit. There were other bits of evidence—shoes, metal clasps, huge buttons for round cuffs, a stickpin of bygone pattern, a reporter's badge with the name of the old *Providence Telegram*, and a crumbling leather pocketbook. Blake examined the latter with care, finding within it several bills of antiquated issue, a celluloid advertising calendar for 1893, some cards with the name "Edwin M. Lillibridge," and a paper covered with pencilled memoranda.

This paper held much of a puzzling nature, and Blake read it carefully at the dim westward window. Its disjointed text included such phrases as the following:

"Prof. Enoch Bowen home from Egypt May 1844—buys old Free-Will Church in July—his archaeological work & studies in occult well known."
"Dr. Drowne of 4th Baptist warns against Starry Wisdom in sermon Dec. 29, 1844."
"Congregation 97 by end of '45."
"1846—3 disappearances—first mention of Shining Trapezohedron."
"7 disappearances 1848—stories of blood sacrifice begin."
"Investigation 1853 comes to nothing—stories of sounds."
"Fr. O'Malley tells of devil-worship with box found in great Egyptian ruins—says they call up something that can't exist in light. Flees a little light, and banished by strong light. Then has to be summoned again. Probably got this from deathbed confession of Francis X. Feeney, who had joined Starry Wisdom in '49. These people say the Shining Trapezohedron shows them heaven & other worlds, & that the Haunter of the Dark tells them secrets in some way."
"Story of Orrin B. Eddy 1857. They call it up by gazing at the crystal, & have a secret language of their own."
"200 or more in cong. 1863, exclusive of men at front."
"Irish boys mob church in 1869 after Patrick Regan's disappearance."
"Veiled article in J. March 14, '72, but people don't talk about it."

"6 disappearances 1876—secret committee calls on Mayor Doyle."
"Action promised Feb. 1877—church closes in April."
"Gang—Federal Hill Boys—threaten Dr —— and vestrymen in May."
"181 persons leave city before end of '77—mention no names."
"Ghost stories begin around 1880—try to ascertain truth of report that no human being has entered church since 1877."
"Ask Lanigan for photograph of place taken 1851."...

Restoring the paper to the pocketbook and placing the latter in his coat, Blake turned to look down at the skeleton in the dust. The implications of the notes were clear, and there could be no doubt but that this man had come to the deserted edifice forty-two years before in quest of a newspaper sensation which no one else had been bold enough to attempt. Perhaps no one else had known of his plan—who could tell? But he had never returned to his paper. Had some bravely suppressed fear risen to overcome him and bring on sudden heart-failure? Blake stooped over the gleaming bones and noted their peculiar state. Some of them were badly scattered, and a few seemed oddly *dissolved* at the ends. Others were strangely yellowed, with vague suggestions of charring. This charring extended to some of the fragments of clothing. The skull was in a very peculiar state—stained yellow, and with a charred aperture in the top as if some powerful acid had eaten through the solid bone. What had happened to the skeleton during its four decades of silent entombment here Blake could not imagine.

Before he realised it, he was looking at the stone again, and letting its curious influence call up a nebulous pageantry in his mind. He saw processions of robed, hooded figures whose outlines were not human, and looked on endless leagues of desert lined with carved, sky-reaching monoliths. He saw towers and walls in nighted depths under the sea, and vortices of space where wisps of black mist floated before thin shimmerings of cold purple haze. And beyond all else he glimpsed an infinite gulf of darkness, where solid and semi-solid forms were known only by their windy stirrings, and cloudy patterns of force seemed to superimpose order on chaos and hold forth a key to all the paradoxes and arcana of the worlds we know.

Then all at once the spell was broken by an access of gnawing, indeterminate panic fear. Blake choked and turned away from the stone, conscious of some formless alien presence close to him and watching him with horrible intentness. He felt entangled with something—something which was not in the stone, but which had looked through it at him—something which would ceaselessly follow him with a cognition that was not physical sight. Plainly, the place was getting on his nerves—as well it might in view of his gruesome find. The light was waning, too, and since he had no illuminant with him he knew he would have to be leaving soon.

It was then, in the gathering twilight, that he thought he saw a faint trace of luminosity in the crazily angled stone. He had tried to look away from it, but some obscure compulsion drew his eyes back. Was there a subtle phosphorescence of radioactivity about the thing? What was it that the dead man's notes had said concerning a *Shining Trapezohedron*? What, anyway, was this abandoned lair of cosmic evil? What had been done here, and what might still be lurking in the bird-shunned shadows? It seemed now as if an elusive touch of foetor had arisen somewhere close by, though its source was not apparent. Blake seized the cover of the long-open box and snapped it down. It moved easily on its alien hinges, and closed completely over the unmistakably glowing stone.

At the sharp click of that closing a soft stirring sound seemed to come from the steeple's eternal blackness overhead, beyond the trapdoor. Rats, without question—the only living things to reveal their presence in this accursed pile since he had entered it. And yet that stirring in the steeple frightened him horribly, so that he plunged almost wildly down the spiral stairs, across the ghoulish nave, into the vaulted basement, out amidst the gathering dusk of the deserted square, and down through the teeming, fear-haunted alleys and avenues of Federal Hill towards the sane central streets and the home-like brick sidewalks of the college district.

During the days which followed, Blake told no one of his expedition. Instead, he read much in certain books, examined long years of newspaper files downtown, and worked feverishly at the cryptogram in that leather volume from the cobwebbed vestry room. The cipher, he soon saw, was no simple one; and after a long period of endeavour he felt sure that its language could not be English, Latin, Greek, French, Spanish, Italian, or German. Evidently he would have to draw upon the deepest wells of his strange erudition.

Every evening the old impulse to gaze westward returned, and he saw the black steeple as of yore amongst the bristling roofs of a distant and half-fabulous world. But now it held a fresh note of terror for him. He knew the heritage of evil lore it masked, and with the knowledge his vision ran riot in queer new ways. The birds of spring were returning, and as he watched their sunset flights he fancied they avoided the gaunt, lone spire as never before. When a flock of them approached it, he thought, they would wheel and scatter in panic confusion—and he could guess at the wild twitterings which failed to reach him across the intervening miles.

It was in June that Blake's diary told of his victory over the cryptogram. The text was, he found, in the dark Aklo language used by certain cults of evil antiquity, and known to him in a halting way through previous researches. The diary is strangely reticent about what Blake deciphered, but he was patently awed and disconcerted by his results. There are references to a Haunter of the Dark awaked by gazing into the Shining Trapezohedron, and insane conjectures about the black gulfs of chaos from which it was called. The being is spoken of as holding all knowledge, and demanding monstrous sacrifices. Some of Blake's entries show fear lest the thing, which he seemed to regard as summoned, stalk abroad; though he adds that the street lights form a bulwark which cannot be crossed.

Of the Shining Trapezohedron he speaks often, calling it a window on all time and space, and tracing its history from the days it was fashioned on dark Yuggoth, before ever the Old Ones brought it to earth. It was treasured and placed in its curious box by the crinoid things of Antarctica, salvaged from their ruins by the serpent-men of Valusia, and peered at aeons later in Lemuria by the first human beings. It crossed strange lands and stranger seas, and sank with Atlantis before a Minoan fisher meshed it in his net and sold it to swarthy merchants from nighted Khem. The Pharaoh Nephren-Ka built around it a temple with a windowless crypt, and did that which caused his name to be stricken from all monuments and records. Then it slept in the ruins of that evil fane which the priests and the new Pharaoh destroyed, till the delver's spade once more brought it forth to curse mankind.

Early in July the newspapers oddly supplement Blake's entries, though in so brief and casual a way that only the diary has called general attention to their contribution. It appears that a new fear had been growing on Federal Hill since a stranger had entered the dreaded church. The Italians whispered of unaccustomed stirrings and bumpings and scrapings in the dark windowless steeple, and called on their priests to banish an entity which haunted their dreams. Something, they said, was constantly watching at a door to see if it were dark enough to venture forth. Press items mentioned the long-standing local superstitions, but failed to shed much light on the earlier background of the horror. It was obvious that the young reporters of today are no antiquarians. In writing of these things in his diary, Blake expresses a curious kind of remorse, and talks of the duty of burying the Shining Trapezohedron and of banishing what he had evoked by letting daylight into the hideous jutting spire. At the same time, however, he displays the dangerous extent of his fascination, and admits a morbid longing—pervading even his dreams—to visit the accursed tower and gaze again into the cosmic secrets of the glowing stone.

Then something in the *Journal* on the morning of July 17 threw the diarist into a veritable fever of horror. It was only a variant of the other half-humorous items about the Federal Hill restlessness, but to Blake it was somehow very terrible indeed. In the night a thunderstorm had put the city's lighting system out of commission for a full hour, and in that black interval the Italians had nearly gone mad with fright. Those living near the dreaded church had sworn that the thing in the steeple had taken advantage of the street lamps' absence and gone down into the body of the church, flopping and bumping around in a viscous, altogether dreadful way. Towards the last it had bumped up to the tower, where there were sounds of the shattering of glass. It could go wherever the darkness reached, but light would always send it fleeing.

When the current blazed on again there had been a shocking commotion in the tower, for even the feeble light trickling through the grime-blackened, louvre-boarded windows was too much for the thing. It had bumped and slithered up into its tenebrous steeple just in time—for a long dose of light would have sent it back into the abyss whence the crazy stranger had called it. During the dark hour praying crowds had clustered round the church in the rain with lighted candles and lamps somehow shielded with folded paper and umbrellas—a guard of light to save the city from the nightmare that stalks in darkness. Once, those nearest the church declared, the outer door had rattled hideously.

But even this was not the worst. That evening in the *Bulletin* Blake read of what the reporters had found. Aroused at last to the whimsical news value of the scare, a pair of them had defied the frantic crowds of Italians and crawled into the church through the cellar window after trying the doors in vain. They found the dust of the vestibule and of the spectral nave ploughed up in a singular way, with bits of rotted cushions and satin pew-linings scattered curiously around. There was a bad odour everywhere, and here and there were bits of yellow stain and patches of what looked like charring. Opening the door to the tower, and pausing a moment at the suspicion of a scraping sound above, they found the narrow spiral stairs wiped roughly clean.

In the tower itself a similarly half-swept condition existed. They spoke of the heptagonal stone pillar, the overturned Gothic chairs, and the bizarre plaster images; though strangely enough the metal box and the old mutilated skeleton were not mentioned. What disturbed Blake the most—except for the hints of stains and charring and bad odours—was the final detail that explained the crashing glass. Every one of the tower's lancet windows was broken, and two of them had been darkened in a crude and hurried way by the stuffing of satin pew linings and cushion horsehair into the spaces between the slanting exterior louver-boards. More satin fragments and bunches of horsehair lay scattered around the newly swept floor, as if someone had been interrupted in the act of restoring the tower to the absolute blackness of its tightly curtained days.

Yellowish stains and charred patches were found on the ladder to the windowless spire, but when a reporter climbed up, opened the horizontally sliding trapdoor, and shot a feeble flashlight beam into the black and strangely foetid space, he saw nothing but darkness, and a heterogeneous litter of shapeless fragments near the aperture. The verdict, of course, was charlatanry. Somebody had played a joke on the superstitious hill-dwellers, or else some fanatic had striven to bolster up their fears for their own supposed good. Or perhaps some of the younger and more sophisticated dwellers had staged an elaborate hoax on the outside world. There was an amusing aftermath when the police sent an officer to verify the reports. Three men in succession found ways of evading the assignment, and the fourth went very reluctantly and returned very soon without adding to the account given by the reporters.

From this point onwards Blake's diary shows a mounting tide of insidious horror and nervous apprehension. He upbraids himself for not doing something, and speculates wildly on the consequences of another electrical breakdown. It has been verified that on three occasions—during thunderstorms—he telephoned the electric light company in a frantic vein and asked that desperate precautions against a lapse of power be taken. Now and then his entries show concern over the failure of the reporters to find the metal box and stone, and the strangely marred old skeleton, when they explored the shadowy tower room. He assumed that these things had been removed—whither, and by whom or what, he could only guess. But his worst fears concerned himself, and the kind of unholy rapport he felt to exist between his mind and that lurking horror in the distant steeple—that monstrous thing of night which his rashness had called out of the ultimate black spaces. He seemed to feel a constant tugging at his will, and callers of that period remember how he would sit abstractedly at his desk and stare out of the west window at that far-off, spire-bristling mound beyond the swirling smoke of the city. His entries dwell monotonously on certain terrible dreams, and of a strengthening of the unholy rapport in his sleep. There is mention of a night when he awakened to find himself fully dressed, outdoors, and headed automatically down College Hill towards the west. Again and again he dwells on the fact that the thing in the steeple knows where to find him.

The week following July 30 is recalled as the time of Blake's partial breakdown. He did not dress, and ordered all his food by telephone. Visitors remarked the cords he kept near his bed, and he said that sleep-walking had forced him to bind his ankles every night with knots which would probably hold or else waken him with the labour of untying.

In his diary he told of the hideous experience which had brought the collapse. After retiring on the night of the 30th he had suddenly found himself groping about in an almost black space. All he could see were short, faint, horizontal streaks of bluish light, but he could smell an overpowering foetor and hear a curious jumble of soft, furtive sounds above him. Whenever he moved he stumbled over something, and at each noise there would come a sort of answering sound from above—a vague stirring, mixed with the cautious sliding of wood on wood.

Once his groping hands encountered a pillar of stone with a vacant top, whilst later he found himself clutching the rungs of a ladder built into the wall, and fumbling his uncertain way upward towards some region of intenser stench where a hot, searing blast beat down against him. Before his eyes a kaleidoscopic range of phantasmal images played, all of them dissolving at intervals into the picture of a vast, unplumbed abyss of night wherein whirled suns and worlds of an even profounder blackness. He thought of the ancient legends of Ultimate Chaos, at whose centre sprawls the blind idiot god Azathoth, Lord of All Things, encircled by his flopping horde of mindless and amorphous dancers, and lulled by the thin monotonous piping of a demoniac flute held in nameless paws.

Then a sharp report from the outer world broke through his stupor and roused him to the unutterable horror of his position. What it was, he never knew—perhaps it was some belated peal from the fireworks heard all summer on Federal Hill as the dwellers hail their various patron saints, or the saints of their native villages in Italy. In any event he shrieked aloud, dropped frantically from the ladder, and stumbled blindly across the obstructed floor of the almost lightless chamber that encompassed him.

He knew instantly where he was, and plunged recklessly down the narrow spiral staircase, tripping and bruising himself at every turn. There was a nightmare flight through a vast cobwebbed nave whose ghostly arches reached up to realms of leering shadow, a sightless scramble through a littered basement, a climb to regions of air and street lights outside, and a mad racing down a spectral hill of gibbering gables, across a grim, silent city of tall black towers, and up the steep eastward precipice to his own ancient door.

On regaining consciousness in the morning he found himself lying on his study floor fully dressed. Dirt and cobwebs covered him, and every inch of his body seemed sore and bruised. When he faced the mirror he saw that his hair was badly scorched, while a trace of strange, evil odour seemed to cling to his upper outer clothing. It was then that his nerves broke down. Thereafter, lounging exhaustedly about in a dressing-gown, he did little but stare from his west window, shiver at the threat of thunder, and make wild entries in his diary.

The great storm broke just before midnight on August 8th. Lightning struck repeatedly in all parts of the city, and two remarkable fireballs were reported. The rain was torrential, while a constant fusillade of thunder brought sleeplessness to thousands. Blake was utterly frantic in his fear for the lighting system, and tried to telephone the company around 1 a.m., though by that time service had been temporarily cut off in the interests of safety. He recorded everything in his diary—the large, nervous, and often undecipherable hieroglyphs telling their own story of growing frenzy and despair, and of entries scrawled blindly in the dark.

He had to keep the house dark in order to see out of the window, and it appears that most of his time was spent at his desk, peering anxiously through the rain across the glistening miles of downtown roofs at the constellation of distant lights marking Federal Hill. Now and then he would fumblingly make an entry in his diary, so that detached phrases such as "The lights must not go"; "It knows where I am"; "I must destroy it"; and "It is calling to me, but perhaps it means no injury this time"; are found scattered down two of the pages.

Then the lights went out all over the city. It happened at 2.12 a.m. according to power-house records, but Blake's diary gives no indication of the time. The entry is merely, "Lights out—God help me." On Federal Hill there were watchers as anxious as he, and rain-soaked knots of men paraded the square and alleys around the evil church with umbrella-shaded candles, electric flashlights, oil lanterns, crucifixes, and obscure charms of the many sorts common to southern Italy. They blessed each flash of lightning, and made cryptical signs of fear with their right hands when a turn in the storm caused the flashes to lessen and finally to cease altogether. A rising wind blew out most of the candles, so that the scene grew threateningly dark. Someone roused Father Merluzzo of Spirito Santo Church, and he hastened to the dismal square to pronounce whatever helpful syllables he could. Of the restless and curious sounds in the blackened tower, there could be no doubt whatever.

For what happened at 2.35 we have the testimony of the priest, a young, intelligent, and well-educated person; of Patrolman William J. Monahan of the Central Station, an officer of the highest reliability who had paused at that part of his beat to inspect the crowd; and of most of the seventy-eight men who had gathered around the church's high bank wall—especially those in the square where the eastward façade was visible. Of course there was nothing which can be proved as being outside the order of Nature. The possible causes of such an event are many. No one can speak with certainty of the obscure chemical processes arising in a vast, ancient, ill-aired, and long-deserted building of heterogeneous contents. Mephitic vapours—spontaneous combustion—pressure of gases born of long decay—any one of numberless phenomena might be responsible. And then, of course, the factor of conscious charlatanry can by no means be excluded. The thing was really quite simple in itself, and covered less than three minutes of actual time. Father Merluzzo, always a precise man, looked at his watch repeatedly.

It started with a definite swelling of the dull fumbling sounds inside the black tower. There had for some time been a vague exhalation of strange, evil odours from the church, and this had now become emphatic and offensive. Then at last there was a sound of splintering wood, and a large, heavy object crashed down in the yard beneath the frowning easterly façade. The tower was invisible now that the candles would not burn, but as the object neared the ground the people knew that it was the smoke-grimed louvre-boarding of that tower's east window.

Immediately afterwards an utterly unbearable foetor welled forth from the unseen heights, choking and sickening the trembling watchers, and almost prostrating those in the square. At the same time the air trembled with a vibration as of flapping wings, and a sudden east-blowing wind more violent than any previous blast snatched off the hats and wrenched the dripping umbrellas of the crowd. Nothing definite could be seen in the candleless night, though some upward-looking spectators thought they glimpsed a great spreading blur of denser blackness against the inky sky—something like a formless cloud of smoke that shot with meteor-like speed towards the east.

That was all. The watchers were half numbed with fright, awe, and discomfort, and scarcely knew what to do, or whether to do anything at all. Not knowing what had happened, they did not relax their vigil; and a moment later they sent up a prayer as a sharp flash of belated lightning, followed by an earsplitting crash of sound, rent the flooded heavens. Half an hour later the rain stopped, and in fifteen minutes more the street lights sprang on again, sending the weary, bedraggled watchers relievedly back to their homes.

The next day's papers gave these matters minor mention in connection with the general storm reports. It seems that the great lightning flash and deafening explosion which followed the Federal Hill occurrence were even more tremendous farther east, where a burst of the singular foetor was likewise noticed. The phenomenon was most marked over College Hill, where the crash awakened all the sleeping inhabitants and led to a bewildered round of speculations. Of those who were already awake only a few saw the anomalous blaze of light near the top of the hill, or noticed the inexplicable upward rush of air which almost stripped the leaves from the trees and blasted the plants in the gardens. It was agreed that the lone, sudden lightning bolt must have struck somewhere in this neighbourhood, though no trace of its striking could afterwards be found. A youth in the Tau Omega fraternity house thought he saw a grotesque and hideous mass of smoke in the air just as the preliminary flash burst, but his observation has not been verified. All of the few observers, however, agree as to the violent gust from the west and the flood of intolerable stench which preceded the belated stroke, whilst evidence concerning the momentary burned odour after the stroke is equally general.

These points were discussed very carefully because of their probable connection with the death of Robert Blake. Students in the Psi Delta house, whose upper rear windows looked into Blake's study, noticed the blurred white face at the westward window on the morning of the 9th, and wondered what was wrong with the expression. When they saw the same face in the same position that evening, they felt worried, and watched for the lights to come up in his apartment. Later they rang the bell of the darkened flat, and finally had a policeman force the door.

The rigid body sat bolt upright at the desk by the window, and when the intruders saw the glassy, bulging eyes, and the marks of stark, convulsive fright on the twisted features, they turned away in sickened dismay. Shortly afterwards the coroner's physician made an examination, and despite the unbroken window reported electrical shock, or nervous tension induced by electrical discharge, as the cause of death. The hideous expression he ignored altogether, deeming it a not improbable result of the profound shock as experienced by a person of such abnormal imagination and unbalanced emotions. He deduced these latter qualities from the books, paintings, and manuscripts found in the apartment, and from the blindly scrawled entries in the diary on the desk. Blake had prolonged his frenzied jottings to the last, and the broken-pointed pencil was found clutched in his spasmodically contracted right hand.

The entries after the failure of the lights were highly disjointed, and legible only in part. From them certain investigators have drawn conclusions differing greatly from the materialistic official verdict, but such speculations have little chance for belief among the conservative. The case of these imaginative theorists has not been helped by the action of superstitious Dr Dexter, who threw the curious box and angled stone—an object certainly self-luminous as seen in the black windowless steeple where it was found—into the deepest channel of Narragansett Bay. Excessive imagination and neurotic unbalance on Blake's part, aggravated by knowledge of the evil bygone cult whose startling traces he had uncovered, form the dominant interpretation given those final frenzied jottings. These are the entries—or all that can be made of them.

"Lights still out—must be five minutes now. Everything depends on lightning. Yaddith grant it will keep up!... Some influence seems beating through it.... Rain and thunder and wind deafen.... The thing is taking hold of my mind....

"Trouble with memory. I see things I never knew before. Other worlds and other galaxies... Dark... The lightning seems dark and the darkness seems light....

"It cannot be the real hill and church that I see in the pitch-darkness. Must be retinal impression left by flashes. Heaven grant the Italians are out with their candles if the lightning stops!

"What am I afraid of? Is it not an avatar of Nyarlathotep, who in antique and shadowy Khem even took the form of man? I remember Yuggoth, and more distant Shaggai, and the ultimate void of the black planets....

"The long, winging flight through the void... cannot cross the universe of light... re-created by the thoughts caught in the Shining Trapezohedron... send it through the horrible abysses of radiance....

"My name is Blake—Robert Harrison Blake of 620 East Knapp Street, Milwaukee, Wisconsin.... I am on this planet....

"Azathoth have mercy!—the lightning no longer flashes—horrible—I can see everything with a monstrous sense that is not sight—light is dark and dark is light... those people on the hill... guard... candles and charms... their priests....

"Sense of distance gone—far is near and near is far. No light—no glass—see that steeple—that tower—window—can hear—Roderick Usher—am mad or going mad—the thing is stirring and fumbling in the tower—I am it and it is I—I want to get out... must get out and unify the forces.... It knows where I am....

"I am Robert Blake, but I see the tower in the dark. There is a monstrous odour... senses transfigured... boarding at that tower window cracking and giving way.... Iä... ngai... ygg....

"I see it—coming here—hell-wind—titan blur—black wings—Yog-Sothoth save me—the three-lobed burning eye..."

THE INTERRUPTION

W.W. Jacobs

I

THE LAST of the funeral guests had gone and Spencer Goddard, in decent black, sat alone in his small, well-furnished study. There was a queer sense of freedom in the house since the coffin had left it; the coffin which was now hidden in its solitary grave beneath the yellow earth. The air, which for the last three days had seemed stale and contaminated, now smelt fresh and clean.

He went to the open window and, looking into the fading light of the autumn day, took a deep breath. He closed the window, and, stooping down, put a match to the fire, and, dropping into his easy chair, sat listening to the cheery crackle of the wood. At the age of thirty-eight he had turned over a fresh page. Life, free and unencumbered, was before him. His dead wife's money was at last his, to spend as he pleased instead of being doled out in reluctant driblets.

He turned at a step at the door and his face assumed the appearance of gravity and sadness it had worn for the last four days. The cook, with the same air of decorous grief, entered the room quietly and, crossing to the mantelpiece placed upon it a photograph.

"I thought you'd like to have it, sir," she said, in a low voice, "to remind you."

Goddard thanked her, and, rising, took it in his hand and stood regarding it. He noticed with satisfaction that his hand was absolutely steady.

"It is a very good likeness—till she was taken ill," continued the woman. "I never saw anybody change so sudden."

"The nature of her disease, Hannah," said her master.

The woman nodded, and, dabbing at her eyes with her handkerchief, stood regarding him. "Is there anything you want?" he inquired, after a time.

She shook her head. "I can't believe she's gone," she said, in a low voice. "Every now and then I have a queer feeling that she's still here—and wanting to tell me something."

"It's your nerves," said her master sharply.

By a great effort Goddard refrained from looking at her.

"Nerves," he said again. "Perhaps you ought to have a little holiday. It has been a great strain upon you."

"You, too, sir," said the woman respectfully. "Waiting on her hand and foot as you have done, I can't think how you stood it. If you'd only had a nurse—"

"I preferred to do it myself, Hannah," said her master. "If I had had a nurse it would have alarmed her."

The woman assented. "And they are always peeking and prying into what doesn't concern them," she added. "Always think they know more than the doctors do."

Goddard turned a slow look upon her. The tall, angular figure was standing in an attitude of respectful attention; the cold slaty-brown eyes were cast down, the sullen face expressionless.

"She couldn't have had a better doctor," he said, looking at the fire again. "No man could have done more for her."

"And nobody could have done more for her than you did, sir," was the reply. "There's few husbands that would have done what you did."

Goddard stiffened in his chair. "That will do, Hannah," he said curtly.

"Or done it so well," said the woman, with measured slowness.

With a strange, sinking sensation, her master paused to regain his control. Then he turned and eyed her steadily. "Thank you," he said, slowly; "you mean well, but at present I cannot discuss it."

For some time after the door had closed behind her he sat in deep thought. The feeling of well-being of a few minutes before had vanished, leaving in its place an apprehension which he refused to consider, but which would not be allayed. He thought over his actions of the last few weeks, carefully, and could remember no flaw. His wife's illness, the doctor's diagnosis, his own solicitous care, were all in keeping with the ordinary. He tried to remember the woman's exact words—her manner. Something had shown him Fear. What?

He could have laughed at his fears next morning. The dining room was full of sunshine and the fragrance of coffee and bacon was in the air. Better still, a worried and commonplace Hannah. Worried over two eggs with false birth certificates, over the vendor of which she became almost lyrical.

"The bacon is excellent," said her smiling master, "so is the coffee; but your coffee always is."

Hannah smiled in return, and, taking fresh eggs from a rosy-cheeked maid, put them before him.

A pipe, followed by a brisk walk, cheered him still further. He came home glowing with exercise and again possessed with that sense of freedom and freshness. He went into the garden—now his own—and planned alterations.

After lunch he went over the house. The windows of his wife's bedroom were open and the room neat and airy. His glance wandered from the made-up bed to the brightly polished furniture. Then he went to the dressing-table and opened the drawers, searching each in turn. With the exception of a few odds and ends they were empty. He went out onto the landing and called for Hannah.

"Do you know whether your mistress locked up any of her things?" he inquired.

"What things?" said the woman.

"Well, her jewellery mostly."

"Oh !" Hannah smiled. "She gave it all to me," she said, quietly.

Goddard checked an exclamation. His heart was beating nervously, but he spoke sternly.

"When?"

"Just before she died—of gastro-enteritis," said the woman.

There was a long silence. He turned and with great care mechanically closed the drawers of the dressing-table. The tilted glass showed him the pallor of his face, and he spoke without turning round.

"That is all right, then," he said, huskily. "I only wanted to know what had become of it. I thought, perhaps, Milly—"

Hannah shook her head. "Milly's all right," she said, with a strange smile. "She's as honest as we are. Is there anything more you want, sir?"

She closed the door behind her with the quietness of the well-trained servant; Goddard, steadying himself with his hand on the rail of the bed, stood looking into the future.

II

The days passed monotonously, as they pass with a man in prison. Gone was the sense of freedom and the idea of a wider life. Instead of a cell, a house with ten rooms—but

Hannah, the jailer, guarding each one. Respectful and attentive, the model servant, he saw in every word a threat against his liberty—his life. In the sullen face and cold eyes he saw her knowledge of power; in her solicitude for his comfort and approval, a sardonic jest. It was the master playing at being the servant. The years of unwilling servitude were over, but she felt her way carefully with infinite zest in the game. Warped and bitter, with a cleverness which had never before had scope, she had entered into her kingdom. She took it little by little, savouring every morsel.

"I hope I've done right, sir," she said one morning. "I have given Milly notice."

Goddard looked up from his paper. "Isn't she satisfactory?" he inquired.

"Not to my thinking, sir," said the woman. "And she says she is coming to see you about it. I told her that would be no good."

"I had better see her and hear what she has to say," said her master.

"Of course, if you wish to," said Hannah; "only, after giving her notice, if she doesn't go I shall. I should be sorry to go—I've been very comfortable here—but it's either her or me."

"I should be sorry to lose you," said Goddard in a hopeless voice.

" Thank you, sir," said Hannah. "I'm sure I've tried to do my best. I've been with you some time now—and I know all your little ways. I expect I understand you better than anybody else would. I do all I can to make you comfortable."

"Very well, I will leave it to you," said Goddard in a voice which strove to be brisk and commanding. "You have my permission to dismiss her."

"There's another thing I wanted to see you about," said Hannah; "my wages. I was going to ask for a rise, seeing that I'm really housekeeper here now."

"Certainly," said her master, considering, "that only seems fair. Let me see—what are you getting?"

"Thirty-six."

Goddard reflected for a moment and then turned with a benevolent smile. "Very well," he said, cordially, "I'll make it forty-two. That's ten shillings a month more."

"I was thinking of a hundred," said Hannah dryly.

The significance of the demand appalled him. "Rather a big jump," he said at last. "I really don't know that I—"

"It doesn't matter," said Hannah. "I thought I was worth it—to you that's all. You know best. Some people might think I was worth *two* hundred. That's a bigger jump, but after all a big jump is better than—"

She broke off and tittered. Goddard eyed her. "than a big drop," she concluded.

Her master's face set. The lips almost disappeared and something came into the pale eyes that was revolting. Still eyeing her, he rose and approached her. She stood her ground and met him eye to eye.

"You are jocular," he said at last.

" Short life and a merry one," said the woman.

"Mine or yours?"

" Both, perhaps," was the reply.

"If—if I give you a hundred," said Goddard, moistening his lips, "that ought to make your life merrier, at any rate."

Hannah nodded. "Merry and long, perhaps," she said slowly. "I'm careful, you know—very careful."

"I am sure you are," said Goddard, his face relaxing. "Careful what I eat and drink, I mean," said the woman, eyeing him steadily.

"That is wise," he said slowly. "I am myself—that is why I am paying a good cook a large salary. But don't overdo things, Hannah; don't kill the goose that lays the golden eggs."

"I am not likely to do that," she said coldly. "Live and let live; that is my motto. Some people have different ones. But I'm careful; nobody won't catch me napping. I've left a letter with my sister, in case."

Goddard turned slowly and in a casual fashion put the flowers straight in a bowl on the table, and, wandering to the window, looked out. His face was white again and his hands trembled.

"To be opened after my death," continued Hannah. "I don't believe in doctors—not after what I've seen of them—I don't think they know enough; so if I die I shall be examined. I've given good reasons."

"And suppose," said Goddard, coming from the window, "suppose she is curious, and opens it before you die?"

"We must chance that," said Hannah, shrugging her shoulders; "but I don't think she will. I sealed it up with sealing wax, with a mark on it."

"She might open it and say nothing about it," persisted her master.

An unwholesome grin spread slowly over Hannah's features. "I should know it soon enough," she declared boisterously, "and so would other people. Lord there would be an upset! Chidham would have something to talk about for once. We should be in the papers—both of us."

Goddard forced a smile. "Dear me !" he said gently. "Your pen seems to be a dangerous weapon, Hannah, but I hope that the need to open it will not happen for another fifty years. You look well and strong."

The woman nodded. "I don't take up my troubles before they come," she said, with a satisfied air; "but there's no harm in trying to prevent them coming. Prevention is better than cure."

"Exactly," said her master; "and, by the way, there's no need for this little financial arrangement to be known by anybody else. I might become unpopular with my neighbours for setting a bad example. Of course, I am giving you this sum because I really think you are worth it."

"I'm sure you do," said Hannah. "I'm not sure I ain't worth more, but this'll do to go on with. I shall get a girl for less than we are paying Milly, and that'll be another little bit extra for me."

"Certainly," said Goddard, and smiled again.

" Come to think of it," said Hannah pausing at the door, "I ain't sure I shall get anybody else; then there'll be more than ever for me. If I do the work I might as well have the money."

Her master nodded, and, left to himself, sat down to think out a position which was as intolerable as it was dangerous. At a great risk he had escaped from the dominion of one woman only to fall, bound and helpless, into the hands of another. However vague and unconvincing the suspicions of Hannah might be, they would be sufficient. Evidence could be unearthed. Cold with fear one moment, and hot with fury the next, he sought in vain for some avenue of escape. It was his brain against that of a cunning, illiterate fool; a fool whose malicious stupidity only added to his danger. And she drank. With largely increased wages she would drink more and his very life might depend upon a hiccuped boast. It was clear that she was enjoying her supremacy; later on her vanity would urge her to display it before others.

He might have to obey the crack of her whip before witnesses, and that would cut off all possibility of escape. He sat with his head in his hands. There must be a way out and he must find it. Soon. He must find it before gossip began; before the changed position of master and servant lent colour to her story when that story became known.

Shaking with fury, he thought of her lean, ugly throat and the joy of choking her life out with his fingers. He started suddenly, and took a quick breath. No, not fingers—a rope.

III

Bright and cheerful outside and with his friends, in the house he was quiet and submissive. Milly had gone, and, if the service was poorer and the rooms neglected, he gave no sign. If a bell remained unanswered he made no complaint, and to studied insolence turned the other cheek of politeness. When at this tribute to her power the woman smiled, he smiled in return. A smile which, for all its disarming softness, left her vaguely uneasy.

"I'm not afraid of you," she said once, with a menacing air.

"I hope not," said Goddard in a slightly surprised voice.

"Some people might be, but I'm not," she declared. "If anything happened to me—"

"Nothing could happen to such a careful woman as you are," he said, smiling again. "You ought to live to ninety—with luck."

It was clear to him that the situation was getting on his nerves. Unremembered but terrible dreams haunted his sleep. Dreams in which some great, inevitable disaster was always pressing upon him, although he could never discover what it was. Each morning he awoke unrefreshed to face another day of torment. He could not meet the woman's eyes for fear of revealing the threat that was in his own.

Delay was dangerous and foolish. He had thought out every move in that contest of wits which was to remove the shadow of the rope from his own neck and place it about that of the woman. There was a little risk, but the stake was a big one. He had but to set the ball rolling and others would keep it on its course. It was time to act.

He came in a little jaded from his afternoon walk, and left his tea untouched. He ate but little dinner, and, sitting hunched up over the fire, told the woman that he had taken a slight chill. Her concern, he felt grimly, might have been greater if she had known the cause.

He was no better next day, and after lunch called in to consult his doctor. He left with a clean bill of health except for a slight digestive derangement, the remedy for which he took away with him in a bottle. For two days he swallowed one tablespoonful three times a day in water, without result, then he took to his bed.

"A day or two in bed won't hurt you," said the doctor. "Show me that tongue of yours again."

But, what is the matter with me, Roberts?" inquired the patient.

The doctor pondered. "Nothing to trouble about—nerves a bit wrong—digestion a little bit impaired. You'll be all right in a day or two."

Goddard nodded. So far, so good; Roberts had not outlived his usefulness. He smiled grimly after the doctor had left at the surprise he was preparing for him. A little rough on Roberts and his professional reputation, perhaps, but these things could not be avoided.

He lay back and visualized the programme. A day or two longer, getting gradually worse, then a little sickness. After that a nervous, somewhat shamefaced patient hinting at things. His food had a queer taste—he felt worse after taking it; he knew it was ridiculous, still—there was some of his beef-tea he had put aside, perhaps the doctor would like to examine it? and the medicine? Secretions, too; perhaps he would like to see those?

Propped on his elbow, he stared fixedly at the wall. There would be a trace—a faint trace—of arsenic in the secretions. There would be more than a trace in the other things. An attempt to poison him would be clearly indicated, and his wife's symptoms had resembled his own—let Hannah get out of the web he was spinning if she could. As for the letter she had threatened him with, let her produce it; it could only recoil upon herself. Fifty letters could not save her from the doom he was preparing for her. It was her life or his, and he would show no mercy. For three days he doctored himself with sedulous care, watching himself anxiously the while. His nerve was going and he knew it. Before him was the strain of the discovery, the arrest, and the trial. The gruesome business of his wife's death. A long business. He would wait no longer, and he would open the proceedings with dramatic suddenness.

It was between nine and ten o'clock at night when he

rang his bell, and it was not until he had rung four times that he heard the heavy steps of Hannah mounting the stairs. "What d'you want?" she demanded, standing in the doorway.

"I'm very ill," he said, gasping. "Run for the doctor. Quick!"

The woman stared at him in genuine amazement. "What, at this time o' night?" she exclaimed. Not likely."

"I'm dying!" said Goddard in a broken voice."

"Not you," she said, roughly. "You'll be better in the morning."

"I'm dying," he repeated. "Go—for—the—doctor."

The woman hesitated. The rain beat in heavy squalls against the window, and the doctor's house was a mile distant on the lonely road. She glanced at the figure on the bed. "I should catch my death o' cold," she grumbled. She stood sullenly regarding him. He certainly looked very ill, and his death would by no means benefit her. She listened, scowling, to the wind and the rain.

"All right," she said at last, and went noisily from the room.

His face set in a mirthless smile, he heard her bustling about below. The front door slammed violently and he was alone. He waited for a few moments and then, getting out of bed, put on his dressing gown and set about his preparations. With a steady hand he added a little white powder to the remains of his beef-tea and to the contents of his bottle of medicine. He stood listening a moment at some faint sound from below, and, having satisfied himself, lit a candle and made his way to Hannah's room. For a space he stood irresolute, looking about him. Then he opened one of the drawers and, placing the broken packet of powder under a pile of clothing at the back, made his way back to bed.

He was disturbed to find that he was trembling with excitement and nervousness. He longed for tobacco, but that was impossible. To reassure himself he began to rehearse his conversation with the doctor, and again he thought over every possible complication. The scene with the woman would be terrible; he would have to be too ill to take any part in it. The less he said the better. Others would do all that was necessary.

He lay for a long time listening to the sound of the wind and the rain. Inside, the house seemed unusually quiet, and with an odd sensation he suddenly realised that it was the first time he had been alone in it since his wife's death. He remembered that she would have to be disturbed. The thought was unwelcome. He did not want her to be disturbed. Let the dead sleep. He sat up in bed and drew his watch from beneath the pillow. Hannah ought to have been back before; in any case she could not be long now. At any moment he might hear her key in the lock. He lay down again and reminded himself that things were shaping well. He had shaped them, and some of the satisfaction of the artist was his.

The silence was oppressive. The house seemed to be listening, waiting. He looked at his watch again and wondered, with a curse, what had happened to the woman. It was clear that the doctor must be out, but that was no reason for her delay. It was close on midnight, and the atmosphere of the house seemed in some strange fashion to be brooding and hostile.

In a lull in the wind he thought he heard footsteps outside, and his face cleared as he sat up listening for the sound of the key in the door below. In another moment the woman would be in the house and the fears engendered by a disordered fancy would have flown. The sound of the steps had ceased, but he could hear no sound of entrance. Until all hope had gone, he sat listening. He was certain he had heard footsteps. Whose?

Trembling and haggard he sat waiting, assailed by a crowd of murmuring fears. One whispered that he had failed and would have to pay the penalty of failing; that he had gambled with Death and lost.

By a strong effort he fought down these fancies and, closing his eyes, tried to compose himself to rest. It was evident now that the doctor was out and that Hannah was waiting to return with him in his car. He was frightening himself for nothing. At any moment he might hear the sound of their arrival.

He heard something else, and, sitting up, suddenly, tried to think what it was and what had caused it. It was a very faint sound—stealthy. Holding his breath, he waited for it to be repeated. He heard it again, the mere ghost of a sound—a whisper of a sound, but significant as most whispers are.

He wiped his brow with his sleeve and told himself firmly that it was nerves, and nothing but nerves; but, against his will, he still listened. He fancied now that the sound came from his wife's room, the other side of the landing. It increased in loudness and became more insistent, but with his eyes fixed on the door of his room he still kept himself in hand, and tried to listen instead to the wind and the rain.

For a time he heard nothing but that. Then there came a scraping, scurrying noise from his wife's room, and a sudden, terrific crash.

With a loud scream his nerve broke, and springing from the bed he sped downstairs and, flinging open the front-door, dashed into the night. The door, caught by the wind, slammed behind him. With his hand holding the garden gate open, ready for further flight, he stood sobbing for breath. His bare feet were bruised and the rain was very cold, but he took no heed. Then he ran a little way along the road and stood for some time, hoping and listening.

He came back slowly. The wind was bitter and he was soaked to the skin. The garden was black and forbidding, and unspeakable horror might be lurking in the bushes. He went up the road again, trembling with cold. Then, in desperation, he passed through the terrors of the garden to the house, only to find the door closed. The porch gave a little protection from the icy rain, but none from the wind, and, shaking in every limb, he leaned in abject misery against the door. He pulled himself together after a time and stumbled round to the back door. Locked! And all the lower windows were shuttered. He made his way back to the porch, and, crouching there in hopeless misery, waited for the woman to return.

IV

He had a dim memory when he awoke of somebody questioning him, and then of being half-pushed, half-carried upstairs to bed. There was something wrong with his head and his chest and he was trembling violently, and very cold. Somebody was speaking.

"You must have taken leave of your senses," said the voice of Hannah. "I thought you were dead."

He forced his eyes to open. "Doctor," he muttered, "Doctor."

"Out on a bad case," said Hannah. "I waited till I was tired of waiting, and then came along. Good thing for you I did. He'll be round first thing this morning. He ought to be here now."

She bustled about, tidying up the room, his leaden eyes following her as she collected the beef-tea and other things on a tray and carried them out.

"Nice thing I did yesterday," she remarked, as she came back. "Left the missus's bedroom window open. When I opened the door this morning I found that beautiful Chippendale glass of hers had blown off the table and smashed to pieces. Did you hear it?"

Goddard made no reply. In a confused fashion he was trying to think. Accident or not, the fall of the glass had served its purpose. Were there such things as accidents? Or was Life a puzzle—a puzzle into which every piece was made to fit? Fear and the wind… no: conscience and the wind… had saved the woman. He must get the powder back from her drawer… before she discovered it and denounced him. The medicine… he must remember not to take it… He was very ill, seriously ill. He must have taken a chill owing to that panic flight into the garden. Why didn't the doctor come? He had come… at last… he was doing something to his chest… it was cold. Again… the doctor… there was something he wanted to tell him. Hannah and a powder… what was it?

Later on he remembered, together with other things that he had hoped to forget. He lay watching an endless procession of memories, broken at times by a glance at the doctor, the nurse, and Hannah, who were all standing near the bed regarding him. They had been there a long time, and they were all very quiet. The last time he looked at Hannah was the first time for months that he had looked at her without loathing and hatred. Then he knew that he was dying.

THE BLACK COURTYARD

Thomas Burke

Nobody saw him. In the late evening of that winter day he came creeping from that riverside courtyard—a courtyard thick with darkness, and alive only with silence and the eyes of blind houses; and nobody saw him. He was slim, and his body in movement was elastic. He walked with a rhythmic padding step. He presented himself to the eye as a heavy overcoat, a soft hat, and a muffler.

That evening, in all parts of London, was an evening of intense darkness; starless and heavy with rain. But in the east the already dark streets were put to confusion by a river-mist. In this mist the lamps were dabs of phosphorescence. The shop lights blessed only a foot of the pavement, and even the torches of the stalls could achieve no more than a luminosity which was no light at all. Belated shoppers moved in and out of the little shops in the form of floating faces. The narrow thoroughfare was populous with the creatures of all nations, but amid the shifting veils of mist one could not know white man from Cingalese, nor yellow man from negro,* nor honest man from skulker. They were no more than spectral shapes of Man.

Perrace, the muffled figure coming from the courtyard, was one of them. Nowhere was the darkness more intense than there. So intense was it that it seemed to have a quality of life. It menaced the eyes and pressed upon the face. Its silence seemed to whisper upon the ears. It was an organism of blackness whose tendrils almost throttled the breath. But to Perrace and his purposes this profusion of darkness was kind.

As he came from the courtyard the river sent to land the howl of a foghorn, and from distant byways came the cries of roysterers. A banjo could be heard; a gramophone; an over-tuned radio. Thick, rough life, and the rumour of unseen life, surged all about him; but Perrace, padding his solitary way, was concerned with death.

He padded along the High Street. He padded up Love Lane. He padded along Cable Street and along Brook Street, and as he passed from one street to another the tempo of his padding increased, and gave him the air of one in flight.

He *was* in flight. He was fleeing not from fear of arrest, but from fear of a courtyard thick with darkness, deaf to noise, and alive only with the eyes of blind houses. Those

* These terms, now understood to be offensive, were commonly used at the time this story was published. 'Cingalese' is an archaic spelling of Singhalese, a people of Sri Lanka.

houses had seen nothing; in that darkness they could not, even unshuttered, have seen; yet their very blindness had shot him with a deeper fear than the fear of capture. They and the courtyard in which they stood were before him now. They were like figures threatening. They seemed to say "We didn't see, but we *know*. And we're going to make you pay." In the effort to shake them from his eyes he padded faster and faster. He turned into Stepney Causeway, and loped along it, and did not fall to his customary rhythm until he came out to the misty glitter and clamour of Commercial Road.

There he paused, uncertain of his next action. But his mind told him that action was imperative: he must not linger; he must not be seen here. He debated by which way he should return home, but so many ways came to his mind that he could not decide upon one for thought of the others. Then, when he had hesitated some two minutes, a string of westward buses, lumbering out of the mist, settled the matter for him. Their presence brought him out of his paralysis; with automatic movements he boarded the first of them and climbed to the top. He sat down with a heavy sigh.

Life on a sudden seemed unaccountably strange. He was still alive, breathing through his nose, seeing with his eyes. Yet his state of being was not the state of being of a few hours ago. He was sitting on a bus; a bus like other buses; but charged to his mind with some intense and un-buslike essence. Like that courtyard and that darkness and those houses, it seemed alive. This was Perrace sitting on the bus—Perrace, himself yet not himself. The same hair, the same eyes, the same hands, the same flow of conscious memory. Yet a Perrace who was a stranger to him.

At the bottom of his mind was a faint feeling, or perhaps a faint hope, that soon he would wake up and find himself warm and comfortable in his bed at Kingsland Road. The top of his mind knew that he wouldn't. He looked down at his overcoat. It was his overcoat, his quite ordinary overcoat. Since the day he bought it he had never really seen it. Now he saw it, and the coat, too, seemed to come to life. He had put it on that afternoon as casually as he always put it on. But that was before the Idea had come to him. He knew that he would not take it off casually. It was now an experienced overcoat; dramatic overcoat; it had been in that courtyard. It might even become a famous overcoat.

At that thought he shivered, and felt sick. Events of the last two hours recurred to him. They had the complexion of that truth which is insistently truth but incomprehensible by human reason. That accursed courtyard had created them.

He recalled the courtyard, and he recalled the dark room, and he recalled the bent, questioning figure of the old man. And he recalled the old man lying still and pulseless on the floor. And he recalled the escape by the window. He recalled how often he had haunted that courtyard, and how often the courtyard had haunted *him*. He recalled how it had set things in his mind. How it had lived there, peacefully malignant, suggesting sin, but never the price of sin. How it had beckoned him to give it the story for which it was made. He recalled the many times when he had looked into it and looked at a certain house, and had thought of the hundreds of notes which the stupid feeble old man was known to hoard; notes which meant so much to one who was out of a job. He recalled how he had planned the affair over drinks in the—what was the name of the place? He recalled how he had first brushed the idea aside—its mere presence had given him a fit of tremors—and how, later, he had gibed at himself for a coward, and screwed himself up to it. He recalled how clear it had been in his mind during the long evening.

It was when he had come to set it to action that it had gone blurred and feverish. Coming out of the courtyard had been like a waking-up. He could not recall entering the house; he could only dimly recall being there. He could not recall what he had started to do; he could recall only what had been done. He could not recall what desk or cupboard or safe he had opened. He could not even recall the contents of the room. He could recall only its darkness and its shape. He could not recall finding the money, nor, if he found it, what he had done with it. He knew only that he had brought none of it away. He could not recall the entrance of the miser to the room; he could recall only the patch on the dark floor.

The two really vivid memories were of going into the courtyard, and of coming out of it. Once or twice he had a feeling that it had never happened, but in the moment of the feeling a dim glow of memory told him that the feeling was merely a reflection of his agonised wish.

He was suffering and making forlorn efforts to escape the suffering. Above the imps of thought that were dancing on his brain hovered the word MURDER. It seemed ludicrous, insane almost, that this word could be fastened to the name Perrace. This Perrace was known to his few acquaintances as a fellow like other fellows. A fellow who had no life beyond the life which society allows to a poor man—the life of a steady worker, a respectable nine-o'clock-to-six-o'clock employee who held no opinions to attract remark, who did nothing today that would be remembered tomorrow, and to whom nothing outside routine ever happened. And now he had broken the bounds of routine and opened its quiet to the claws of peril and dread.

Never again would he sleep securely. Never again would he walk the streets carelessly. Life and death had broken in upon his coma, and he, who had hitherto faced only the shadow of them, must now, through the memory of a black courtyard, face the reality. And he was not ready to face it. He had acted before he had reached the mood for action. He was unprepared. He hadn't *meant* to do it. Yet they would brand him, and if they seized him they would talk about him as though he were an animal, and not Perrace, the ordinary, likeable fellow. And then they would kill him.

He had always been assured, as most of us are, that while other men might commit murder, he, Perrace, never could.

He had read in newspapers of men who committed murder, but he had read of them as monsters, remote creatures of another plane and another state; not as fellow-creatures of the world he lived in. They were not men who rode in buses and worked in offices and were sometimes out of a job, and sat in tea shops and went to whist drives and did a bit of gardening on Saturday afternoons. They were Murderers; something apart.

Yet this night he had been presented in that courtyard with himself in that shape, a self which he knew was his but which he could not recognise; a self from which he revolted. Perrace, the ordinary likeable fellow, turned within an hour into a creature who belonged in that affrighting gallery in the basement of Tussaud's. It was ludicrous. It was like a tale of a millionaire forging a cheque for five pounds. But a persistent spot in his brain said: "Yes—but true." His quiescent mind said: "It isn't. It isn't. I didn't do it. I didn't." His active mind drowned it with "You did. You did. You may not have meant to, but you did."

Under these conflicting mental revolutions he suffered a loathing of his existence, and a bilious horror of the black courtyard. It was beginning to torment him. It danced in his mind, and his mind interpreted it to his sight and his body as clammy shadows touching the skin. In that long ride through Stepney, Aldgate and the City, he saw, wherever he looked, a courtyard thick with darkness, deaf to noise and alive only with the eyes of blind houses. A courtyard that might tempt a man and encourage him to all manner of enormities and then turn upon him.

He left the bus at the Bank and caught a last bus for Shoreditch. He was aware that he moved rationally and spoke rationally, but this behaviour, he knew, came from the last automatic movements of his real self. That self, the self he had known these thirty years, was now lying numb and bemused. It seemed to be fading from him, his being was slowly passing into possession of a new stranger-self.

He did not like this new self, and fought against surrendering to it. But there was no question of his surrendering. It was insistently taking possession of him a nervous, feverish self that had crept out of a courtyard thick with darkness and deaf to noise. He wondered whether all murderers were possessed like this. From their behaviour in court he felt that they were not. Murder seemed to make them stronger instead of weaker, more callous instead of more sensitive.

In his room at Kingsland Road he took off his overcoat and hung it on a coat hanger. From the other side of the room he turned to look at it. It seemed to look back at him. He took off his boots and looked at them, and they too seemed different from other boots. Mighty and terrible boots. At any moment, he foolishly felt, coat and boots might become articulate. The sight of them began to fret his already fretted mind. He gathered them up and stowed them into a cupboard. For the next half-hour he padded about the room.

From time to time he brushed his arm across his eyes. Somewhere on his retina was the image of a black courtyard. He went to the mirror to see if he could find it. Then realised his own folly, and gave a weak laugh, and again felt sick. Under this sickness he crept to the bed and fell on it, and, not expecting sleep, slept. But in the sleep he was aware that he was sleeping on the stones of a black courtyard.

He awoke as Perrace, to a few shreds of his own self not yet destroyed; but in a few seconds, when fully awake, he realised that he was no longer Perrace. He was a creature out of a black courtyard, and he existed only in relation to that courtyard. He was its prisoner.

Overriding the memory of last night's affair was the more awful presence of this manifestation. He was in the world, but he was enclosed from it. He could see it only through the shadows of his courtyard.

He strove to shoulder it away by movement. He got up and exercised himself. He plunged his head and neck into cold water. He went over himself with a rough towel. He felt too sick to eat the breakfast his landlady had prepared, but he drank two cups of tea and nibbled some bread. At ten o'clock he went out and walked wherever the streets led him.

Throughout the day he loafed about the main streets of the poorer quarters. He wandered from Oxford Street to St John's Wood, from there to Camden Town, then to Finsbury Park, to Highgate, to Islington, to Euston Road, to Charing Cross, Waterloo Road, to Kennington,

Camberwell, Peckham. After some hours of walking at his gentle padding pace, his mind cleared and things began to adjust themselves. In the light he regained something of his old self; a little of the everyday confidence he had known before yesterday. He began to feel that he had exaggerated the affair and his own fears. In the afternoon sun the black courtyard seemed far away in distance and in time and in conception. Neither the morning papers nor the evening papers carried a line about that courtyard. No doubt in a day or two it would fade from his mind as other incidents faded from the mind. Within a month he would perhaps have to make an effort to recall anything about that courtyard. It might be weeks yet before the secret was discovered, and there would be nothing by which they could connect it with him. In momentary facetiousness the thought occurred to him that anyway it was his first offence.

But when night came upon the city he learned that the courtyard was only beginning its work upon him. He had not noted the approach of dusk, and he was walking along Rye Lane, Peckham, when the horror descended. The haunting took material shape. He was certain that it was Rye Lane. He had seen its name on a plate at a corner. Yet, turning suddenly from a brilliant shop-window, he found that he was not in Rye Lane. Shops and lights had disappeared. He was in that black courtyard.

He could feel its darkness upon his face; he could hear its crowding silence; he could see the sightless eyes of its houses. A dry choking seized his throat. He turned in panic to get out of the place. He tore through the courtyard, and down the entrance alley. As he ran, he was aware of shouts and noises. Dimly he saw scared faces about him, and heard the grinding of brakes. He had a vision of a lorry striking his shoulder, of a bus driver making a scowling face. But they were phantasmagoria floating across the fact of the black courtyard, and he gave them no attention. Every nerve of him was centred on getting out of the courtyard.

But he was not to get out of it. He was its prisoner. He thought he had got out of it, but, on crossing the road and taking the first turning, he found he was in it again. There it was, in Peckham, clear to the eye—a riverside courtyard thick with darkness. This time he fought his way out of it, and stood at its entrance gasping. Real people moving along Rye Lane passed him as shadows, and an elfin voice came out of the air—"How's a chap get like that so early in the evening? Quick work eh?"

The words, faint as an echo in a valley, suggested something to him, though for some time he could not locate the suggestion. Then it came to him in clear terms—a drink. A drink was what he wanted. He hadn't had any drink or any food all day. A drink might rid him of this horror. But the idea of a drink brought a crowded, noisy bar; and he could not face a crowded, noisy bar. He wondered whether he might find a quiet side-street place nearby.

A little bland-faced man was passing the mouth of the alley. He stopped him.

"Er—could you tell me if there's a quiet little bar anywhere near here? Little place a respectable man can go to?"

The bland-faced man looked at him. "Yes. But a respectable man can go anywhere, can't he? Still, if you want a quiet place, go up here and take the first on the left."

He thanked the bland-faced man, and went swiftly up the half-lit road. Projecting from the corner of the first turning on the left he saw a signboard—*The Anchor and Hope.* He saw it as a portent. Reaching the first turning, he went to the left, anticipating the soothing effect of the drink. He went to the left, and walked into a courtyard thick with darkness and deaf to noise.

He came out of it cursing the bland-faced man, and sobbing. He fell into a loping run.

He pressed his fingers to his eyes, and rubbed his face. He uttered automatic noises. His voice said " Damn—damn—damn," and many coarser words.

In a long blue-lit street his breathing made him pause. Looking about him, he saw that the street was a street and its lamps were lamps. He took off his hat and rubbed his hands round his head. Nerves, he told himself. Nerves; just nerves. That's what it was. That courtyard wasn't there. Couldn't be there. An attack of nerves. He was just *seeing* it. Well, he wouldn't see it. It wasn't there at all. It was just nerves. Nerves. Nerves.

But with that discovery he learned that he had admitted another enemy. He had admitted a word, and the word, once admitted, pattered on his brain until even the haunting of the courtyard seemed less horrible. It walked with his feet, and beat with his pulse, and floated before his eyes. Nerves... Nerves... Nerves... Nerves. The shape of the word, as it spelt its letters before him, was of something spidery and ghastly. The sound of it became like a wail from an asylum. Nerves... Nerves... Nerves... Or like the last rush of breath from a dying old man. Nerves... Nerves... Nerves... Eugh... Eugh... Eugh.

"You better go home," he told himself.

"You better go home. That's the best place."

He went home. Somehow he found his way back to Kingsland Road. He went by buses that glided through one black courtyard after another, and he walked through black courtyards. In a shop in one of these courtyards he bought a quart bottle of stout, and at last he came to his room in a black courtyard, and the room itself was a black courtyard.

He sat on the bed in that courtyard and said, "Oh... Oh..." and "Oh, dear... Oh, dear..." He poured a glass of the stout, and drank it off. It soothed him, and within a few minutes the room began to resume the features of his old room. He drank another glass, and sat with hands limply hanging over knees. "I must be going mad. I must be going mad. Oh, if only..." He drank another glass; and soon the stout, working upon the exhaustion of the day's walk, brought sleepiness. It brought, too, the complete removal of the courtyard. As he sat on the bed, it faded from eye and mind, and all that he could see resolved itself into his own familiar room.

But in sleep it came back. It came back in all its detail. The courtyard itself, the shuttered house, the dark room, the bent old man. They danced and whirled about his consciousness. They were figures. They were colours. They were sounds and smells. They changed their form; they changed their character; they shifted from solid to vapour. But always, whatever their form or figuration, in their impact upon the brain they were black courtyard, shuttered house, dark room, bent old man. It seemed that he had not finished with them. It seemed that they were beckoning him. At times their attitude penetrated to his consciousness as friendly and encouraging. It seemed that there was something they wanted of him. But when he awoke, he awoke with a moan and a gasp and a sensation of choking.

The day repeated the yesterday. In the thin winter sunlight he was safe, but once the night had come the courtyard fastened upon him and enclosed him. London was one black courtyard. Beyond it he could see gleaming tram-cars and buses, and blazing shops, and streets crowded with faces dull or bright. But he could reach none of them. He could not get out. He could only pad round and round his courtyard, moaning.

Late in the evening, an idea came to him. "See a doctor." Somewhere in the everlasting black courtyard, a few paces back, he had noted a brass plate. With some trouble he found it again, and fifteen minutes later he was sitting in a pleasant consulting room. The atmosphere of the room, the furniture, the bright fire, the dog's-eared back-numbers of illustrated papers, restored him to a sense of everyday. Here were peace and warmth; nothing foolish, it seemed, could live here. It was a haven of sanity and sense to which the sailing courtyard could not penetrate.

By the time the doctor came in he was collected and calm. He gave a fictitious name and address as easily as though it were his own, and began to state his case.

"Know anything about nerves, doctor?"

"A good deal of the little we can know. What's the trouble?"

"Haunted."

"Mmmm. I see. Being followed, eh?"

"Oh, no. No. Not that. But... wherever I go I see a dark courtyard. A dark courtyard. It seems to close me in, like. Even Regent Street becomes a dark courtyard. Black."

"Yes. Well, there's lots of dark courtyards in London. You *would* see a lot if you go about much. There's one or two off Regent Street."

"Yes, but... It's everywhere. Even at home. Though I feel all right here. This is the first place I've been free of it for two days. It don't seem able to get at me here. Perhaps it can't come where there's strong people. I was wondering if you could give me some—" His voice broke. His eyes were staring past the doctor. "Oh, God—look—it's there. It's there!"

He was half-way from his chair, his hand pointing to something behind the doctor. "The window. I can see it outside the window."

The doctor did not look towards the window. He kept his eyes on his patient. "What is it you're seeing?"

"It's there—outside the window-the black courtyard. All dark. And little houses."

"Yes, yes. Of course. I know."

"What d'you mean—yes, yes? Look yourself. Look through that window. Tell me what's really there."

"A dark courtyard. With little houses."

"You—you—You playing with me? Humouring me? Or—"

"Of course not, man. If I look out of that window I can see a dark courtyard with little houses. Same as you can. And everybody else. I've been seeing it every night since I've been here—these twelve years."

"It's there, then?"

"Of course it's there. Now then—sit down. Take it easy. Let's try the old reflexes."

There was a ten-minute examination. The doctor went to his desk and made some notes. He turned to the patient. "What you want is a change. Complete change and rest.

You're just on the edge of a breakdown. But before you can get anything out of change and rest you must get this thing off your mind. You've got a dark courtyard on your mind. Something unpleasant must have happened to you in a dark courtyard. Well, the right thing to do is to go back to that courtyard, and—"

"Go *back!*"

"Yes. Don't look so scared, man. It's the cleanest way. Go back to that identical courtyard and those little houses. At night. And face whatever it's got. Go over it all again in the identical spot. Challenge it."

"You don't know what you're asking."

"Yes I do. I'm asking you to make a drastic effort. It's the only way. Nerves are like mad dogs. Run away, and they'll get you. Face 'em, and you're all right. You must go back to that place. At night, mind you. Face it out. And if you face it and go over whatever happened there, you'll probably find that the second experience will cancel the effect of the first. A mental medicine."

" I don't think I could. You don't understand. You wouldn't—"

"You can do it. If you make yourself. Anyway, try to. Get as far as you can. I can suggest nothing else. *I* can't rid you of this thing. Only yourself can do that. Nervous troubles can only be cured by the patient. The doctor can't cure 'em."

For five nights more he lived with his horror. Through the orchestration of his waking and sleeping life it recurred and persisted like a main theme gone wild. Life, once an affair of light beat and homely tune, had become a fugue upon a black courtyard. And it seemed that there was no stopping it. Nothing he could do would obliterate it. Memory operated upon nothing else. It carried it and dandled it and frisked it under his very eyes, until his surface and his core were a black courtyard at midnight.

It was not until his whole being had become a scream of "What can I do? What can I do?" that he saw the only thing to do. A perilous thing, certainly, but a thing that would lead at least to escape from *this*. He felt that he could live no longer with it. If, then, death was the only escape, he must take that way. But not by the river or the gas-fire. Those ways were certain and fixed. The doctor's way was almost equally certain of ending in disaster, but it was the "almost" that decided him to take it.

If the police were waiting for him; expecting him, as a bungling amateur, to follow the false popular tradition and return to the place—well, that way of ending, hideous as it was, could be no worse than this present horror. And it was possible… it might be that they were not waiting for him. He had searched each day the morning and evening papers, but never a line had he seen about any discovery in any riverside court. It might be that nothing had become known. It might be that the doctor's advice was not only sound but safe; that this one secret visit would indeed ease him of his burden. And that he might not only lose burden and danger of the law's penalty, but win the money he had forgotten to bring away. Suppose he risked it?

With that, resolution came to him. His spirits rose. His nerves ceased their jangling. He would risk it, and he would go that night. It seemed a propitious night—the exact week from *the* night and it would at least mean action and a result of some sort.

So at ten o'clock that night he went. In Kingsland Road the air was clear, but by the river there was again a mist, and again he passed through its streets as no more than a heavy overcoat, a soft hat, and a muffler. He found himself strangely careless of what might be waiting for him, and he walked with his usual padding step. He felt in good health—confident and strong; and when he came to the little street from which the alley led, he went lightly along it. He turned swiftly into the alley, and thence came once more into a courtyard thick with darkness, deaf to noise, and alive only with the eyes of blind houses.

For some seconds he stood still. But he saw nothing to alarm him, and heard nothing, and with quick, quiet steps he moved to the house in the corner.

There he waited. He looked round the court—challenged it, dared it. It made no demonstration. It did not threaten him. It did not frighten him. It was a court only, like other courts. Now that he was there, it seemed well disposed towards him. He wondered how he could have been so foolish as to let it weigh upon him. He must have been out of sorts last week.

He turned again to the little house. Yes; this was where he had stood, just at this shutter, just above this grating that made a right-angle with the basement window. He bent to the grating and listened. No clear sound at all came to him—only a whispering wave of silence. He touched the grating, and found it as loose as he had left it last week. It would lift easily. He lifted it, and as he lifted it a shaft of memory lit his mind.

He stood with it in his hand, and remembered that this was exactly how he had stood a week ago when he had come over faint. Exactly—the same attitude, the same finger of the left hand supporting the grating, the same movement of the right arm towards the window, the same—

And then he found himself in action. He had not directed himself to this action, but he *was* in action. He was underneath the grating, crouching in the tiny aperture before the window. His knife was working on the catch of the window. The catch slid back. With delicate fingers he lowered the window, and within four seconds he was in the house.

He switched on his torch, and its darting light showed him a dirty unkempt kitchen. But here the shaft of memory blurred and faded. He could not recall this kitchen. He moved the torch and it showed him a door and a staircase. He could not recall that staircase; but even while trying to recall it he found himself ascending it with his rhythmic padding. He reached the top and saw a passage leading to the front door, and in the passage two other doors, and another staircase. This again was strange to him, but he found himself on those stairs, going softly up, and he found himself in another and tinier passage, also with two doors. He found himself trying the handle of one of them, and working upon its lock with a wire key. And then he found the door open and himself in the room.

He darted his torch about the room and saw a chest, and a bureau, and a copper box. He went first to the chest, worked upon its lock, and rooted among its contents. He was blank of all thought and all feeling; blank of all memory of repeating last week; blank of all concern of the dead old man. He was just an organism of action. At the bottom of the chest his hand touched a packet that rustled. He brought it out, and his torch showed him what it was. He thrust it into his pocket, and dived again, and found another and another. Pound notes in packets. The chest yielded three more packets.

When he felt that he had exhausted it, he turned to the bureau. A few twists of his wire key opened it, and he dived his hand into its drawers. His hand found more and more, and he filled his pockets with them.

It was just when he was turning from the bureau to the copper box that he heard a sound. Scarcely a noise; just that faint disturbance of the air which is made by the presence of a living creature. He turned his torch flat to the floor, and with an undirected movement reached to the fireplace. His hand found a fire iron. As his fingers closed upon it, he moved swiftly and shot the beam of the torch at arm's length towards the door. It showed, just inside the door, the bent figure of an old man.

At that sight he knew what he had to do. Something that he had not been ready to do before, but for which he was now ready.

The old man made a faint cluck and shuffled three paces towards him. Perrace took one pace, and met him. From behind his back the fire iron came down on the bent head—one, two—the old man fell—three, four.

He dropped the fire iron and stepped back. His breath came out in a long rush, and with it came all the weight of fear that had been his burden. In that moment some immaterial shuttles seemed to readjust themselves, and bring into being a Perrace that was himself, but stronger. He was conscious of elation. No courtyard now could hold any terrors for him. He had rounded upon his haunting and materialised it. The live idea he had killed, as he had killed the old man. It was now a dead fact.

He shot the light of the torch upon the old man to satisfy himself that the thing was fully done; then switched off the torch, buttoned his coat, and gently felt his way down the stairs.

He came out from the basement window into a courtyard thick with darkness, and alive only with silence and the eyes of blind houses. This time it said nothing to him. He scarcely noticed it. It was just a place where he had cleared up something that had puzzled him. He padded from it into the alley, and so into the misted side streets, and melted into other narrow streets until he appeared in firm shape at Fenchurch Street Station. There, mixing with the crowd coming from a late Tilbury train, he took a taxi to Soho, and from Soho another taxi to Euston. From Euston he took a bus to Dalston, and from there he walked home.

In his room he made a close examination of his clothes, and found that he had been lucky. He stowed his money away in a suitcase and two boxes, and softly whistled a little tune. He went to bed, and slept better than he had slept for many weeks.

He slept until ten o'clock, when his landlady woke him to tell him that two important-looking men wanted to see him.

THE PORTENT OF THE SHADOW

E. Nesbit

THIS IS NOT an artistically rounded off ghost story and nothing is explained in it; and there seems to be no reason why any of it should have happened. But that is no reason why it should not be told. You must have noticed that all the real ghost stories you ever come close to are like this in these respects: no explanation, no logical coherence. Here is the story.

❦

There were three of us—and another. But she had fainted suddenly at the second extra of the Christmas Dance, and had been put to bed in the dressing room next to the room which we three shared. It had been one of those jolly old-fashioned dances, where nearly everybody stays the night, and the big country house is stretched to its utmost containing power; guests harbouring on sofas, couches, cots, and even mattresses on the floor. Some of the young men, even, I believe, slept on the great dining table. We had talked of our partners, as girls will, and then the stillness of the Manor House, broken only by the whisper of the wind in the cedar branches, and the scraping of their lean fingers against our window panes, had pricked us to such a luxurious confidence in our surroundings of bright chintz and candle-flame and firelight, that we had dared to talk of ghosts—in which, said we all, we did not believe one bit. We had told the story of the phantom coach, and the horribly strange bed, and the lady in the sacque, and the house in Berkeley Square. Not one of us believed in ghosts, but my heart, at least, seemed to leap to my throat and choke me, when a tap came to our door—a tap faint, but not to be mistaken.

"Who's there?" said the youngest of us, craning a lean neck towards the door. It opened slowly—and I give you my word the instant of suspense that followed is still reckoned among my life's least confident moments. Almost at once the door opened fully, and Miss Eastwich, my aunt's housekeeper, companion and general standby, looked in on us.

We all said "Come in," but she stood there. She was, at all normal hours, the most silent woman I have ever known. She stood and looked at us, and shivered a little. So did we—for in those days corridors were not warmed by hot-water pipes, and the air from the door was keen.

"I saw your light," she said at last, "and I thought it

was late for you to be up—after all this gaiety. I thought perhaps—" her glance turned towards the door of the dressing room.

"No," I said, "she's fast asleep." I should have added a "goodnight," but the youngest of us forestalled my speech. She did not know Miss Eastwich as we others did. Did not know how her persistent silence had built a wall round her, a wall that no one dared to break down with the commonplaces of talk or the littlenesses of mere human relationship. Miss Eastwich's silence had taught us to treat her as a machine, and as other than a machine we never dreamed of treating her. But the youngest of us had seen Miss Eastwich for the first time that day. She was young and crude and ill-balanced, and the victim of blind calf-like impulse. She was also the heiress of a rich tallow-chandler, but that has nothing to do with this part of the story. She jumped up from the hearthrug, her unsuitably rich silk, lace-trimmed dressing gown falling back from her lean neck, and ran to the door, and put an arm round Miss Eastwich's prim lisse-encircled neck. I gasped. I should as soon have dared embrace Cleopatra's Needle.

"Come in," said the youngest of us, "come in and get warm. There's lots of cocoa left." She drew Miss Eastwich in and shut the door.

The vivid light of pleasure in the housekeeper's pale eyes went through my heart like a knife. It would have been so easy to put an arm round her neck if one had only thought she wanted it. But it was not I who had thought that, and, indeed, my arm might not have brought the light invoked by the lean arm of the youngest of us.

"Now," the youngest went on eagerly, "you shall have the very biggest, nicest chair, and the cocoa pot's here on the hob as hot as hot, and we've all been telling ghost stories, only we don't believe in them a bit, and when you get warm you ought to tell one too."

Miss Eastwich, that model of decorum and decently done duties, tell a ghost story! The child was mad!

"You're sure I'm not in your way?" Miss Eastwich said, stretching her hands to the blaze. I wondered whether housekeepers have fires in their rooms even at Christmas time.

"Not a bit." I said it and I hope I said it as warmly as I felt it. "I—Miss Eastwich—I'd have asked you to come in other times—only I didn't think you'd care for girls' chatter."

The third girl, who was really of no account, and that's why I have not said anything about her before, poured cocoa for our guest; I put my fleecy Madeira shawl round her shoulders. I could not think of anything else to do for her, and I suddenly found myself wishing desperately to do something. The smile she gave us was quite pretty. People can smile prettily at 40 or 50, or even later, though girls don't realise this. It occurred to me, and this was another knife-thrust, that I had never seen Miss Eastwich smile—a real smile—before. The pale smiles of dutiful acquiescence were not of the same blood as this dimpling, happy transfiguring look.

"This is very pleasant," she said, and it seemed to me that I had never before heard her real voice. It did not please me to think that at the cost of cocoa and fire and my arms round her neck I might have heard this new voice any time these six years.

"We've been telling ghost stories," I said. "The worst of it is we don't believe in ghosts. No one anyone knows has ever seen one."

"It's always what somebody told somebody who told somebody, you know," said the youngest of us. "And you can't believe that, can you?"

"What the soldier said is not evidence," said Miss Eastwich. Will it be believed that the little Dickens quotation pierced me more keenly than the new smile or the new voice?

"And all ghost stories are so beautifully rounded off—a murder committed on the spot—or a hidden treasure or a warning—I think that makes them harder to believe. The most horrid ghost story I ever heard was one that was quite silly."

"Tell it."

"I can't—it doesn't sound anything to tell. Mrs Eastwich ought to tell one."

"Oh, do!" said the youngest of us, and her salt-cellars loomed dark as she stretched her neck eagerly and laid an entreating arm on our guest's knee.

"The only thing that I ever knew of was—was hearsay," she said slowly, "at least half of it was."

I knew she would tell her story, and I knew she had never before told it, and I knew she was only telling it now because she was proud, and this seemed the only way to pay for the fire and the cocoa and the laying of that thin arm round her neck.

"Don't tell it," I said suddenly, "I know you'd rather not."

"I daresay it would bore you," she said meekly, and the youngest of us, who after all did not understand everything, glared resentfully at me.

"We should just *love* it," she said, "*Do* tell us. Never mind if it isn't a real proper fixed-up story. I'm certain anything *you* think ghostly would be quite too beautifully horrid for anything."

Miss Eastwich finished her cocoa and reached up to set the cup on the mantelpiece.

"It can't do any harm," she said to herself, "they don't believe in ghosts, and it wasn't exactly a ghost either. And they're all over twenty—they're not babies." There was a breathing time of hush and expectancy. The fire crackled and the gas flared higher because the billiard lights had been put out. We heard the steps and voices of the men going along the corridors.

"It is really hardly worth telling," Miss Eastwich said doubtfully, shading her faded face from the fire with her thin hand.

We all said, "Go on; oh, go on, do!"

"Well," she said, "twenty years ago, and more than that, I had two friends, and I loved them more than anything in the world. And they married each other."

She paused, and I knew just in what way she had loved each of them. The youngest of us said. "How awfully nice for you! Do go on."

She patted the youngest's shoulder, and I was glad that I had understood what the youngest of all hadn't. She went on.

"Well, after they married I didn't see much of them for a year or two, and then he wrote and asked me to come and stay, because his wife was ill, and I should cheer her up, and cheer him up as well, for it was a gloomy house, and he himself was growing gloomy too."

I knew as she spoke that she had every line of that letter by heart.

"Well, I went. The address was in Lee, near London, and in those days there were streets and streets of new villa-houses growing up round old brick mansions standing in their own grounds, with red walls round, you know, and a sort of flavour of coaching days and post-chaises and Blackheath highwaymen about them. He had said the house was gloomy, and it was called 'The Firs,' and I imagined my cab going through a dark winding shrubbery and drawing up in front of one of those sedate old square houses. Instead, we drew up in front of a large, smart villa, with iron railings, gay encaustic tiles leading from the iron gate to the stained-glass-panelled door, and for shrubbery, only a few stunted cypresses and acubas in the tiny front garden. But inside it was all warm and welcoming. He met me at the door.

She was gazing into the fire, and I knew she had forgotten us. But the youngest girl of all still thought that it was to us she was telling her story.

"He met me at the door," she said again, "and thanked me for coming, and asked me to forgive the past."

"What past?" asked that high priestess of the *inapropos*, the youngest of all.

"Oh, I suppose he meant because they hadn't invited me before, or something," said Miss Eastwich, worriedly. "But it's a very dull story, I find, after all, and—"

"Do go on," I said. Then I kicked the youngest of us and got up to rearrange Miss Eastwich's shawl, and said in blatant dumb show, over the shawled shoulders:

"Shut up, you little idiot!"

After another silence the housekeeper's new voice went on:

"They were very glad to see me, and I was very glad to be there. You girls now have such troops of friends, but these two were all I had, all I had ever had. Mabel wasn't exactly ill, only weak and excitable. I thought he seemed more ill than she did. She went to bed early, and before she went, she asked me to keep him company through his last pipe, so we went into the dining room and sat in the two armchairs on each side of the fireplace. They were covered with green leather, I remember. There were bronze groups of horses and a black marble clock on the mantelpiece—all wedding presents. He poured out some whisky for himself, but he hardly touched it. He sat looking into the fire.

At last I said: 'What's wrong? Mabel looks as well as you could expect.'

"He said 'Yes, but I don't know from one day to another that she won't begin to notice something wrong. That's why I wanted you to come. You were always so sensible and strong-minded, and Mabel's like a little bird, or a flower.'

"I said 'Yes, of course,' and waited for him to go on. I thought he must be in debt or in trouble of some sort. So I just waited.

Presently he said: 'Margaret, this is a very peculiar house.' He always called me Margaret; you see, we'd been such old friends. I told him I thought the house was very pretty, and fresh, and homelike, only a little too new, but that fault would mend with time.

He said: 'It is new; that's just it. We're the first people who've ever lived in it. If it were an old house, Margaret, I should think it was haunted.'

"I asked if he had seen anything. 'No,' he said, 'not yet.'

"'Heard, then?' said I.

"'No, nor heard either,' he said, 'but there's a sort of feeling, I can't describe it. I've seen nothing and I've heard nothing, but I've been so near to seeing and hearing! Just not, that's all. And something follows me about—only when I turn round there's never anything but my shadow. And I always feel that I *shall* see the thing, or hear it, next minute; but I never do, not quite, it's always just not visible.'

"I thought he'd been working rather hard, and I tried to cheer him up by making light of all this. 'It was just nerves,' I said. Then he said he had thought I could help him, and did I think anyone he had wronged could have laid a curse on him, and did I believe in curses? I said I didn't, and the only person anyone could have said he had wronged forgave him freely, I knew, if there was anything to forgive. So I told him this too."

It was I, not the youngest of us, who knew the name of that person wronged and forgiving.

"So then I said 'He ought to take Mabel away from the house and have a complete change.' But he said, 'No, Mabel had got everything in order, and he could never manage to get her away just now without explaining everything, and above all,' he said, 'she mustn't guess there's anything wrong. I daresay I shall not feel quite such a lunatic now you're here.'

"So we said 'Good-night.'"

"Is that all the story?" said the third girl, striving to convey that even as it stood it was a good story.

"That is only the beginning," said Miss Eastwich. "Whenever I was alone with him, he used to tell me the same thing over and over again, and at first when I began to notice things I tried to think that it was his talk that had upset my nerves. The odd thing was that it wasn't only at night—but in broad daylight, and particularly on the stairs and passages. On the staircase the feeling used to be so awful that I have had to bite my lips till they bled, to keep myself from running up the stairs at full speed. Only I knew if I did I should go mad at the top. There was always something behind me—exactly as he had said—something that one could just not see. And a sound that one could just not hear. There was a long corridor at the top of the house. I have sometimes almost seen something—you know how one sees things without looking—but if I turned round it seemed as if the thing dropped and melted into my shadow. There was a little window at the end of the corridor.

"Downstairs there was another corridor, something like it, with a cupboard at one end and the kitchen at the other. One night I went down into the kitchen to warm some milk for Mabel. The servants had gone to bed. As I stood by the fire waiting for the milk to boil I glanced through the open door and along the passage. I never could keep my eyes on what I was doing, in that house. The cupboard door was partly open; they used to keep empty bottles and things in it. And as I looked I knew that now it was not going to be 'almost' any more. Yet I said 'Mabel?' not because I thought it could be Mabel who was crouching down there, half in and half out of the cupboard. The thing was grey at first and then it was black. And when I whispered 'Mabel,' it seemed to sink down till it lay like a pool of ink on the floor, and then its edges drew in, and it seemed to flow, like ink, when you tilt up the paper you have spilt it on, and it flowed into the cupboard till it was all gathered into the shadow there. I saw it go quite plainly. The gas was full on in the kitchen. I screamed aloud, but even then I'm thankful to say I had enough sense to upset the boiling milk, so that when he came downstairs three steps at a time, I had the excuse for my scream of a scalded hand. The explanation was satisfactory to Mabel, but next night he said: 'Why didn't you tell me? It was that cupboard. All the horror of the house comes out of that. Tell me, have you seen anything yet? Or is it only the nearly seeing and nearly hearing still?'

"I said 'You must tell me first what you've seen.' He told me, and his eyes wandered as he spoke to the shadows by the curtains, and I turned up all three gaslights and lit the candles on the mantelpiece. Then we looked at each other and said we were both mad, and thanked God that Mabel was at least sane. For what he had seen was what I had seen.

"After that I hated to be alone with a shadow, because at any moment I might see something that would crouch and sink and lie like a black pool and then slowly draw itself into the shadow that was nearest. Often that shadow was my own. The thing came first at night, but afterwards there was no hour safe from it. I saw it at dawn, and at noon, in the dusk and in the firelight, and always it crouched and sank, and was a pool that flowed into some shadow and became part of it. And always I saw it with a straining of the eyes, a pricking and aching. It seemed as though I could only just see it, as if my sight, to see it, had to be strained to the uttermost.

"And still the sound was in the house, the sound that I could just not hear. At last one morning early I did hear it. It was close behind me, and it was only a sigh. It was worse than the thing that crept among the shadows.

"I don't know how I bore it. I couldn't have borne it if I hadn't been so fond of them both. But I knew in my heart that if he had no one to whom he could speak openly he would go mad, or tell Mabel. His was not a very strong character. Very sweet and kind and gentle, but not strong. He was always easily led. So I stayed on and bore up, and we were very cheerful and made little jokes and tried to be amusing when Mabel was with us. But when we were alone we did not try to be amusing.

"And sometimes a day or two would go by without our seeing or hearing anything, and we should perhaps have fancied that we had fancied what we had seen and heard, only there was always the feeling of there being something about the house that one could just not hear and not see. Sometimes we used to try not to talk about it, but generally we talked of nothing else at all. And the weeks went by, and Mabel's baby was born. The nurse and the doctor said that both mother and child were doing well. He and I sat late in the dining room that night. We had neither of us seen or heard anything for three days—our anxiety about Mabel was lessened. We talked of the future: it seemed then so much brighter than the past. We arranged that the moment she was fit to be moved he should take her away to the sea, and I should superintend the moving of their furniture into the new house he had already chosen. He was gayer than I had seen him since his marriage—almost like his old self. When I said 'good night' to him he said a lot of things about my having been a comfort to them both. I hadn't done anything much of course, but still I am glad he said that.

"Then I went upstairs—almost for the first time without that feeling of something following me. I listened at Mabel's room. Everything was quiet. I went on towards my own room, and in an instant I felt that there *was* something behind me. I turned. It was crouching there: it sank, and the black fluidness of it seemed to be sucked under the floor of Mabel's room.

"I went back. I opened the door a listening inch. All was still. And then I heard a sigh—close behind me. I opened the door and went in. The nurse and the baby were asleep. Mabel was asleep, too; she looked so pretty, like a tired child—the baby was cuddled up into one of her arms with its tiny head against her side. I prayed then that Mabel might never know the terrors that he and I had known—that those little ears might never hear any but pretty sounds, those dear eyes never see any but pretty sights. I did not dare to pray for a long time after that. Because my prayer was answered. She never saw, never heard anything more in this world. And now I could do nothing more for him or for her.

"When they had put her in her coffin I lighted wax candles round her, and laid the horrible white flowers that people will send, near to her, and then I saw he had followed me. I took his hand to lead him away.

"At the door we both turned. It seemed to us that we heard a sigh. He would have sprung to her side in I don't know what mad glad hope. But at that instant we both saw it. Between us and the coffin, first grey, then black, it crouched an instant, then sank and liquefied, and was gathered together and drawn till it ran into the nearest shadow. And the nearest shadow was the shadow of Mabel's coffin. I left the next day. His mother came. She had never liked me."

Miss Eastwich paused. I think she had quite forgotten us.

"Didn't you see him again?" asked the youngest of all.

"Only once," Miss Eastwich answered, "and something black crouched then between him and me. But it was only his second wife crying beside his coffin. It's not a cheerful story, is it? And it doesn't lead anywhere. I've never told anyone else. I think it was seeing his daughter that brought it all back."

She looked toward the dressing room door. "Mabel's baby," said the youngest of all.

"Yes, and exactly like Mabel, only with his eyes."

The youngest of all had Miss Eastwich's hands and was petting them.

Suddenly the woman wrenched her hands away and stood at her gaunt height, hands clenched, eyes straining. She was looking at something that we could not see, and I know now what the man in the Bible meant when he said "the hair of my flesh stood up—"

What she saw seemed not quite to reach the height of the dressing room door handle. Her eyes following it down, down, widened and widened. Mine followed hers, and all the nerves of my eyes seemed strained to the uttermost—and I almost saw—or did I quite see? I can't be certain. But we all heard the long-drawn, quivering sigh. And to each of us it seemed to be breathed just behind each.

It was I who caught up the candle—it dropped wax all over my trembling hands—it was I who was dragged by Miss Eastwich to the side of the girl who had fainted during the second extra. But it was the youngest of all whose lean arms were round the housekeeper when we turned away, and that have been round her many a time since in the new home where she keeps house for the youngest of us all.

The doctor, who came in the morning, said that Mabel's daughter had died of heart disease, which she inherited from her mother. That was what made her faint during the second extra. But I have sometimes wondered whether she may not have inherited something from her father. I have never been able to forget the look on her dead face.

THE SECOND GENERATION

Algernon Blackwood

SOMETIMES, in a moment of sharp experience, comes that vivid flash of insight that makes a platitude suddenly seem a revelation—its full content is abruptly realised. "Ten years *is* a long time, yes," he thought, as he walked up the drive to the great Kensington house where she still lived.

Ten years—long enough, at any rate, for her to have married and for her husband to have died. More than that he had not heard, in the outlandish places where life had cast him in the interval. He wondered whether there had been any children. All manner of thoughts and questions, confused a little, passed across his mind. He was well-to-do now, though probably his entire capital did not amount to her income for a single year. He glanced at the huge, forbidding mansion. Yet that pride was false which had made of poverty an insuperable obstacle. He saw it now. He had learned values in his long exile.

But he was still ridiculously timid. This confusion of thought, of mental images rather, was due to a kind of fear, since worship ever is akin to awe. He was as nervous as a boy going up for a *viva voce*; and with the excitement was also that unconquerable sinking—that horrid shrinking sensation that excessive shyness brings. Why in the world had he come? Why had he telegraphed the very day after his arrival in England? Why had he not sent a tentative, tactful letter, feeling his way a little?

Very slowly he walked up the drive, feeling that if a reasonable chance of escape presented itself he would almost take it. But all the windows stared so hard at him that retreat was really impossible now; and though no faces were visible behind the curtains, all had seen him, possibly she herself—his heart beat absurdly at the extravagant suggestion. Yet it was odd—he felt so certain of being seen, and that someone watched him. He reached the wide stone steps that were clean as marble, and shrank from the mark his boots must make upon their spotlessness. In desperation, then, before he could change his mind, he touched the bell. But he did not hear it ring—mercifully; that irrevocable sound must have paralysed him altogether. If no one came to answer, he might still leave a card in the letter box and slip away. Oh, how utterly he despised himself for such a thought! A man of thirty with such a chicken heart was not fit to protect a child, much less a woman. And he recalled with a little stab of pain that the man she married had been noted for his courage, his determined action, his inflexible firmness in various public situations, head and shoulders above lesser men. What presumption on his own part ever to dream…! He remembered, too, with no apparent reason in particular, that this man had a grown-up son already, by a former marriage.

And still no one came to open that huge, contemptuous door with its so menacing, so hostile air. His back was to it, as he carelessly twirled his umbrella, but he 'felt' its sneering expression behind him while it looked him up and down. It seemed to push him away. The entire mansion focused its message through that stern portal: little timid men are not welcomed here.

How well he remembered the house! How often in years gone by had he not stood and waited just like this, trembling with delight and anticipation, yet terrified lest the bell should be answered and the great door actually swung wide! Then, as now, he would have run, had he dared. He was still afraid; his worship was so deep. But in all these years of exile in wild places, farming, mining, working for the position he had at last attained, her face and the memory of her gracious presence had been his comfort and support, his only consolation, though never his actual joy. There was so little foundation for it all, yet her smile and the words she had spoken to him from time to time in friendly conversation had clung, inspired, kept him going. For he knew them all by heart. And, more than once, in foolish optimistic moods, he had imagined, greatly daring, that she possibly had meant more…

He touched the bell a second time—with the point of his umbrella. He meant to go in, carelessly as it were, saying as lightly as might be, "Oh, I'm back in England again—if you haven't *quite* forgotten my existence—I could not forgo the pleasure of saying 'How-do-you-do?' and hearing that you are well…," and the rest; then presently bow himself easily out—into the old loneliness again. But he would at least have seen her; he would have heard her voice, and looked into her gentle, amber eyes; he would have touched her hand. She might even ask him to come in another day and see her! He had rehearsed it all a hundred times, as certain feeble temperaments do rehearse such scenes. And he came rather well out of that rehearsal, though always with an aching heart, the old great yearnings unfulfilled. All the way across the Atlantic he had thought about it, though with lessening confidence as the time drew near. The very night of his arrival in London he wrote; then, tearing up the letter (after sleeping over it), he had telegraphed next morning, asking if she would be in. He signed his surname—such a very common name, alas! but surely she would know—and her reply, "Please call 4.30," struck him as rather oddly worded. Yet here he was.

There was a rattle of the big door knob, that aggressive, hostile knob that thrust out at him insolently like a fist of bronze. He started, angry with himself for doing so. But the door did not open. He became suddenly conscious of the wilds he had lived in for so long; his clothes were hardly fashionable; his voice probably had a twang in it, and he used tricks of speech that must betray the rough life so recently left. What would she think of him—now? He looked much older, too. And how brusque it was to have telegraphed like that! He felt awkward, gauche, tongue-tied, hot and cold by turns. The sentences, so carefully rehearsed, fled beyond recovery.

Good heavens—the door was open! It had been open for some minutes. It moved on big hinges noiselessly. He acted automatically—just like an automaton; he heard himself asking if her ladyship was at home, though his voice was nearly inaudible. The next moment he was standing in the great, dim hall, so poignantly familiar, and the remembered perfume almost made him sway. He did not hear the door close, but he knew. He was caught. The butler betrayed an instant's surprise—or was it overwrought imagination again?—when he gave his name. It seemed to him—though only later did he grasp the significance of that curious intuition—that the man had expected another caller instead. The man took his card respectfully and disappeared. These flunkeys, of course, were so marvellously trained. He was too long accustomed to straight question and straight answer; but here, in the Old Country, privacy was jealously guarded with such careful ritual.

And, almost immediately, the butler returned with his expressionless face again, and showed him into the large drawing room on the ground floor that he knew so well. Tea was on the table—tea for one. He felt puzzled. "If you will have tea first, sir, her ladyship will see you afterwards," was what he heard. And though his breath came thickly, he asked the question that forced itself up and out. Before he knew what he was saying he asked it: "Is she ill?" Oh, no, her ladyship was "quite well, thank you, sir. If you will have tea first, sir, her ladyship will see you afterwards." The horrid formula was repeated, word for word. He sank into an armchair and mechanically poured out his own tea. What he felt he did not exactly know. It seemed so unusual, so utterly unexpected, so unnecessary, too. Was it a special attention, or was it merely casual? That it could mean anything else did not occur to him. How was she busy, occupied—not here to give him tea? He could not understand it. It seemed such a farce having tea alone like this; it was like waiting for an audience, it was like a doctor's or a dentist's room. He felt bewildered, ill at ease, cheap.... But after ten years in primitive lands... perhaps London usages had changed in some extraordinary manner. He recalled his first amazement at the motor-omnibuses, taxicabs, and electric tubes. All were new. London was otherwise than when he left it. Piccadilly and the Marble Arch themselves had altered. And, with his reflection, a shade more confidence stole in. She knew that he was there; and presently she would come in and speak with him, explaining everything by the mere fact of her delicious presence. He was ready for the ordeal; he would see her—and drop out again. It was worth all manner of pain, even of mortification. He was in her house, drinking her tea, sitting in a chair she used herself perhaps. Only—he would never dare to say a word or make a sign that might betray his changeless secret. He still felt the boyish worshipper, worshipping in dumbness from a distance, one of a group of many others like himself. Their dreams had faded, his had continued, that was the difference. Memories tore and raced and poured upon him. How sweet and gentle she had always been to him! He used to wonder sometimes.... Once, he remembered, he had rehearsed a declaration—but, while rehearsing, the big man had come in and captured her, though he had only read the definite news long after by chance in the Arizona paper...

He gulped his tea down. His heart alternately leaped and stood still. A sort of numbness held him most of that dreadful interval, and no clear thought came at all. Every ten seconds his head turned towards the door that rattled, seemed to move, yet never opened. But any moment now it *must* open, and he would be in her very presence, breathing the same air with her. He would see her, charge himself with her beauty once more to the brim, and then go out again into the wilderness—the wilderness of life—without her, and not for a mere ten years but for always. She was so utterly beyond his reach. He felt like a backwoodsman. He was a backwoodsman.

For one thing only was he duly prepared, though he thought about it little enough: she would, of course, have changed. The photograph he owned, cut from an illustrated paper, was not true now. It might even be a little shock perhaps. He must remember that. Ten years cannot pass over a woman without—

Before he knew it, then, the door was open, and she was advancing quietly towards him across the thick carpet that deadened sound. With both hands outstretched she came, and with the sweetest welcoming smile upon her parted lips he had seen in any human face. Her eyes were soft with joy. His whole heart leaped within him; for the instant he saw her it all flashed clear as sunlight—that she knew and understood. She had always known, had always understood. Speech came easily to him in a flood, had he needed it, but he did not need it. It was all so adorably easy, simple, natural, and true. He just took her hands—those welcoming, outstretched hands—in both of his own, and led her to the nearest sofa. He was not even surprised at himself. Inevitably, out of depths of truth, this meeting came about. And he uttered a little foolish commonplace, because he feared the huge revulsion that his sudden glory brought, and loved to taste it slowly:

"So you live here still?"

"Here, and here," she answered softly, touching his heart, and then her own. "I am attached to this house, too, because *you* used to come and see me here, and because it was here I waited so long for you, and still wait. I shall never leave it—unless you change. You see, we live together here."

He said nothing. He leaned forward to take and hold her. The abrupt knowledge of it all somehow did not seem abrupt—as though he had known it always; and the complete disclosure did not seem disclosure either—rather as though she told him something he had inexplicably left unrealized, yet not forgotten. He felt absolutely master of himself, yet, in a curious sense, outside of himself at the same time. His arms were already open—when she gently held her hands up to prevent. He heard a faint sound outside the door.

"But you are free," he cried, his great passion breaking out and flooding him, yet most oddly well controlled, "and I—"

She interrupted him in the softest, quietest whisper he had ever heard:

"You are not free, as I am free—not yet."

The sound outside came suddenly closer. It was a step. There was a faint click on the handle of the door. In a flash, then, came the dreadful shock that overwhelmed him—the abrupt realization of the truth that was somehow horrible—that Time, all these years, had left no mark upon her and that *she had not changed*. Her face was as young as when he saw her last.

With it there came cold and darkness into the great room that turned it instantly otherwise. He shivered with cold, but an alien, unaccountable cold. Some great shadow dropped upon the entire earth, and though but a second could have passed before the handle actually turned, and the other person entered, it seemed to him like several minutes. He heard her saying this amazing thing that was question, answer, and forgiveness all in one. This, at least, he divined before the ghastly interruption came:

"But, George—if you had only spoken—!"

With ice in his blood he heard the butler saying that her ladyship would be "pleased" to see him if he had finished his tea and would be "so good as to bring the papers and documents upstairs with him." He had just sufficient control of certain muscles to stand upright and murmur that he would come. He rose from a sofa that held no one but himself. But, at once, he staggered. He really did not know exactly then what happened, or how he managed to stammer out the medley of excuses and semi-explanations that battered their way through his brain and issued somehow in definite words from his lips. Somehow or other he accomplished it. The sudden attack, the faintness, the collapse! ... He vaguely remembered afterwards—with amazement too—the suavity of the butler, as he suggested telephoning for a doctor, and that he just managed to forbid it, refusing the offered glass of brandy as well, and that he contrived to stumble into the taxicab and give his hotel address, with a final explanation that he would call another day and "bring the papers." It was quite clear that his telegram had been attributed to someone else—someone "with papers"—perhaps a solicitor or architect. His name was such an ordinary one. There were so many Smiths. It was also clear that she whom he had come to see and *had* seen, no longer lived here,—in the flesh…

And, just as he left the hall he had the vision—mere fleeting glimpse it was—of a tall, slim, girlish figure on the stairs asking if anything was wrong, and realized vaguely through his atrocious pain that she was, of course, the wife of the son who had inherited…

AFTERWARD

Edith Wharton

I

"OH, THERE *IS* ONE, of course, but you'll never know it."

The assertion, laughingly flung out six months earlier in a bright June garden, came back to Mary Boyne with a sharp perception of its latent significance as she stood, in the December dusk, waiting for the lamps to be brought into the library.

The words had been spoken by their friend Alida Stair, as they sat at tea on her lawn at Pangbourne, in reference to the very house of which the library in question was the central, the pivotal "feature." Mary Boyne and her husband, in quest of a country place in one of the southern or south-western counties, had, on their arrival in England, carried their problem straight to Alida Stair, who had successfully solved it in her own case; but it was not until they had rejected, almost capriciously, several practical and judicious suggestions that she threw out: "Well, there's Lyng, in Dorsetshire. It belongs to Hugo's cousins, and you can get it for a song."

The reason she gave for its being obtainable on these terms—its remoteness from a station, its lack of electric light, hot-water pipes, and other vulgar necessities—were exactly those pleading in its favour with two romantic Americans perversely in search of the economic drawbacks which were associated, in their tradition, with unusual architectural felicities.

"I should never believe I was living in an old house unless I was thoroughly uncomfortable," Ned Boyne, the more extravagant of the two, had jocosely insisted; "the least hint of 'convenience' would make me think it had been bought out of an exhibition, with the pieces numbered, and set up again." And they had proceeded to enumerate, with humorous precision, their various suspicions and exactions, refusing to believe that the house their cousin recommended was *really* Tudor till they learned it had no heating system, or that the village church was literally in the grounds till she assured them of the deplorable uncertainty of the water supply.

"It's too uncomfortable to be true!" Edward Boyne had continued to exult as the avowal of each disadvantage was successively wrung from her; but he had cut short his rhapsody to ask, with a relapse to distrust: "And the ghost?

You've been concealing from us the fact that there is no ghost!"

Mary, at the moment, had laughed with him, yet almost with her laugh, being possessed of several sets of independent perceptions, had noted a sudden flatness of tone in Alida's answering hilarity.

"Oh, Dorsetshire's full of ghosts, you know."

"Yes, yes; but that won't do. I don't want to have to drive ten miles to see somebody else's ghost. I want one of my own on the premises. *Is* there a ghost at Lyng?"

His rejoinder had made Alida laugh again, and it was then that she had flung back tantalizingly: "Oh, there *is* one, of course, but you'll never know it."

"Never know it?" Boyne pulled her up. "But what in the world constitutes a ghost except the fact of its being known for one?"

"I can't say. But that's the story."

"That there's a ghost, but that nobody knows it's a ghost?"

"Well—not till afterward, at any rate."

"Till afterward?"

"Not till long, long afterward."

"But if it's once been identified as an unearthly visitant, why hasn't its *signalement* been handed down in the family? How has it managed to preserve its incognito?"

Alida could only shake her head. "Don't ask me. But it has."

"And then suddenly—" Mary spoke up as if from some cavernous depth of divination—"suddenly, long afterward, one says to one's self, '*That was it?*'"

She was oddly startled at the sepulchral sound with which her question fell on the banter of the other two, and she saw the shadow of the same surprise flit across Alida's pupils. "I suppose so. One just has to wait."

"Oh, hang waiting!" Ned broke in. "Life's too short for a ghost who can only be enjoyed in retrospect. Can't we do better than that, Mary?"

But it turned out that in the event they were not destined to, for within three months of their conversation with Mrs Stair they were established at Lyng, and the life they had yearned for, to the point of planning it out in all its daily details, had actually begun for them.

It was to sit, in the thick December dusk, by just such a wide-hooded fireplace, under just such black oak rafters, with the sense that beyond the mullioned panes the downs were darkened to a deeper solitude: it was for the ultimate indulgence of such sensations that Mary Boyne, abruptly exiled from New York by her husband's business, had endured for nearly fourteen years the soul-deadening ugliness of a Middle Western town, and that Boyne had ground on doggedly at his engineering till, with a suddenness that still made her blink, the prodigious windfall of the Blue Star Mine had put them at a stroke in possession of life and the leisure to taste it. They had never for a moment meant their new state to be one of idleness; but they meant to give themselves only to harmonious activities. She had her vision of painting and gardening (against a background of grey walls), he dreamed of the production of his long-planned book on the "Economic Basis of Culture"; and with such absorbing work ahead no existence could be too sequestered: they could not get far enough from the world, or plunge deep enough into the past.

Dorsetshire had attracted them from the first by a semblance of remoteness out of all proportion to its geographical position. But to the Boynes it was one of the ever-recurring wonders of the whole incredibly compressed island—a nest of counties, as they put it—that for the production of its effects so little of a given quality went so far: that so few miles made a distance, and so short a distance a difference.

"It's that," Ned had once enthusiastically explained, "that gives such depth to their effects, such relief to their least contrasts. They've been able to lay the butter so thick on every exquisite mouthful."

The butter had certainly been laid on thick at Lyng: the old house, hidden under a shoulder of the downs, had almost all the finer marks of commerce with a protracted past. The mere fact that it was neither large nor exceptional made it, to the Boynes, abound the more completely in its special charm—the charm of having been for centuries a deep, dim reservoir of life. The life had probably not been of the most vivid order: for long periods, no doubt, it had fallen as noiselessly into the past as the quiet drizzle of autumn fell, hour after hour, into the fish pond between the yews; but these back-waters of existence sometimes breed, in their sluggish depths, strange acuities of emotion, and Mary Boyne had felt from the first the occasional brush of an intenser memory.

The feeling had never been stronger than on this December afternoon when, waiting in the library for the lamps to come, she rose from her seat and stood among the shadows of the hearth. Her husband had gone off, after luncheon, for one of his long tramps on the downs. She had noticed of late that he preferred to go alone; and, in the tried security of their personal relations, had been driven to conclude that his book was bothering him, and that he needed the afternoons to turn over in solitude the problems left from the morning's work. Certainly the book was not going as smoothly as she thought it would, and there were lines of perplexity between his eyes such as had never been there in his engineering days. He had often looked then fagged to the verge of illness, but the native demon of "worry" had never branded his brow. Yet the few pages he had so far read to her—the introduction, and a summary of the opening chapter—showed a firm hold on his subject, and increasing confidence in his powers.

The fact threw her into deeper perplexity, since, now that he had done with "business" and its disturbing contingencies, the one other possible source of anxiety was eliminated. Unless it were his health, then? But physically he had gained since they had come to Dorsetshire, grown robuster, ruddier and fresher-eyed. It was only within a week that she had felt in him the undefinable change which made her restless in his absence, and as tongue-tied in his presence as though it were *she* who had a secret to keep from him!

The thought that there *was* a secret somewhere between them struck her with a sudden smart rap of wonder, and she looked about her down the long room.

"Can it be the house?" she mused.

The room itself might have been full of secrets. They seemed to be piling themselves up, as evening fell, like the layers and layers of velvet shadow dropping from the low ceiling, the books, the smoke-blurred sculpture of the hearth.

"Why, of course—the house is haunted!" she reflected.

The ghost—Alida's imperceptible ghost—after figuring largely in the banter of their first month or two at Lyng, had been gradually left aside as too ineffectual for imaginative use. Mary had, indeed, as became the tenant of a haunted house, made the customary inquiries among her rural neighbours, but, beyond a vague, "They do say so, Ma'am," the villagers had nothing to impart. The elusive spectre had apparently never had sufficient identity for a legend to crystallise about it, and after a time the Boynes had laughingly set the matter down to their profit and-loss account, agreeing that Lyng was one of the few houses good enough in itself to dispense with supernatural enhancements.

"And I suppose, poor ineffectual demon, that's why it beats its beautiful wings in vain in the void," Mary had laughingly concluded.

"Or, rather," Ned answered, in the same strain, "why, amid so much that's ghostly, it can never affirm its separate existence as *the* ghost." And thereupon their invisible housemate had finally dropped out of their references, which were numerous enough to make them soon unaware of the loss.

Now, as she stood on the hearth, the subject of their earlier curiosity revived in her with a new sense of its meaning—a sense gradually acquired through daily contact with the scene of the lurking mystery. It was the house itself, of course, that possessed the ghost-seeing faculty, that communed visually but secretly with its own past; if one could only get into close enough communion with the house, one might surprise its secret, and acquire the ghost-sight on one's own account. Perhaps, in his long hours in this very room, where she never trespassed till the afternoon, her husband *had* acquired it already, and was silently carrying about the weight of whatever it had revealed to him. Mary was too well versed in the code of the spectral world not to know that one could not talk about the ghosts one saw: to do so was almost as great a breach of taste as to name a lady in a club. But this explanation did not really satisfy her. “What, after all, except for the fun of the shudder,” she reflected, “would he really care for any of their old ghosts?” And thence she was thrown back once more on the fundamental dilemma: the fact that one’s greater or less susceptibility to spectral influences had no particular bearing on the case, since, when one *did* see a ghost at Lyng, one did not know it.

“Not till long afterward,” Alida Stair had said. Well, supposing Ned *had* seen one when they first came, and had known only within the last week what had happened to him? More and more under the spell of the hour, she threw back her searching thoughts to the early days of their tenancy, but at first only to recall a gay confusion of unpacking, settling, arranging of books, and calling to each other from remote corners of the house as, treasure after treasure, it revealed itself to them. It was in this particular connection that she presently recalled a certain soft afternoon of the previous October, when, passing from the first rapturous flurry of exploration to a detailed inspection of the old house, she had pressed (like a novel heroine) a panel that opened on a narrow corkscrew flight of stairs leading to a flat ledge of the roof—the roof which, from below, seemed to slope away on all sides too abruptly for any but practised feet to scale.

The view from this hidden coign was enchanting, and she had flown down to snatch Ned from his papers and give him the freedom of her discovery. She remembered still how, standing at her side, he had passed his arm about her while their gaze flew to the long tossed horizon-line of the downs, and then dropped contentedly back to trace the arabesque of yew hedges about the fish pond, and the shadow of the cedar on the lawn.

"And now the other way," he had said, turning her about within his arm; and closely pressed to him, she had absorbed, like some long, satisfying draft, the picture of the grey-walled court, the squat lions on the gates, and the lime avenue reaching up to the highroad under the downs.

It was just then, while they gazed and held each other, that she had felt his arm relax, and heard a sharp "Hullo!" that made her turn to glance at him.

Distinctly, yes, she now recalled she had seen, as she glanced, a shadow of anxiety, of perplexity, rather, fall across his face; and, following his eyes, had beheld the figure of a man—a man in loose, greyish clothes, as it appeared to her—who was sauntering down the lime avenue to the court with the doubtful gait of a stranger who seeks his way. Her short-sighted eyes had given her but a blurred impression of slightness and greyness, with something foreign, or at least unlocal, in the cut of the figure or its dress; but her husband had apparently seen more—seen enough to make him push past her with a sharp "Wait!" and dash down the twisting stairs without pausing to give her a hand.

A slight tendency to dizziness obliged her, after a provisional clutch at the chimney against which they had been leaning, to follow him down more cautiously; and when she had reached the landing she paused again, for a less definite reason, leaning over the oak banister to strain her eyes through the silence of the brown, sun-flecked depths. She lingered there till, somewhere in those depths, she heard the closing of a door; then, mechanically impelled, she went down the shallow flights of steps till she reached the lower hall.

The front door stood open on the mild sunlight of the court, and hall and court were empty. The library door was open, too, and after listening in vain for any sound of voices within she crossed the threshold, and found her husband alone, vaguely fingering the papers on his desk.

He looked up, as if surprised at her entrance, but the shadow of anxiety had passed from his face, leaving it even, as she fancied, a little brighter and clearer than usual.

"What was it? Who was it?" she asked.

"Who?" he repeated, with the surprise still all on his side.

"The man we saw coming toward the house."

He seemed to reflect. "The man? Why, I thought I saw Peters; I dashed after him to say a word about the stable drains, but he had disappeared before I could get down."

"Disappeared? But he seemed to be walking so slowly when we saw him."

Boyne shrugged his shoulders. "So I thought; but he must have got up steam in the interval. What do you say to our trying a scramble up Meldon Steep before sunset?"

That was all. At the time the occurrence had been less than nothing; had, indeed, been immediately obliterated by the magic of their first vision from Meldon Steep, a height which they had dreamed of climbing ever since they had first seen its bare spine heaving itself above the low roof of Lyng. Doubtless it was the mere fact of the other incident's having occurred on the very day of their ascent to Meldon that had kept it stored away in the fold of memory from which it now emerged; for in itself it had no mark of the portentous. At the moment there could have been nothing more natural than that Ned should dash himself from the roof in the pursuit of dilatory tradesmen. It was the period when they were always on the watch for one or the other of the specialists employed about the place; always lying in wait for them, and dashing out at them with questions, reproaches or reminders. And certainly in the distance the grey figure had looked like Peters.

Yet now, as she reviewed the scene, she felt her husband's explanation of it to have been invalidated by the look of anxiety on his face. Why had the familiar appearance of Peters made him anxious? Why, above all, if it was of such prime necessity to confer with that authority on the subject of the stable drains, had the failure to find him produced such a look of relief? Mary could not say that any one of these considerations had occurred to her at the time, yet, from the promptness with which they now marshalled themselves at her summons, she had a sudden sense that they must all along have been there, waiting their hour.

II

Weary with her thoughts, she moved to the window. The library was now quite dark, and she was surprised to see how much faint light the outer world still held.

As she peered out into it across the court, a figure shaped itself far down the perspective of bare limes: it looked a mere blot of deeper grey in the greyness, and for an instant, as it moved toward her, her heart thumped to the thought "It's the ghost!"

She had time, in that long instant, to feel suddenly that the man of whom, two months earlier, she had a brief distant vision from the roof, was now, at his predestined hour, about to reveal himself as *not* having been Peters; and her spirit sank under the impending fear of the disclosure. But almost with the next tick of the clock the figure, gaining substance and character, showed itself even to her weak sight as her husband's; and she turned to meet him, as he entered, with the confession of her folly.

"It's really too absurd," she laughed out, "but I never *can* remember!"

"Remember what?" Boyne questioned as they drew together.

"That when one sees the Lyng ghost one never knows it."

Her hand was on his sleeve, and he kept it there, but with no response in his gesture or in the lines of his preoccupied face.

"Did you think you'd seen it?" he asked, after an appreciable interval.

"Why, I actually took *you* for it, my dear, in my mad determination to spot it!"

"Me—just now?" His arm dropped away, and he turned from her with a faint echo of her laugh. "Really, dearest, you'd better give it up, if that's the best you can do."

"Oh, yes, I give it up. Have *you*?" she asked, turning round on him abruptly.

The parlour-maid had entered with letters and a lamp, and the light struck up into Boyne's face as he bent above the tray she presented.

"Have *you*?" Mary perversely insisted, when the servant had disappeared on her errand of illumination.

"Have I what?" he rejoined absently, the light bringing out the sharp stamp of worry between his brows as he turned over the letters.

"Given up trying to see the ghost." Her heart beat a little at the experiment she was making.

Her husband, laying his letters aside, moved away into the shadow of the hearth.

"I never tried," he said, tearing open the wrapper of a newspaper.

"Well, of course," Mary persisted, "the exasperating thing

is that there's no use trying, since one can't be sure till so long afterward."

He was unfolding the paper as if he had hardly heard her; but after a pause, during which the sheets rustled spasmodically between his hands, he looked up to ask, "Have you any idea *how long*?"

Mary had sunk into a low chair beside the fireplace. From her seat she glanced over, startled, at her husband's profile, which was projected against the circle of lamplight.

"No; none. Have *you*?" she retorted, repeating her former phrase with an added keenness of intention.

Boyne crumpled the paper into a bunch, and then, inconsequently, turned back with it toward the lamp.

"Lord, no! I only meant," he explained, with a faint tinge of impatience, "is there any legend, any tradition, as to that?"

"Not that I know of," she answered; but the impulse to add "What makes you ask?" was checked by the re-appearance of the parlour-maid with tea and a second lamp.

With the dispersal of shadows, and the repetition of the daily domestic office, Mary Boyne felt herself less oppressed by that sense of something mutely imminent which had darkened her afternoon. For a few moments she gave herself to the details of her task, and when she looked up from it she was struck to the point of bewilderment by the change in her husband's face. He had seated himself near the farther lamp, and was absorbed in the perusal of his letters; but was it something he had found in them, or merely the shifting of her own point of view, that had restored his features to their normal aspect? The longer she looked the more definitely the change affirmed itself. The lines of tension had vanished, and such traces of fatigue as lingered were of the kind easily attributable to steady mental effort. He glanced up, as if drawn by her gaze, and met her eyes with a smile.

"I'm dying for my tea, you know; and here's a letter for you," he said.

She took the letter he held out in exchange for the cup she proffered him, and, returning to her seat, broke the seal with the languid gesture of the reader whose interests are all enclosed in the circle of one cherished presence.

Her next conscious motion was that of starting to her feet, the letter falling to them as she rose, while she held out to her husband a newspaper clipping.

"Ned! What's this? What does it mean?"

He had risen at the same instant, almost as if hearing her cry before she uttered it; and for a perceptible space of time he and she studied each other, like adversaries watching for an advantage, across the space between her chair and his desk.

"What's what? You fairly made me jump!" Boyne said at length, moving toward her with a sudden, half-exasperated laugh. The shadow of apprehension was on his face again, not now a look of fixed foreboding, but a shifting vigilance of lips and eyes that gave her the sense of his feeling himself invisibly surrounded.

Her hand shook so that she could hardly give him the clipping.

"This article—from the *Waukesha Sentinel*—that a man named Elwell has brought suit against you—that there was something wrong about the Blue Star Mine. I can't understand more than half."

They continued to face each other as she spoke, and to her astonishment she saw that her words had the almost immediate effect of dissipating the strained watchfulness of his look.

"Oh, *that*!" He glanced down the printed slip, and then folded it with the gesture of one who handles something harmless and familiar. "What's the matter with you this afternoon, Mary? I thought you'd got bad news."

She stood before him with her undefinable terror subsiding slowly under the reassurance of his tone.

"You knew about this, then—it's all right?"

"Certainly I knew about it; and it's all right."

"But what *is* it? I don't understand. What does this man accuse you of?"

"Pretty nearly every crime in the calendar." Boyne had tossed the clipping down, and thrown himself comfortably into an armchair near the fire. "Do you want to hear the story? It's not particularly interesting—just a squabble over interests in the Blue Star."

"But who is this Elwell? I don't know the name."

"Oh, he's a fellow I put into it—gave him a hand up. I told you all about him at the time."

"I daresay. I must have forgotten." Vainly she strained back among her memories. "But if you helped him, why does he make this return?"

"Probably some shyster lawyer got hold of him and talked him over. It's all rather technical and complicated. I thought that kind of thing bored you."

His wife felt a sting of compunction. Theoretically, she deprecated the American wife's detachment from her husband's professional interests, but in practice she had always found it difficult to fix her attention on Boyne's report of the transactions in which his varied interests involved him. Besides, she had felt during their years of exile that, in a community where the amenities of living could be obtained only at the cost of efforts as arduous as her husband's professional labours, such brief leisure as he and she could command should be used as an escape from immediate preoccupations, a flight to the life they always dreamed of living. Once or twice, now that this new life had actually drawn its magic circle about them, she had asked herself if she had done right; but hitherto such conjectures had been no more than the retrospective excursions of an active fancy. Now, for the first time, it startled her a little to find how little she knew of the material foundation on which her happiness was built.

She glanced at her husband, and was again reassured by the composure of his face; yet she felt the need of more definite grounds for her reassurance.

"But doesn't this suit worry you? Why have you never spoken to me about it?"

He answered both questions at once. "I didn't speak of it at first because it *did* worry me—annoyed me, rather. But it's all ancient history now. Your correspondent must have got hold of a back number of the *Sentinel*."

She felt a quick thrill of relief. "You mean it's over? He's lost his case?"

There was a just perceptible delay in Boyne's reply. "The suit's been withdrawn—that's all."

But she persisted, as if to exonerate herself from the inward charge of being too easily put off. "Withdrawn it because he saw he had no chance?"

"Oh, he had no chance," Boyne answered.

She was still struggling with a dimly felt perplexity at the back of her thoughts.

"How long ago was it withdrawn?"

He paused, as if with a slight return of his former uncertainty. "I've just had the news now; but I've been expecting it."

"Just now—in one of your letters?"

"Yes; in one of my letters."

She made no answer, and was aware only, after a short interval of waiting, that he had risen, and, strolling across the room, had placed himself on the sofa at her side. She felt him, as he did so, pass an arm about her, she felt his hand seek hers and clasp it, and turning slowly, drawn by the warmth of his cheek, she met his smiling eyes.

"It's all right—it's all right?" she questioned, through the flood of her dissolving doubts; and "I give you my word it never was righter!" he laughed back at her, holding her close.

III

One of the strangest things she was afterward to recall out of all the next day's incredible strangeness was the sudden and complete recovery of her sense of security.

It was in the air when she woke in her low-ceilinged, dusky room; it went with her downstairs to the breakfast table, flashed out at her from the fire, and reduplicated itself from the flanks of the urn and the sturdy flutings of the Georgian teapot. It was as if, in some roundabout way, all her diffused fears of the previous day, with their moment of sharp concentration about the newspaper article—as if this dim questioning of the future, and startled return upon the past—had between them liquidated the arrears of some haunting moral obligation. If she had indeed been careless of her husband's affairs, it was, her new state seemed to prove, because her faith in him instinctively justified such carelessness; and his right to her faith had now affirmed itself in the very face of menace and suspicion. She had never seen him more untroubled, more naturally and unconsciously himself, than after the cross-examination to which she had subjected him: it was almost as if he had been aware of her lurking doubts, and had wanted the air cleared as much as she did.

It was as clear, thank Heaven!, as the bright outer light that surprised her almost with a touch of summer when she issued from the house for her daily round of the gardens. She had left Boyne at his desk, indulging herself, as she passed the library door, by a last peep at his quiet face, where he bent, pipe in mouth, above his papers; and now she had her own morning's task to perform. The task involved, on such charmed winter days, almost as much loitering about the different quarters of her demesne as if spring were already at work. There were such endless possibilities still before her, such opportunities to bring out the latent graces of the old place, without a single irreverent touch of alteration, that the winter was all too short to plan what spring and autumn executed. And her recovered sense of safety gave, on this particular morning, a peculiar zest to her progress through the sweet still place. She went first to the kitchen garden, where the espaliered pear trees drew complicated patterns on the walls, and pigeons were fluttering and preening about the silvery-slated roof of their cot. There was something wrong about the piping of the hothouse, and she was expecting an authority from Dorchester, who was to drive out between trains and make a diagnosis of the boiler. But when she dipped into the damp heat of the greenhouses, among the spiced scents and waxy pinks and reds of old-fashioned exotics—even the flora of Lyng was in the note!—she learned that the great man had not arrived, and, the day being too rare to waste in an artificial atmosphere, she came out again and paced slowly along the springy turf of the bowling green to the gardens behind the house. At their farther end rose a grass terrace, commanding, looking across the fish pond and yew hedges, a view of the long house front, with its twisted chimney stacks and blue roof angles all drenched in the pale gold moisture of the air.

Seen thus, across the level tracery of the yews, it sent her, from open windows and hospitably smoking chimneys, the look of some warm human presence, of a mind slowly ripened on a sunny wall of experience. She had never before had such a sense of her intimacy with it, such a conviction that its secrets were all beneficent, kept, as they said to children, "for one's good," such a trust in its power to gather up her life and Ned's into the harmonious pattern of the long, long story it sat there weaving in the sun.

She heard steps behind her, and turned, expecting to see the gardener accompanied by the engineer from Dorchester. But only one figure was in sight, that of a youngish slightly built man, who, for reasons she could not on the spot have given, did not remotely resemble her preconceived notion of an authority on hot-house boilers. The newcomer, on seeing her, lifted his hat, and paused with the air of a gentleman—perhaps a traveller—who wishes to make it known that his intrusion is involuntary. Lyng occasionally attracted the more cultivated traveller, and Mary half-expected to see the stranger dissemble a camera, or justify his presence by producing it. But he made no gesture of any sort, and after a moment she asked, in a tone responding to the courteous hesitation of his attitude: "Is there any one you wish to see?"

"I came to see Mr Boyne," he replied. His intonation, rather than his accent, was faintly American, and Mary, at the familiar note, looked at him more closely. The brim of his soft felt hat cast a shade on his face, which, thus obscured, wore to her short-sighted gaze a look of seriousness, as of a person arriving "on business," and civilly but firmly aware of his rights.

Past experience had made her equally sensible to such claims; but she was jealous of her husband's morning hours, and doubtful of his having given anyone the right to intrude on them.

"Have you an appointment with my husband?" she asked.

The visitor hesitated, as if unprepared for the question.

"I think he expects me," he replied.

It was Mary's turn to hesitate. "You see this is his time for work: he never sees any one in the morning."

He looked at her a moment without answering; then, as if accepting her decision, he began to move away. As he turned, Mary saw him pause and glance up at the peaceful house-front. Something in his air suggested weariness and disappointment, the dejection of the traveller who has come from far off and whose hours are limited by the time-table. It occurred to her that if this were the case her refusal might have made his errand vain, and a sense of compunction caused her to hasten after him.

"May I ask if you have come a long way?"

He gave her the same grave look. "Yes—I have come a long way."

"Then, if you'll go to the house, no doubt my husband will see you now. You'll find him in the library."

She did not know why she had added the last phrase, except from a vague impulse to atone for her previous inhospitality. The visitor seemed about to express his thanks, but her attention was distracted by the approach of the gardener with a companion who bore all the marks of being the expert from Dorchester.

"This way," she said, waving the stranger to the house; and an instant later she had forgotten him in the absorption of her meeting with the boiler-maker.

The encounter led to such far-reaching results that the engineer ended by finding it expedient to ignore his train, and Mary was beguiled into spending the remainder of the morning in absorbed confabulation among the flower-pots. When the colloquy ended, she was surprised to find that it was nearly luncheon-time, and she half expected, as she hurried back to the house, to see her husband coming out to meet her. But she found no one in the court but an under-gardener raking the gravel, and the hall, when she entered it, was so silent that she guessed Boyne to be still at work.

Not wishing to disturb him, she turned into the drawing room, and there, at her writing table, lost herself in renewed calculations of the outlay to which the morning's conference had pledged her. The knowledge that she could permit herself such follies had not yet lost its novelty; and somehow, in contrast to the vague fears of the previous days, it now seemed an element of her recovered security, of the sense that, as Ned had said, things in general had never been "righter."

She was still luxuriating in a lavish play of figures when the parlour maid, from the threshold, roused her with an inquiry as to the expediency of serving luncheon. It was one of their jokes that Trimmle announced luncheon as if she were divulging a state secret, and Mary, intent upon her papers, merely murmured an absent-minded assent.

She felt Trimmle wavering doubtfully on the threshold as if in rebuke of such unconsidered assent; then her retreating steps sounded down the passage, and Mary, pushing away her papers, crossed the hall and went to the library door. It was still closed, and she wavered in her turn, disliking to disturb her husband, yet anxious that he should not exceed his normal measure of work. As she stood there, balancing her impulses, the esoteric Trimmle returned with the announcement of luncheon, and Mary, thus impelled, opened the library door.

Boyne was not at his desk, and she peered about her, expecting to discover him before the bookshelves, somewhere down the length of the room; but her call brought no response, and gradually it became clear to her that he was not there.

She turned back to the parlour maid.

"Mr Boyne must be upstairs. Please tell him that luncheon is ready."

Trimmle appeared to hesitate between the obvious duty of obedience and an equally obvious conviction of the foolishness of the injunction laid on her. The struggle resulted in her saying: "If you please, Madam, Mr Boyne's not upstairs."

"Not in his room? Are you sure?"

"I'm sure, Madam."

Mary consulted the clock. "Where is he, then?"

"He's gone out," Trimmle announced, with the superior air of one who has respectfully waited for the question that a well-ordered mind would have put first.

Mary's conjecture had been right, then. Boyne must have gone to the gardens to meet her, and since she had missed him, it was clear that he had taken the shorter way by the south door, instead of going round to the court. She crossed the hall to the French window opening directly on the yew garden, but the parlour maid, after another moment of inner conflict, decided to bring out: "Please, Madam, Mr Boyne didn't go that way."

Mary turned back. "Where *did* he go? And when?"

"He went out of the front door, up the drive, Madam." It was a matter of principle with Trimmle never to answer more than one question at a time.

"Up the drive? At this hour?" Mary went to the door herself, and glanced across the court through the tunnel of bare limes. But its perspective was as empty as when she had scanned it on entering.

"Did Mr Boyne leave no message?"

Trimmle seemed to surrender herself to a last struggle with the forces of chaos.

"No, Madam. He just went out with the gentleman."

"The gentleman? What gentleman?" Mary wheeled about, as if to front this new factor.

"The gentleman who called, Madam," said Trimmle resignedly.

"When did a gentleman call? Do explain yourself, Trimmle!"

Only the fact that Mary was very hungry, and that she wanted to consult her husband about the greenhouses, would have caused her to lay so unusual an injunction on her attendant; and even now she was detached enough to note in Trimmle's eye the dawning defiance of the respectful subordinate who has been pressed too hard.

"I couldn't exactly say the hour, Madam, because I didn't let the gentleman in," she replied, with an air of discreetly ignoring the irregularity of her mistress's course.

"You didn't let him in?"

"No, Madam. When the bell rang I was dressing, and Agnes—"

"Go and ask Agnes, then," said Mary.

Trimmle still wore her look of patient magnanimity. "Agnes would not know, Madam, for she had unfortunately burnt her hand in trimming the wick of the new lamp from town"—Trimmle, as Mary was aware, had always been opposed to the new lamp—"and so Mrs Dockett sent the kitchen maid instead."

Mary looked again at the clock. "It's after two! Go and ask the kitchen maid if Mr Boyne left any word."

She went into luncheon without waiting, and Trimmle presently brought her there the kitchen maid's statement that the gentleman had called about eleven o'clock, and that Mr Boyne had gone out with him without leaving any message. The kitchen-maid did not even know the caller's name, for he had written it on a slip of paper, which he had folded and handed to her, with the injunction to deliver it at once to Mr Boyne.

Mary finished her luncheon, still wondering, and when it was over, and Trimmle had brought the coffee to the drawing room, her wonder had deepened to a first faint tinge of disquietude. It was unlike Boyne to absent himself without explanation at so unwonted an hour, and the difficulty of identifying the visitor whose summons he had apparently obeyed made his disappearance the more unaccountable. Mary Boyne's experience as the wife of a busy engineer, subject to sudden calls and compelled to keep irregular hours, had trained her to the philosophic acceptance of surprises; but since Boyne's withdrawal from business he had adopted a Benedictine regularity of life. As if to make up for the dispersed and agitated years, with their "stand-up" lunches, and dinners rattled down to the joltings of the dining cars, he cultivated the last refinements of punctuality and monotony, discouraging his wife's fancy for the unexpected, and declaring that to a delicate taste there were infinite gradations of pleasure in the recurrences of habit.

Still, since no life can completely defend itself from the unforeseen, it was evident that all Boyne's precautions would sooner or later prove unavailable, and Mary concluded that he had cut short a tiresome visit by walking with his caller to the station, or at least accompanying him for part of the way.

This conclusion relieved her from farther preoccupation, and she went out herself to take up her conference with the gardener. Thence she walked to the village post office, a mile or so away; and when she turned toward home the early twilight was setting in.

She had taken a footpath across the downs, and as Boyne, meanwhile, had probably returned from the station by the highroad, there was little likelihood of their meeting. She felt sure, however, of his having reached the house before her; so sure that, when she entered it herself, without even pausing to inquire of Trimmle, she made directly for the library. But the library was still empty, and with an unwonted exactness of visual memory she observed that the papers on her husband's desk lay precisely as they had lain when she had gone in to call him to luncheon.

Then of a sudden she was seized by a vague dread of the unknown. She had closed the door behind her on entering, and as she stood alone in the long silent room her dread seemed to take shape and sound, to be there breathing and lurking among the shadows. Her short-sighted eyes strained through them, half-discerning an actual presence, something aloof, that watched and knew; and in the recoil from that intangible presence she threw herself on the bell rope and gave it a sharp pull.

The sharp summons brought Trimmle in precipitately with a lamp, and Mary breathed again at this sobering reappearance of the usual.

"You may bring tea if Mr Boyne is in," she said, to justify her ring.

"Very well, Madam. But Mr Boyne is not in," said Trimmle, putting down the lamp.

"Not in? You mean he's come back and gone out again?"

"No, Madam. He's never been back."

The dread stirred again, and Mary knew that now it had her fast.

"Not since he went out with—the gentleman?"

"Not since he went out with the gentleman."

"But who *was* the gentleman?" Mary insisted, with the shrill note of someone trying to be heard through a confusion of noises.

"That I couldn't say, Madam." Trimmle, standing there by the lamp, seemed suddenly to grow less round and rosy, as though eclipsed by the same creeping shade of apprehension.

"But the kitchen maid knows—wasn't it the kitchen maid who let him in?"

"She doesn't know either, Madam, for he wrote his name on a folded paper."

Mary, through her agitation, was aware that they were both designating the unknown visitor by a vague pronoun, instead of the conventional formula which, till then, had kept their allusions within the bounds of conformity. And at the same moment her mind caught at the suggestion of the folded paper.

"But he must have a name! Where's the paper?"

She moved to the desk, and began to turn over the documents that littered it. The first that caught her eye was an unfinished letter in her husband's hand, with his pen lying across it, as though dropped there at a sudden summons.

"My dear Parvis"—who was Parvis?—"I have just received your letter announcing Elwell's death, and while I suppose there is now no further risk of trouble, it might be safer—"

She tossed the sheet aside, and continued her search; but no folded paper was discoverable among the letters and pages of manuscript which had been swept together in a heap, as if by a hurried or a startled gesture.

"But the kitchen maid *saw* him. Send her here," she commanded, wondering at her dulness in not thinking sooner of so simple a solution.

Trimmle vanished in a flash, as if thankful to be out of the room, and when she reappeared, conducting the agitated underling, Mary had regained her self-possession, and had her questions ready.

The gentleman was a stranger, yes—that she understood. But what had he said? And, above all, what had he looked like? The first question was easily enough answered, for the disconcerting reason that he had said so little—had merely asked for Mr Boyne, and, scribbling something on a bit of paper, had requested that it should at once be carried in to him.

"Then you don't know what he wrote? You're not sure it *was* his name?"

The kitchen maid was not sure, but supposed it was, since he had written it in answer to her inquiry as to whom she should announce.

“And when you carried the paper in to Mr Boyne, what did he say?”

The kitchen maid did not think that Mr Boyne had said anything, but she could not be sure, for just as she had handed him the paper and he was opening it, she had become aware that the visitor had followed her into the library, and she had slipped out, leaving the two gentlemen together.

“But then, if you left them in the library, how do you know that they went out of the house?”

This question plunged the witness into a momentary inarticulateness, from which she was rescued by Trimmle, who, by means of ingenious circumlocutions, elicited the statement that before she could cross the hall to the back passage she had heard the two gentlemen behind her, and had seen them go out of the front door together.

“Then, if you saw the strange gentleman twice, you must be able to tell me what he looked like.”

But with this final challenge to her powers of expression it became clear that the limit of the kitchen maid’s endurance had been reached. The obligation of going to the front door to “show in” a visitor was in itself so subversive of the fundamental order of things that it had thrown her faculties into hopeless disarray, and she could only stammer out, after various panting efforts: “His hat, mum, was different-like, as you might say—”

"Different? How different?" Mary flashed out, her own mind, in the same instant, leaping back to an image left on it that morning, and then lost under layers of subsequent impressions.

"His hat had a wide brim, you mean? and his face was pale—a youngish face?" Mary pressed her, with a white-lipped intensity of interrogation. But if the kitchen maid found any adequate answer to this challenge, it was swept away for her listener down the rushing current of her own convictions. The stranger—the stranger in the garden! Why had Mary not thought of him before? She needed no one now to tell her that it was he who had called for her husband and gone away with him. But who was he, and why had Boyne obeyed him?

IV

It leaped out at her suddenly, like a grin out of the dark, that they had often called England so little—"such a confoundedly hard place to get lost in."

A confoundedly hard place to get lost in! That had been her husband's phrase. And now, with the whole machinery of official investigation sweeping its flashlights from shore to shore, and across the dividing straits; now, with Boyne's name blazing from the walls of every town and village, his portrait (how that wrung her!) hawked up and down the country like the image of a hunted criminal; now the little compact populous island, so policed, surveyed and administered, revealed itself as a Sphinx-like guardian of abysmal mysteries, staring back into his wife's anguished eyes as if with the wicked joy of knowing something they would never know!

In the fortnight since Boyne's disappearance there had been no word of him, no trace of his movements. Even the usual misleading reports that raise expectancy in tortured bosoms had been few and fleeting. No one but the kitchen maid had seen Boyne leave the house, and no one else had seen "the gentleman" who accompanied him. All inquiries in the neighbourhood failed to elicit the memory of a stranger's presence that day in the neighbourhood of Lyng. And no one had met Edward Boyne, either alone or in company, in any of the neighbouring villages, or on the road across the downs, or at either of the local railway stations. The sunny English noon had swallowed him as completely as if he had gone out into Cimmerian night.

Mary, while every official means of investigation was working at its highest pressure, had ransacked her husband's papers for any trace of antecedent complications, of entanglements or obligations unknown to her, that might throw a ray into the darkness. But if any such had existed in the background of Boyne's life, they had vanished like the slip of paper on which the visitor had written his name. There remained no possible thread of guidance except—if it were indeed an exception—the letter which Boyne had apparently been in the act of writing when he received his mysterious summons. That letter, read and reread by his wife, and submitted by her to the police, yielded little enough to feed conjecture.

"I have just heard of Elwell's death, and while I suppose there is now no farther risk of trouble, it might be safer—" That was all. The "risk of trouble" was easily explained by the newspaper clipping which had apprised Mary of the suit brought against her husband by one of his associates in the Blue Star enterprise. The only new information conveyed by the letter was the fact of its showing Boyne, when he wrote it, to be still apprehensive of the results of the suit, though he had told his wife that it had been withdrawn, and though the letter itself proved that the plaintiff was dead. It took several days of cabling to fix the identity of the "Parvis" to whom the fragment was addressed, but even after these inquiries had shown him to be a Waukesha lawyer, no new facts concerning the Elwell suit were elicited. He appeared to have had no direct concern in it, but to have been conversant with the facts merely as an acquaintance, and possible intermediary; and he declared himself unable to guess with what object Boyne intended to seek his assistance.

This negative information, sole fruit of the first fortnight's search, was not increased by a jot during the slow weeks that followed. Mary knew that the investigations were still being carried on, but she had a vague sense of their gradually slackening, as the actual march of time seemed to slacken.

It was as though the days, flying horror-struck from the shrouded image of the one inscrutable day, gained assurance as the distance lengthened, till at last they fell back into their normal gait. And so with the human imaginations at work on the dark event. No doubt it occupied them still, but week by week and hour by hour it grew less absorbing, took up less space, was slowly but inevitably crowded out of the foreground of consciousness by the new problems perpetually bubbling up from the cloudy caldron of human experience.

Even Mary Boyne's consciousness gradually felt the same lowering of velocity. It still swayed with the incessant oscillations of conjecture; but they were slower, more rhythmical in their beat. There were even moments of weariness when, like the victim of some poison which leaves the brain clear, but holds the body motionless, she saw herself domesticated with the Horror, accepting its perpetual presence as one of the fixed conditions of life.

These moments lengthened into hours and days, till she passed into a phase of stolid acquiescence. She watched the routine of daily life with the incurious eye of a savage on whom the meaningless processes of civilisation make but the faintest impression. She had come to regard herself as part of the routine, a spoke of the wheel, revolving with its motion; she felt almost like the furniture of the room in which she sat, an insensate object to be dusted and pushed about with the chairs and tables. And this deepening apathy held her fast at Lyng, in spite of the entreaties of friends and the usual medical recommendation of "change." Her friends supposed that her refusal to move was inspired by the belief that her husband would one day return to the spot from which he had vanished, and a beautiful legend grew up about this imaginary state of waiting. But in reality she had no such belief: the depths of anguish enclosing her were no longer lighted by flashes of hope. She was sure that Boyne would never come back, that he had gone out of her sight as completely as if Death itself had waited that day on the threshold. She had even renounced, one by one, the various theories as to his disappearance which had been advanced by the press, the police, and her own agonised imagination. In sheer lassitude her mind turned from these alternatives of horror, and sank back into the blank fact that he was gone.

No, she would never know what had become of him—no one would ever know. But the house *knew*; the library in which she spent her long lonely evenings knew. For it was here that the last scene had been enacted, here that the stranger had come, and spoken the word which had caused Boyne to rise and follow him. The floor she trod had felt his tread; the books on the shelves had seen his face; and there were moments when the intense consciousness of the old dusky walls seemed about to break out into some audible revelation of their secret. But the revelation never came, and she knew it would never come. Lyng was not one of the garrulous old houses that betray the secrets entrusted to them. Its very legend proved that it had always been the mute accomplice, the incorruptible custodian, of the mysteries it had surprised. And Mary Boyne, sitting face to face with its silence, felt the futility of seeking to break it by any human means.

V

"I don't say it *wasn't* straight, and yet I don't say it *was* straight. It was business."

Mary, at the words, lifted her head with a start, and looked intently at the speaker.

When, half an hour before, a card with "Mr Parvis" on it had been brought up to her, she had been immediately aware that the name had been a part of her consciousness ever since she had read it at the head of Boyne's unfinished letter. In the library she had found awaiting her a small sallow man with a bald head and gold eyeglasses, and it sent a tremor through her to know that this was the person to whom her husband's last known thought had been directed.

Parvis, civilly, but without vain preamble—in the manner of a man who has his watch in his hand—had set forth the object of his visit. He had "run over" to England on business, and finding himself in the neighbourhood of Dorchester had not wished to leave it without paying his respects to Mrs Boyne; and without asking her, if the occasion offered, what she meant to do about Bob Elwell's family.

The words touched the spring of some obscure dread in Mary's bosom. Did her visitor, after all, know what Boyne had meant by his unfinished phrase? She asked for an elucidation of his question, and noticed at once that he seemed surprised at her continued ignorance of the subject. Was it possible that she really knew as little as she said?

"I know nothing—you must tell me," she faltered out; and her visitor thereupon proceeded to unfold his story. It threw, even to her confused perceptions, and imperfectly initiated vision, a lurid glare on the whole hazy episode of the Blue Star Mine. Her husband had made his money in that brilliant speculation at the cost of "getting ahead" of someone less alert to seize the chance; and the victim of his ingenuity was young Robert Elwell, who had "put him on" to the Blue Star scheme.

Parvis, at Mary's first cry, had thrown her a sobering glance through his impartial glasses.

"Bob Elwell wasn't smart enough, that's all; if he had been, he might have turned round and served Boyne the same way. It's the kind of thing that happens every day in business. I guess it's what the scientists call the survival of the fittest—see?" said Mr Parvis, evidently pleased with the aptness of his analogy.

Mary felt a physical shrinking from the next question she tried to frame: it was as though the words on her lips had a taste that nauseated her.

"But then—you accuse my husband of doing something dishonourable?"

Mr Parvis surveyed the question dispassionately. "Oh, no, I don't. I don't even say it wasn't straight." He glanced up and down the long lines of books, as if one of them might have supplied him with the definition he sought. "I don't say it *wasn't* straight, and yet I don't say it *was* straight. It was business." After all, no definition in his category could be more comprehensive than that.

Mary sat staring at him with a look of terror. He seemed to her like the indifferent emissary of some evil power.

"But Mr Elwell's lawyers apparently did not take your view, since I suppose the suit was withdrawn by their advice."

"Oh, yes; they knew he hadn't a leg to stand on, technically. It was when they advised him to withdraw the suit that he got desperate. You see, he'd borrowed most of the money he lost in the Blue Star, and he was up a tree. That's why he shot himself when they told him he had no show."

The horror was sweeping over Mary in great deafening waves.

"He shot himself? He killed himself because of *that*?"

"Well, he didn't kill himself, exactly. He dragged on two months before he died." Parvis emitted the statement as unemotionally as a gramophone grinding out its "record."

"You mean that he tried to kill himself, and failed? And tried again?"

"Oh, he didn't have to *try* again," said Parvis grimly.

They sat opposite each other in silence, he swinging his eyeglasses thoughtfully about his finger, she, motionless, her arms stretched along her knees in an attitude of rigid tension.

"But if you knew all this," she began at length, hardly able to force her voice above a whisper, "how is it that when I wrote you at the time of my husband's disappearance you said you didn't understand his letter?"

Parvis received this without perceptible embarrassment: "Why, I didn't understand it—strictly speaking. And it wasn't the time to talk about it, if I had. The Elwell business was settled when the suit was withdrawn. Nothing I could have told you would have helped you to find your husband."

Mary continued to scrutinise him. "Then why are you telling me now?"

Still Parvis did not hesitate. "Well, to begin with, I supposed you knew more than you appear to—I mean about the circumstances of Elwell's death. And then people are talking of it now; the whole matter's been raked up again. And I thought if you didn't know you ought to."

She remained silent, and he continued: "You see, it's only come out lately what a bad state Elwell's affairs were in. His wife's a proud woman, and she fought on as long as she could, going out to work, and taking sewing at home when she got too sick—something with the heart, I believe. But she had his mother to look after, and the children, and she broke down under it, and finally had to ask for help. That called attention to the case, and the papers took it up, and a subscription was started. Everybody out there liked Bob Elwell, and most of the prominent names in the place are down on the list, and people began to wonder why—"

Parvis broke off to fumble in an inner pocket. "Here," he continued, "here's an account of the whole thing from the *Sentinel*—a little sensational, of course. But I guess you'd better look it over."

He held out a newspaper to Mary, who unfolded it slowly, remembering, as she did so, the evening when, in that same room, the perusal of a clipping from the *Sentinel* had first shaken the depths of her security.

As she opened the paper, her eyes, shrinking from the glaring headlines, "Widow of Boyne's Victim Forced to Appeal for Aid," ran down the column of text to two portraits inserted in it. The first was her husband's, taken from a photograph made the year they had come to England. It was the picture of him that she liked best, the one that stood on the writing table upstairs in her bedroom. As the eyes in the photograph met hers, she felt it would be impossible to read what was said of him, and closed her lids with the sharpness of the pain.

"I thought if you felt disposed to put your name down—" she heard Parvis continue.

She opened her eyes with an effort, and they fell on the other portrait. It was that of a youngish man, slightly built, with features somewhat blurred by the shadow of a projecting hat brim. Where had she seen that outline before? She stared at it confusedly, her heart hammering in her ears. Then she gave a cry.

"This is the man—the man who came for my husband!"

She heard Parvis start to his feet, and was dimly aware that she had slipped backward into the corner of the sofa, and that he was bending above her in alarm. She straightened herself, and reached out for the paper, which she had dropped.

"It's the man! I should know him anywhere!" she persisted in a voice that sounded to her own ears like a scream.

Parvis's answer seemed to come to her from far off, down endless fog-muffled windings.

"Mrs Boyne, you're not very well. Shall I call somebody? Shall I get a glass of water?"

"No, no, no!" She threw herself toward him, her hand frantically clutching the newspaper. "I tell you, it's the man! I *know* him! He spoke to me in the garden!"

Parvis took the journal from her, directing his glasses to the portrait. "It can't be, Mrs Boyne. It's Robert Elwell."

"Robert Elwell?" Her white stare seemed to travel into space. "Then it was Robert Elwell who came for him."

"Came for Boyne? The day he went away from here?" Parvis's voice dropped as hers rose. He bent over, laying a fraternal hand on her, as if to coax her gently back into her seat. "Why, Elwell was dead! Don't you remember?"

Mary sat with her eyes fixed on the picture, unconscious of what he was saying.

"Don't you remember Boyne's unfinished letter to me—the one you found on his desk that day? It was written just after he'd heard of Elwell's death." She noticed an odd shake in Parvis's unemotional voice. "Surely you remember!" he urged her.

Yes, she remembered: that was the profoundest horror of it. Elwell had died the day before her husband's disappearance; and this was Elwell's portrait; and it was the portrait of the man who had spoken to her in the garden. She lifted her head and looked slowly about the library.

The library could have borne witness that it was also the portrait of the man who had come in that day to call Boyne from his unfinished letter. Through the misty surgings of her brain she heard the faint boom of half-forgotten words—words spoken by Alida Stair on the lawn at Pangbourne before Boyne and his wife had ever seen the house at Lyng, or had imagined that they might one day live there.

"This was the man who spoke to me," she repeated.

She looked again at Parvis. He was trying to conceal his disturbance under what he probably imagined to be an expression of indulgent commiseration; but the edges of his lips were blue. "He thinks me mad; but I'm not mad," she reflected; and suddenly there flashed upon her a way of justifying her strange affirmation.

She sat quiet, controlling the quiver of her lips, and waiting till she could trust her voice; then she said, looking straight at Parvis: "Will you answer me one question, please? When was it that Robert Elwell tried to kill himself?"

"When—when?" Parvis stammered.

"Yes; the date. Please try to remember."

She saw that he was growing still more afraid of her. "I have a reason," she insisted.

"Yes, yes. Only I can't remember. About two months before, I should say."

"I want the date," she repeated.

Parvis picked up the newspaper. "We might see here," he said, still humouring her. He ran his eyes down the page. "Here it is. Last October—the—"

She caught the words from him. "The 20th, wasn't it?" With a sharp look at her, he verified. "Yes, the 20th. Then you *did* know?"

"I know now." Her gaze continued to travel past him. "Sunday, the 20th—that was the day he came first."

Parvis's voice was almost inaudible. "Came *here* first?"

"Yes."

"You saw him twice, then?"

"Yes, twice." She just breathed it at him. "He came first on the 20th of October. I remember the date because it was the day we went up Meldon Steep for the first time." She felt a faint gasp of inward laughter at the thought that but for that she might have forgotten.

Parvis continued to scrutinise her, as if trying to intercept her gaze.

"We saw him from the roof," she went on. "He came down the lime avenue toward the house. He was dressed just as he is in that picture. My husband saw him first. He was frightened, and ran down ahead of me; but there was no one there. He had vanished."

"Elwell had vanished?" Parvis faltered.

"Yes." Their two whispers seemed to grope for each other. "I couldn't think what had happened. I see now. He *tried* to come then; but he wasn't dead enough—he couldn't reach us. He had to wait for two months to die; and then he came back again—and Ned went with him."

She nodded at Parvis with the look of triumph of a child who has worked out a difficult puzzle. But suddenly she lifted her hands with a desperate gesture, pressing them to her temples.

"Oh, my God! I sent him to Ned—I told him where to go! I sent him to this room!" she screamed.

She felt the walls of books rush toward her, like inward falling ruins; and she heard Parvis, a long way off, through the ruins, crying to her, and struggling to get at her. But she was numb to his touch, she did not know what he was saying. Through the tumult she heard but one clear note, the voice of Alida Stair, speaking on the lawn at Pangbourne.

"You won't know till afterward," it said. "You won't know till long, long afterward."

CHANGE

Arthur Machen

“Here,” said old Mr Vincent Rimmer, fumbling in the pigeonholes of his great and ancient bureau, “is an oddity which may interest you.”

He drew a sheet of paper out of the dark place where it had been hidden, and handed it to Reynolds, his curious guest. The oddity was an ordinary sheet of notepaper, of a sort which has long been popular; a bluish grey with slight flecks and streaks of a darker blue embedded in its substance. It had yellowed a little with age at the edges. The outer page was blank; Reynolds laid it open, and spread it out on the table beside his chair. He read something like this:

a aa e ee i e ee
aa i o e ee o
ee ee i aa o oo o
a o a a e i ee
e o i ee a e i

Reynolds scanned it with stupefied perplexity.

"What on earth is it?" he said. "Does it mean anything? Is it a cypher, or a silly game, or what?"

Mr Rimmer chuckled. "I thought it might puzzle you," he remarked. "Do you happen to notice anything about the writing; anything out of the way at all?"

Reynolds scanned the document more closely.

"Well, I don't know that there is anything out of the way in the script itself. The letters are rather big, perhaps, and they are rather clumsily formed. But it's difficult to judge handwriting by a few letters, repeated again and again. But, apart from the writing, what is it?"

"That's a question that must wait a bit. There are many strange things related to that bit of paper. But one of the strangest things about it is this: that it is intimately connected with the Darren Mystery."

"What Mystery did you say? The Darren Mystery? I don't think I ever heard of it."

"Well, it was a little before your time. And, in any case, I don't see how you could have heard of it. There were, certainly, some very curious and unusual circumstances in the case, but I don't think that they were generally known, and if they were known, they were not understood. You won't wonder at that, perhaps, when you consider that the bit of paper before you was one of those circumstances."

"But what exactly happened?"

"That is largely a matter of conjecture. But, anyhow, here's the outside of the case, for a beginning. Now, to start with, I don't suppose you've ever been to Meirion? Well, you should go. It's a beautiful county, in West Wales, with a fine sea coast, and some very pleasant places to stay at, and none of them too large or too popular. One of the smallest of these places, Trenant, is just a village. There is a wooded height above it called the Allt; and down below, the church, with a Celtic cross in the churchyard, a dozen or so of cottages, a row of lodging houses on the slope round the corner, a few more cottages dotted along the road to Meiros, and that's all. Below the village are marshy meadows where the brook that comes from the hills spreads abroad, and then the dunes, and the sea, stretching away to the Dragon's Head in the far east and enclosed to the west by the beginnings of the limestone cliffs. There are fine, broad sands all the way between Trenant and Porth, the market town, about a mile and a half away, and it's just the place for children.

"Well, just forty-five years ago, Trenant was having a very successful season. In August there must have been eighteen or nineteen visitors in the village. I was staying in Porth at the time, and, when I walked over, it struck me that the Trenant beach was quite crowded—eight or nine children castle-building and learning to swim, and looking for shells, and all the usual diversions. The grown-up people sat in groups on the edge of the dunes and read and gossiped, or took a turn towards Porth, or perhaps tried to catch prawns in the rock pools at the other end of the sands. Altogether a very pleasant, happy scene in its simple way, and, as it was a beautiful summer, I have no doubt they all enjoyed themselves very much. I walked to Trenant and back three or four times, and I noticed that most of the children were more or less in charge of a very pretty dark girl, quite young, who seemed to advise in laying out the ground plan of the castle, and to take off her stockings and tuck up her skirts—we thought a lot of Legs in those days—when the bathers required supervision. She also indicated the kinds of shells which deserved the attention of collectors: an extremely serviceable girl.

"It seemed that this girl, Alice Hayes, was really in charge of the children—or of the greater part of them. She was a sort of nursery governess or lady of all work to Mrs Brown, who had come down from London in the early part of July with Miss Hayes and little Michael, a child of eight, who refused to recover nicely from his attack of measles. Mr Brown had joined them at the end of the month with the two elder children, Jack and Rosamund. Then, there were the Smiths, with their little family, and the Robinsons with their three; and the fathers and mothers, sitting on the beach every morning, got to know each other very easily. Mrs Smith and Mrs Robinson soon appreciated Miss Hayes's merits as a child-herd; they noticed that Mrs

Brown sat placid and went on knitting in the sun, quite safe and unperturbed, while they suffered from recurrent alarms. Jack Smith, though barely fourteen, would be seen dashing through the waves, out to sea, as if he had quite made up his mind to swim to the Dragon's Head, about twenty miles away, or Jane Robinson, in bright pink, would appear suddenly right away among the rocks of the point, ready to vanish into the perilous unknown round the corner. Hence, alarums and excursions, tiring expeditions of rescue and remonstrance, through soft sand or over slippery rocks under a hot sun. And then these ladies would discover that certain of their offspring had entirely disappeared or were altogether missing from the landscape; and dreadful and true tales of children who had driven tunnels into the sand and had been overwhelmed therein rushed to the mind. And all the while Mrs Brown sat serene, confident in the overseership of her Miss Hayes. So, as was to be gathered, the other two took counsel together. Mrs Brown was approached, and something called an arrangement was made, by which Miss Hayes undertook the joint mastership of all three packs, greatly to the ease of Mrs Smith and Mrs Robinson.

It was about this time, I suppose, that I got to know this group of holidaymakers. I had met Smith, whom I knew slightly in town, in the streets of Porth, just as I was setting out for one of my morning walks. We strolled together to Trenant on the firm sand down by the water's edge, and introductions went round, and so I joined the party, and sat with them, watching the various diversions of the children and the capable superintendence of Miss Hayes.

"Now there's a queer thing about this little place," said Brown, a genial man, connected, I believe, with Lloyd's. "Wouldn't you say this was as healthy a spot as any you could find? Well sheltered from the north, southern aspect, never too cold in winter, fresh sea breeze in summer: what could you have more?"

"Well," I replied, "it always agrees with me very well: a little relaxing, perhaps, but I like being relaxed. Isn't it a healthy place, then? What makes you think so?"

"I'll tell you. We have rooms in Govan Terrace, up there on the hillside. The other night I woke up with a coughing fit. I got out of bed to get a drink of water, and then had a look out of the windows to see what sort of night it was. I didn't like the look of those clouds in the south-west after sunset the night before. As you can see, the upper windows of Govan Terrace command a good many of the village houses. And, do you know, there was a light in almost every house? At two o'clock in the morning. Apparently the village is full of sick people. But who would have thought it?"

We were sitting a little apart from the rest. Smith had brought a London paper from Porth and he and Robinson had their heads together over the City article. The three women were knitting and talking hard, and down by the blue, creaming water Miss Hayes and her crew were playing happily in the sunshine.

"Do you mind," I said to Brown, "if I swear you to secrecy? A limited secrecy: I don't want you to speak of this to any of the village people. They wouldn't like it. And have you told your wife or any of the party about what you saw?"

"As a matter of fact, I haven't said a word to anybody. Illness isn't a very cheerful topic for a holiday, is it? But what's up? You don't mean to say there's some sort of epidemic in the place that they're keeping dark? I say! That would be awful. We should have to leave at once. Think of the children."

"Nothing of the kind. I don't think that there's a single case of illness in the place—unless you count old Thomas Evans, who has been in what he calls a decline for thirty years. You won't say anything? Then I'm going to give you a shock. The people have a light burning in their houses all night to keep out the fairies."

I must say it was a success. Brown looked frightened. Not of the fairies; most certainly not; rather at the reversion of his established order of things. He occupied his business in the City; he lived in an extremely comfortable house at Addiscombe; he was a keen though sane adherent of the Liberal Party; and in the world between these points there was no room at all either for fairies or for people who believed in fairies. The latter were almost as fabulous to him as the former, and still more objectionable.

“Look here!” he said at last. “You’re pulling my leg. Nobody believes in fairies. They haven’t for hundreds of years. Shakespeare didn’t believe in fairies. He says so.”

I let him run on. He implored me to tell him whether it was typhoid, or only measles, or even chickenpox. I said at last:

“You seem very positive on the subject of fairies. Are you sure there are no such things?”

“Of course I am,” said Brown, very crossly.

“How do you know?”

It is a shocking thing to be asked a question like that, to which, be it observed, there is no answer. I left him seething dangerously.

“Remember,” I said, “not a word of lit windows to anybody; but if you are uneasy as to epidemics, ask the doctor about it.”

He nodded his head glumly. I knew he was drawing all sorts of false conclusions; and for the rest of our stay I would say that he did not seek me out—until the last day of his visit. I had no doubt that he put me down as a believer in fairies and a maniac; but it is, I consider, good for men who live between the City and Liberal politics and Addiscombe to be made to realize that there is a world elsewhere. And, as it happens, it was quite true that most of the Trenant people believed in the fairies and were horribly afraid of them.

But this was only an interlude. I often strolled over and joined the party. And I took up my freedom with the young members by contributing posts and a tennis net to the beach sports. They had brought down rackets and balls, in the vague idea that they might be able to get a game somehow and somewhere, and my contribution was warmly welcomed. I helped Miss Hayes to fix the net, and she marked out the court, with the help of many suggestions from the elder children, to which she did not pay the slightest attention. I think the constant disputes as to whether the ball was "in" or "out" brightened the game, though Wimbledon would not have approved. And sometimes the elder children accompanied their parents to Porth in the evening and watched the famous Japanese Jugglers or Pepper's Ghost at the Assembly Rooms, or listened to the Mysterious Musicians at the De Barry Gardens—and altogether everybody had, you would say, a very jolly time.

It all came to a dreadful end. One morning when I had come out on my usual morning stroll from Porth, and had got to the camping ground of the party at the edge of the dunes, I found somewhat to my surprise that there was nobody there. I was afraid that Brown had been in part justified in his dread of concealed epidemics, and that some of the children had "caught something" in the village. So I walked up in the direction of Govan Terrace, and found Brown standing at the bottom of his flight of steps, and looking very much upset.

I hailed him.

"I say," I began, "I hope you weren't right, after all.

None of the children down with measles, or anything of that sort?"

"It's something worse than measles. We none of us know what has happened. The doctor can make nothing of it. Come in, and we can talk it over."

Just then a procession came down the steps leading from a house a few doors further on. First of all there was the porter from the station, with a pile of luggage on his truck. Then came the two elder Smith children, Jack and Millicent, and finally Mr and Mrs Smith. Mr Smith was carrying something wrapped in a bundle in his arms.

"Where's Bob?" He was the youngest; a brave, rosy little man of five or six.

"Smith's carrying him," murmured Brown. "What's happened? Has he hurt himself on the rocks? I hope it's nothing serious."

I was going forward to make my enquiries, but Brown put a hand on my arm and checked me. Then I looked at the Smith party more closely, and I saw at once that there was something very much amiss. The two elder children had been crying, though the boy was doing his best to put up a brave face against disaster—whatever it was. Mrs Smith had drawn her veil over her face, and stumbled as she walked, and on Smith's face there was a horror as of ill dreams.

"Look," said Brown in his low voice.

Smith had half-turned, as he set out with his burden to walk down the hill to the station. I don't think he knew we were there; I don't think any of the party had noticed us as we stood on the bottom step, half-hidden by a blossoming shrub. But as he turned uncertainly, like a man in the dark, the wrappings fell away a little from what he carried, and I saw a little wizened, yellow face peering out; malignant, deplorable.

I turned helplessly to Brown, as that most wretched procession went on its way and vanished out of sight.

"What on earth has happened? That's not Bobby. Who is it?"

"Come into the house," said Brown, and he went before me up the long flight of steps that led to the terrace.

There was a shriek and a noise of thin, shrill, high-pitched laughter as we came into the lodging house.

"That's Miss Hayes in blaspheming hysterics," said Brown grimly. "My wife's looking after her. The children are in the room at the back. I daren't let them go out by themselves in this awful place." He beat with his foot on the floor and glared at me, awestruck, a solid man shaken.

"Well," he said at last, "I'll tell you what we know; and as far as I can make out, that's very little. However.... You know Miss Hayes, who helps Mrs Brown with the children, had more or less taken over the charge of the lot; the young Robinsons and the Smiths, too. You've seen how well she looks after them all on the sands in the morning. In the afternoon she's been taking them inland for a change. You know there's beautiful country if you go a little way inland;

rather wild and woody; but still very nice; pleasant and shady. Miss Hayes thought that the all-day glare of the sun on the sands might not be very good for the small ones, and my wife agreed with her. So they took their teas with them and picnicked in the woods and enjoyed themselves very much, I believe. They didn't go more than a couple of miles or three at the outside; and the little ones used to take turns in a go-cart. They never seemed too tired.

"Yesterday at lunch they were talking about some caves at a place called the Darren, about two miles away. My children seemed very anxious to see them, and Mrs Probert, our landlady, said they were quite safe, so the Smiths and Robinsons were called in, and they were enthusiastic, too; and the whole party set off with their tea-baskets, and candles and matches, in Miss Hayes's charge. Somehow they made a later start than usual, and from what I can make out they enjoyed themselves so much in the cool dark cave, first of all exploring, and then looking for treasure, and winding up with tea by candlelight, that they didn't notice how the time was going—nobody had a watch—and by the time they'd packed up their traps and come out from underground, it was quite dark. They had a little trouble making out the way at first, but not very much, and came along in high spirits, tumbling over molehills and each other, and finding it all quite an adventure.

"They had got down in the road there, and were sorting themselves out into the three parties, when somebody called out: 'Where's Bobby Smith?' Well, he wasn't there. The usual story; everybody thought he was with somebody else. They were all mixed up in the dark, talking and laughing and shrieking at the top of their voices, and taking everything for granted—I suppose it was like that. But poor little Bob was missing. You can guess what a scene there was. Everybody was much too frightened to scold Miss Hayes, who had no doubt been extremely careless, to say the least of it—not like her. Robinson pulled us together. He told Mrs Smith that the little chap would be perfectly all right: there were no precipices to fall over and no water to fall into, the way they'd been, that it was a warm night, and the child had had a good stuffing tea, and he would be as right as rain when they found him. So we got a man from the farm, with a lantern, and Miss Hayes to show us exactly where they'd been, and Smith and Robinson and I went off to find poor Bobby, feeling a good deal better than at first. I noticed that the farm man seemed a good deal put out when we told him what had happened and where we were going. 'Got lost in the Darren,' he said, 'indeed, that is a pity.' That set Smith off at once; and he asked Williams what he meant; what was the matter with the place? Williams said there was nothing the matter with it at all whatever but it was 'a tiresome place to be in after dark.' That reminded me of what you were saying a couple of weeks ago about the people here. 'Some damned superstitious nonsense,' I said to myself, and thanked God it was nothing worse. I thought the fellow might be going to tell us of a masked bog or something like that. I gave Smith a hint in a whisper as to where the land lay; and we went on, hoping to come on little Bob any minute. Nearly all the way we were going through open fields without any cover or bracken or anything of that sort, and Williams kept twirling his lantern, and Miss Hayes and the rest of us called out the child's name; there didn't seem much chance of missing him.

"However, we saw nothing of him—till we got to the Darren. It's an odd sort of place, I should think. You're in an ordinary field, with a gentle upward slope, and you come to a gate, and down you go into a deep, narrow valley; a regular nest of valleys as far as I could make out in the dark, one leading into another, and the sides covered with trees. The famous caves were on one of these steep slopes, and, of course, we all went in. They didn't stretch far; nobody could have got lost in them, even if the candles gave out. We searched the place thoroughly, and saw where the children had had their tea: no signs of Bobby. So we went on down the valley between the woods, till we came to where it opens out into a wide space, with one tree growing all alone in the middle. And then we heard a miserable whining noise, like some little creature that's got hurt. And there under the tree was—what you saw poor Smith carrying in his arms this morning.

"It fought like a wild cat when Smith tried to pick it up, and jabbered some unearthly sort of gibberish. Then Miss

Hayes came along and seemed to soothe it; and it's been quiet ever since. The man with the lantern was shaking with terror; the sweat was pouring down his face."

I stared hard at Brown. "And," I thought to myself, "you are very much in the same condition as Williams."

Brown was obviously overcome with dread. We sat there in silence.

"Why do you say 'it'?" I asked. "Why don't you say 'him'?"

"You saw."

"Do you mean to tell me seriously that you don't believe that child you helped to bring home was Bobby? What does Mrs Smith say?"

"She says the clothes are the same. I suppose it must be Bobby. The doctor from Porth says the child must have had a severe shock. I don't think he knows anything about it."

He stuttered over his words, and said at last: "I was thinking of what you said about the lighted windows. I hoped you might be able to help. Can you do anything? We are leaving this afternoon; all of us. Is there nothing to be done?"

"I am afraid not."

I had nothing else to say. We shook hands and parted without more words.

The next day I walked over to the Darren. There was something fearful about the place, even in the haze of a golden afternoon. As Brown had said, the entrance and the disclosure of it were sudden and abrupt. The fields of the approach held no hint of what was to come. Then, past the gate, the ground fell violently away on every side, grey rocks of an ill shape pierced through it, and the ash trees on the steep slopes overshadowed all. The descent was into silence, without the singing of a bird, into a wizard shade. At the farther end, where the wooded heights retreated somewhat, there was the open space, or circus, of turf; and in the middle of it a very ancient, twisted thorn tree, beneath which the party in the dark had found the little creature that whined and cried out in unknown speech. I turned about, and on my way back I entered the caves, and lit the carriage candle I had brought with me. There was nothing much to see—I never think there is much to see in caves. There was the place where the children and others before them had taken their tea, with a ring of blackened stones within which many fires of twigs had been kindled. In caves or out of caves, townsfolk in the country are always alike in leaving untidy and unseemly litter behind; and here were the usual scraps of greasy paper, daubed with smears of jam and butter, the half-eaten sandwich, and the gnawed crust. Amidst all this nastiness I saw a piece of folded notepaper, and in sheer idleness picked it up and opened it. You have just seen it. When I asked you if you saw anything peculiar about the writing, you said that the letters were rather big and clumsy. The reason of that is that they were written by a child. I don't think you examined the back of the second leaf. Look: "Rosamund"—Rosamund Brown, that is. And beneath; there, in the corner.

Reynolds looked, and read, and gaped aghast.

"That was—her other name; her name in the dark."

"Name in the dark?"

"In the dark night of the Sabbath. That pretty girl had caught them all. They were in her hands, those wretched children, like the clay images she made. I found one of those things, hidden in a cleft of the rocks, near the place where they had made their fire. I ground it into dust beneath my feet."

"And I wonder what her name was?"

"They called her, I think, the Bridegroom and the Bride."

"Did you ever find out who she was, or where she came from?"

"Very little. Only that she had been a mistress at the Home for Christian Orphans in North Tottenham, where there was a hideous scandal some years before."

"Then she must have been older than she looked, according to your description."

"Possibly."

They sat in silence for a few minutes. Then Reynolds said:

"But I haven't asked you about this formula, or whatever you may call it—all these vowels, here. Is it a cypher?"

"No. But it is really a great curiosity, and it raises some extraordinary questions, which are outside this particular case. To begin with—and I am sure I could go much farther back than my beginning, if I had the necessary scholarship—I once read an English rendering of a Greek manuscript of the second or third century—I won't be certain which. It's a long time since I've seen the thing. The translator and editor of it was of the opinion that it was a Mithraic Ritual; but I have gathered that weightier authorities are strongly inclined to discredit this view. At any rate, it was no doubt an initiation rite into some mystery; possibly it had Gnostic connections; I don't know. But our interest lies in this, that one of the stages or portals, or whatever you call them, consisted almost exactly of that formula you have in your hand. I don't say that the vowels and double vowels are in the same order; I don't think the Greek manuscript has any *ae*s or *aa*s. But it is perfectly clear that the two documents are of the same kind and have the same purpose. And, advancing a little in time from the Greek manuscript, I don't think it is very surprising that the final operation of an incantation in mediæval and later magic consisted of this wailing on vowels arranged in a certain order.

"But here is something that is surprising. A good many years ago I strolled one Sunday morning into a church in Bloomsbury, the headquarters of a highly respectable sect. And in the middle of a very dignified ritual there rose quite suddenly, without preface or warning, this very sound, a wild wail of vowels. The effect was astounding, anyhow; whether it was terrifying or merely funny is a matter of taste. You'll have guessed what I heard: they call it 'speaking with tongues,' and they believe it to be a heavenly language. And I need scarcely say that they mean very well. But the problem is: how did a congregation of solid Scotch Presbyterians hit on that queer, ancient and not over-sanctified method of expressing spiritual emotion? It is a singular puzzle.

"And that woman? That is not by any means so difficult. The good Scotchmen—I can't think how they did it—got hold of something that didn't belong to them: she was in her own tradition. And, as they say down there: *asakai dasa*: the darkness is undying."

LUELLA MILLER

Mary Wilkins Freeman

CLOSE TO THE VILLAGE STREET stood the one-story house in which Luella Miller, who had an evil name in the village, had dwelt. She had been dead for years, yet there were those in the village who, in spite of the clearer light which comes on a vantage-point from a long-past danger, half believed in the tale which they had heard from their childhood. In their hearts, although they scarcely would have owned it, was a survival of the wild horror and frenzied fear of their ancestors who had dwelt in the same age with Luella Miller. Young people even would stare with a shudder at the old house as they passed, and children never played around it as was their wont around an untenanted building. Not a window in the old Miller house was broken: the panes reflected the morning sunlight in patches of emerald and blue, and the latch of the sagging front door was never lifted, although no bolt secured it. Since Luella Miller had been carried out of it, the house had had no tenant except one friendless old soul who had no choice between that and the far-off shelter of the open sky. This old woman, who had survived her kindred and friends, lived in the house one week, then one morning no smoke came out of the chimney, and a body of neighbours, a score strong, entered and found her dead in her bed. There were dark whispers as to the cause of her death, and there were those who testified to an expression of fear so exalted that it showed forth the state of the departing soul upon the dead face. The old woman had been hale and hearty when she entered the house, and in seven days she was dead; it seemed that she had fallen a victim to some uncanny power. The minister talked in the pulpit with covert severity against the sin of superstition; still the belief prevailed. Not a soul in the village but would have chosen the almshouse rather than that dwelling. No vagrant, if he heard the tale, would seek shelter beneath that old roof, unhallowed by nearly half a century of superstitious fear.

There was only one person in the village who had actually known Luella Miller. That person was a woman well over eighty, but a marvel of vitality and unextinct youth. Straight as an arrow, with the spring of one recently let loose from the bow of life, she moved about the streets, and she always went to church, rain or shine. She had never married, and had lived alone for years in a house across the road from Luella Miller's.

This woman had none of the garrulousness of age, but never in all her life had she ever held her tongue for any will save her own, and she never spared the truth when she essayed to present it. She it was who bore testimony to the life, evil, though possibly wittingly or designedly so, of Luella Miller, and to her personal appearance. When this old woman spoke—and she had the gift of description, although her thoughts were clothed in the rude vernacular of her native village—one could seem to see Luella Miller as she had really looked. According to this woman, Lydia Anderson by name, Luella Miller had been a beauty of a type rather unusual in New England. She had been a slight, pliant sort of creature, as ready with a strong yielding to fate and as unbreakable as a willow. She had glimmering lengths of straight, fair hair, which she wore softly looped round a long, lovely face. She had blue eyes full of soft pleading, little slender, clinging hands, and a wonderful grace of motion and attitude.

"Luella Miller used to sit in a way nobody else could if they sat up and studied a week of Sundays," said Lydia Anderson, "and it was a sight to see her walk. If one of them willows over there on the edge of the brook could start up and get its roots free of the ground, and move off, it would go just the way Luella Miller used to. She had a green shot silk she used to wear, too, and a hat with green ribbon streamers, and a lace veil blowing across her face and out sideways, and a green ribbon flyin' from her waist.

That was what she came out bride in when she married Erastus Miller. Her name before she was married was Hill. There was always a sight of "l's" in her name, married or single. Erastus Miller was good lookin', too, better lookin' than Luella. Sometimes I used to think that Luella wa'n't so handsome after all. Erastus just about worshiped her. I used to know him pretty well. He lived next door to me, and we went to school together. Folks used to say he was waitin' on me, but he wa'n't. I never thought he was except once or twice when he said things that some girls might have suspected meant somethin'. That was before Luella came here to teach the district school. It was funny how she came to get it, for folks said she hadn't any education, and that one of the big girls, Lottie Henderson, used to do all the teachin' for her, while she sat back and did embroidery work on a cambric pocket-handkerchief. Lottie Henderson was a real smart girl, a splendid scholar, and she just set her eyes by Luella, as all the girls did. Lottie would have made a real smart woman, but she died when Luella had been here about a year—just faded away and died: nobody knew what ailed her. She dragged herself to that schoolhouse and helped Luella teach till the very last minute. The committee all knew how Luella didn't do much of the work herself, but they winked at it. It wa'n't long after Lottie died that Erastus married her. I always thought he hurried it up because she wa'n't fit to teach. One of the big boys used to help her after Lottie died, but he hadn't much government, and the school didn't do very well, and Luella might have had to give it up, for the committee couldn't have shut their eyes to things much longer. The boy that helped her was a real honest, innocent sort of fellow, and he was a good scholar, too. Folks said he overstudied, and that was the reason he was took crazy the year after Luella married, but I don't know. And I don't know what made Erastus Miller go into consumption of the blood the year after he was married: consumption wa'n't in his family. He just grew weaker and weaker, and went almost bent double when he tried to wait on Luella, and he spoke feeble, like an old man. He worked terrible hard till the last trying to save up a little to leave Luella. I've seen him out in the worst storms on a wood-sled—he used to cut and sell wood—and he was hunched up on top lookin' more dead than alive. Once I couldn't stand it: I went over and helped him pitch some wood on the cart—I was always strong in my arms. I wouldn't stop for all he told me to, and I guess he was glad enough for the help. That was only a week before he died. He fell on the kitchen floor while he was gettin' breakfast. He always got the breakfast and let Luella lay abed. He did all the sweepin' and the washin' and the ironin' and most of the cookin'. He couldn't bear to have Luella lift her finger, and she let him do for her. She lived like a queen for all the work she did. She didn't even do her sewin'. She said it made her shoulder ache to sew, and poor Erastus's sister Lily used to do all her sewin'. She wa'n't able to, either;

she was never strong in her back, but she did it beautifully. She had to, to suit Luella, she was so dreadful particular. I never saw anythin' like the fagottin' and hemstitchin' that Lily Miller did for Luella. She made all Luella's weddin' outfit, and that green silk dress, after Maria Babbit cut it. Maria she cut it for nothin', and she did a lot more cuttin' and fittin' for nothin' for Luella, too. Lily Miller went to live with Luella after Erastus died. She gave up her home, though she was real attached to it and wa'n't a mite afraid to stay alone. She rented it and she went to live with Luella right away after the funeral."

Then this old woman, Lydia Anderson, who remembered Luella Miller, would go on to relate the story of Lily Miller. It seemed that on the removal of Lily Miller to the house of her dead brother, to live with his widow, the village people first began to talk. This Lily Miller had been hardly past her first youth, and a most robust and blooming woman, rosy-cheeked, with curls of strong, black hair overshadowing round, candid temples and bright dark eyes. It was not six months after she had taken up her residence with her sister-in-law that her rosy colour faded and her pretty curves became wan hollows. White shadows began to show in the black rings of her hair, and the light died out of her eyes, her features sharpened, and there were pathetic lines at her mouth, which yet wore always an expression of utter sweetness and even happiness. She was devoted to her sister; there was no doubt that she loved her with her whole heart, and was perfectly content in her service. It was her sole anxiety lest she should die and leave her alone.

"The way Lily Miller used to talk about Luella was enough to make you mad and enough to make you cry," said Lydia Anderson. "I've been in there sometimes toward the last when she was too feeble to cook and carried her some blanc-mange or custard—somethin' I thought she might relish, and she'd thank me, and when I asked her how she was, say she felt better than she did yesterday, and asked me if I didn't think she looked better, dreadful pitiful, and say poor Luella had an awful time takin' care of her and doin' the work—she wa'n't strong enough to do anythin'—when all the time Luella wa'n't liftin' her finger and poor Lily didn't get any care except what the neighbours gave her, and Luella eat up everythin' that was carried in for Lily. I had it real straight that she did. Luella used to just sit and cry and do nothin'. She did act real fond of Lily, and she pined away considerable, too. There was those that thought she'd go into a decline herself. But after Lily died, her Aunt Abby Mixter came, and then Luella picked up and grew as fat and rosy as ever. But poor Aunt Abby begun to droop just the way Lily had, and I guess somebody wrote to her married daughter, Mrs Sam Abbot, who lived in Barre, for she wrote her mother that she must leave right away and come and make her a visit, but Aunt Abby wouldn't go. I can see her now. She was a real good-lookin' woman, tall and large, with a big, square face and a high forehead that looked of itself kind of benevolent and good. She just tended out on Luella as if she had been a baby, and when her married daughter sent for her she wouldn't stir one inch. She'd always thought a lot of her daughter, too, but she said Luella needed her and her married daughter didn't. Her daughter kept writin' and writin', but it didn't do any good. Finally she came, and when she saw how bad her mother looked, she broke down and cried and all but went on her knees to have her come away. She spoke her mind out to Luella, too. She told her that she'd killed her husband and everybody that had anythin' to do with her, and she'd thank her to leave her mother alone. Luella went into hysterics, and Aunt Abby was so frightened that she called me after her daughter went. Mrs Sam Abbot she went away fairly cryin' out loud in the buggy, the neighbours heard her, and well she might, for she never saw her mother again alive. I went in that night when Aunt Abby called for me, standin' in the door with her little green-checked shawl over her head. I can see her now. 'Do come over here, Miss Anderson,' she sung out, kind of gasping for breath. I didn't stop for anythin'. I put over as fast as I could, and when I got there, there was Luella laughin' and cryin' all together, and Aunt Abby trying to hush her, and all the time she herself was white as a sheet and shakin' so she could hardly stand. 'For the land sakes, Mrs Mixter,' says I, 'you look worse than she does. You ain't fit to be up out of your bed.'

"'Oh, there ain't anythin' the matter with me,' says she. Then she went on talkin' to Luella. 'There, there, don't, don't, poor little lamb,' says she. 'Aunt Abby is here. She ain't goin' away and leave you. Don't, poor little lamb.'

"'Do leave her with me, Mrs Mixter, and you get back to bed,' says I, for Aunt Abby had been layin' down considerable lately, though somehow she contrived to do the work.

"'I'm well enough,' says she. 'Don't you think she had better have the doctor, Miss Anderson?'

"'The doctor,' says I, 'I think *you* had better have the doctor. I think you need him much worse than some folks I could mention.' And I looked right straight at Luella Miller laughin' and cryin' and goin' on as if she was the centre of all creation. All the time she was actin' so—seemed as if she was too sick to sense anythin'—she was keepin' a sharp lookout as to how we took it out of the corner of one eye. I see her. You could never cheat me about Luella Miller. Finally I got real mad and I run home and I got a bottle of valerian I had, and I poured some boilin' hot water on a handful of catnip, and I mixed up that catnip tea with most half a wineglass of valerian, and I went with it over to Luella's. I marched right up to Luella, a-holdin' out of that cup, all smokin'. 'Now,' says I, 'Luella Miller, '*You swaller this!*'

"'What is—what is it, oh, what is it?' she sort of screeches out. Then she goes off a-laughin' enough to kill.

"'Poor lamb, poor little lamb,' says Aunt Abby, standin' over her, all kind of tottery, and tryin' to bathe her head with camphor.

"'*You swaller this right down*,' says I. And I didn't waste any ceremony. I just took hold of Luella Miller's chin and I tipped her head back, and I caught her mouth open with laughin', and I clapped that cup to her lips, and I fairly hollered at her: 'Swaller, swaller, swaller!' and she gulped it right down. She had to, and I guess it did her good. Anyhow, she stopped cryin' and laughin' and let me put her to bed, and she went to sleep like a baby inside of half an hour. That was more than poor Aunt Abby did. She lay awake all that night and I stayed with her, though she tried not to have me; said she wa'n't sick enough for watchers. But I stayed, and I made some good cornmeal gruel and I fed her a teaspoon every little while all night long. It seemed to me as if she was jest dyin' from bein' all wore out. In the mornin' as soon as it was light I run over to the Bisbees and sent Johnny Bisbee for the doctor. I told him to tell the doctor to hurry, and he come pretty quick. Poor Aunt Abby didn't seem to know much of anythin' when he got there. You couldn't hardly tell she breathed, she was so used up. When the doctor had gone, Luella came into the room lookin' like a baby in her ruffled nightgown. I can see her now. Her eyes were as blue and her face all pink and white like a blossom, and she looked at Aunt Abby in the bed sort of innocent and surprised. 'Why,' says she, 'Aunt Abby ain't got up yet?'

"'No, she ain't,' says I, pretty short.

"'I thought I didn't smell the coffee,' says Luella.

"'Coffee,' says I. 'I guess if you have coffee this mornin' you'll make it yourself.'

"'I never made the coffee in all my life,' says she, dreadful astonished. 'Erastus always made the coffee as long as he lived, and then Lily she made it, and then Aunt Abby made it. I don't believe I *can* make the coffee, Miss Anderson.'

"'You can make it or go without, jest as you please,' says I.

"Ain't Aunt Abby goin' to get up?' says she.

"'I guess she won't get up,' says I, 'sick as she is.' I was gettin' madder and madder. There was somethin' about that little pink-and-white thing standin' there and talkin' about coffee, when she had killed so many better folks than she was, and had jest killed another, that made me feel 'most as if I wished somebody would up and kill her before she had a chance to do any more harm.

"'Is Aunt Abby sick?' says Luella, as if she was sort of aggrieved and injured.

"'Yes,' says I, 'she's sick, and she's goin' to die, and then you'll be left alone, and you'll have to do for yourself and wait on yourself, or do without things.' I don't know but I was sort of hard, but it was the truth, and if I was any harder than Luella Miller had been I'll give up. I ain't never been sorry that I said it. Well, Luella, she up and had hysterics again at that, and I jest let her have 'em. All I did was to bundle her into the room on the other side of the entry where Aunt Abby couldn't hear her, if she wa'n't past it—I don't know but she was—and set her down hard in a chair and told her not to come back into the other room, and she minded. She had her hysterics in there till she got tired. When she found out that nobody was comin' to coddle her and do for her she stopped. At least I suppose she did. I had all I could do with poor Aunt Abby tryin' to keep the breath of life in her. The doctor had told me that she was dreadful low, and give me some very strong medicine to give to her in drops real often, and told me real particular about the nourishment. Well, I did as he told me real faithful till she wa'n't able to swaller any longer. Then I had her daughter sent for. I had begun to realize that she wouldn't last any time at all. I hadn't realized it before, though I spoke to Luella the way I did. The doctor he came, and Mrs Sam Abbot, but when she got there it was too late; her mother was dead. Aunt Abby's daughter just give one look at her mother layin' there, then she turned sort of sharp and sudden and looked at me.

"'Where is she?' says she, and I knew she meant Luella.

"'She's out in the kitchen,' says I. 'She's too nervous to see folks die. She's afraid it will make her sick.'

"The Doctor he speaks up then. He was a young man. Old Doctor Park had died the year before, and this was a young fellow just out of college. 'Mrs Miller is not strong,' says he, kind of severe, 'and she is quite right in not agitating herself.'

"'You are another, young man; she's got her pretty claw on you,' thinks I, but I didn't say anythin' to him. I just said over to Mrs Sam Abbot that Luella was in the kitchen, and Mrs Sam Abbot she went out there, and I went, too, and I never heard anythin' like the way she talked to Luella Miller. I felt pretty hard to Luella myself, but this was more than I ever would have dared to say. Luella she was too scared to go into hysterics. She jest flopped. She seemed to jest shrink away to nothin' in that kitchen chair, with Mrs Sam Abbot standin' over her and talkin' and tellin' her the truth. I guess the truth was most too much for her and no mistake, because Luella presently actually did faint away, and there wa'n't any sham about it, the way I always suspected there was about them hysterics. She fainted dead away and we had to lay her flat on the floor, and the Doctor he came runnin' out and he said somethin' about a weak heart dreadful fierce to Mrs Sam Abbot, but she wa'n't a mite scared. She faced him jest as white as even Luella was layin' there lookin' like death and the Doctor feelin' of her pulse.

"'Weak heart,' says she, 'weak heart; weak fiddlesticks! There ain't nothin' weak about that woman. She's got strength enough to hang on to other folks till she kills 'em. Weak? It was my poor mother that was weak: this woman killed her as sure as if she had taken a knife to her.'

“But the Doctor he didn’t pay much attention. He was bendin’ over Luella layin’ there with her yellow hair all streamin’ and her pretty pink-and-white face all pale, and her blue eyes like stars gone out, and he was holdin’ on to her hand and smoothin’ her forehead, and tellin’ me to get the brandy in Aunt Abby’s room, and I was sure as I wanted to be that Luella had got somebody else to hang on to, now Aunt Abby was gone, and I thought of poor Erastus Miller, and I sort of pitied the poor young Doctor, led away by a pretty face, and I made up my mind I’d see what I could do.

“I waited till Aunt Abby had been dead and buried about a month, and the Doctor was goin’ to see Luella steady and folks were beginnin’ to talk; then one evenin’, when I knew the Doctor had been called out of town and wouldn’t be round, I went over to Luella’s. I found her all dressed up in a blue muslin with white polka dots on it, and her hair curled jest as pretty, and there wa’n’t a young girl in the place could compare with her. There was somethin’ about Luella Miller seemed to draw the heart right out of you, but she didn’t draw it out of *me*. She was settin’ rocking in the chair by her sittin’-room window, and Maria Brown had gone home. Maria Brown had been in to help her, or rather to do the work, for Luella wa’n’t helped when she didn’t do anythin’. Maria Brown was real capable and she didn’t have any ties; she wa’n’t married, and lived alone, so she’d offered. I couldn’t see why she should do the work any more than Luella; she wa’n’t any too strong; but she seemed to think she could and Luella seemed to think so, too, so she went over and did all the work—washed, and ironed, and baked, while Luella sat and rocked. Maria didn't live long afterward. She began to fade away just the same fashion the others had. Well, she was warned, but she acted real mad when folks said anythin': said Luella was a poor, abused woman, too delicate to help herself, and they'd ought to be ashamed, and if she died helpin' them that couldn't help themselves she would—and she did.

"'I s'pose Maria has gone home,' says I to Luella, when I had gone in and sat down opposite her.

"'Yes, Maria went half an hour ago, after she had got supper and washed the dishes,' says Luella, in her pretty way.

"'I suppose she has got a lot of work to do in her own house to-night,' says I, kind of bitter, but that was all thrown away on Luella Miller. It seemed to her right that other folks that wa'n't any better able than she was herself should wait on her, and she couldn't get it through her head that anybody should think it *wa'n't* right.

"'Yes,' says Luella, real sweet and pretty, 'yes, she said she had to do her washin' to-night. She has let it go for a fortnight along of comin' over here.'

"'Why don't she stay home and do her washin' instead of comin' over here and doin' *your* work, when you are just as well able, and enough sight more so, than she is to do it?' says I.

“Then Luella she looked at me like a baby who has a rattle shook at it. She sort of laughed as innocent as you please. ‘Oh, I can’t do the work myself, Miss Anderson,’ says she. ‘I never did. Maria *has* to do it.’

“Then I spoke out: ‘Has to do it!’ says I. ‘Has to do it!’ She don’t have to do it, either. Maria Brown has her own home and enough to live on. She ain’t beholden to you to come over here and slave for you and kill herself.’

“Luella she jest set and stared at me for all the world like a doll-baby that was so abused that it was comin’ to life.

“‘Yes,’ says I, ‘she’s killin’ herself. She’s goin’ to die just the way Erastus did, and Lily, and your Aunt Abby. You’re killin’ her jest as you did them. I don’t know what there is about you, but you seem to bring a curse,’ says I. ‘You kill everybody that is fool enough to care anythin’ about you and do for you.’

“She stared at me and she was pretty pale.

“‘And Maria ain’t the only one you’re goin’ to kill,’ says I. ‘You’re goin’ to kill Doctor Malcom before you’re done with him.’

“Then a red colour came flamin’ all over her face. ‘I ain’t goin’ to kill him, either,’ says she, and she begun to cry.

“‘Yes, you *be*!’ says I. Then I spoke as I had never spoke before. You see, I felt it on account of Erastus. I told her that she hadn’t any business to think of another man after she’d been married to one that had died for her: that she was a dreadful woman; and she was, that’s true enough, but sometimes I have wondered lately if she knew it—if she wa'n't like a baby with scissors in its hand cuttin' everybody without knowin' what it was doin'.

"Luella she kept gettin' paler and paler, and she never took her eyes off my face. There was somethin' awful about the way she looked at me and never spoke one word. After a while I quit talkin' and I went home. I watched that night, but her lamp went out before nine o'clock, and when Doctor Malcom came drivin' past and sort of slowed up he see there wa'n't any light and he drove along. I saw her sort of shy out of meetin' the next Sunday, too, so he shouldn't go home with her, and I begun to think mebbe she did have some conscience after all. It was only a week after that that Maria Brown died—sort of sudden at the last, though everybody had seen it was comin'. Well, then there was a good deal of feelin' and pretty dark whispers. Folks said the days of witchcraft had come again, and they were pretty shy of Luella. She acted sort of offish to the Doctor and he didn't go there, and there wa'n't anybody to do anythin' for her. I don't know how she *did* get along. I wouldn't go in there and offer to help her—not because I was afraid of dyin' like the rest, but I thought she was just as well able to do her own work as I was to do it for her, and I thought it was about time that she did it and stopped killin' other folks. But it wa'n't very long before folks began to say that Luella herself was goin' into a decline jest the way her husband, and Lily, and Aunt Abby and the others had, and I saw myself that she looked pretty bad. I used to see her goin' past from the store with a bundle as if she could hardly crawl, but I remembered how Erastus used to wait and 'tend when he couldn't hardly put one foot before the other, and I didn't go out to help her.

"But at last one afternoon I saw the Doctor come drivin' up like mad with his medicine chest, and Mrs Babbit came in after supper and said that Luella was real sick.

"'I'd offer to go in and nurse her,' says she, 'but I've got my children to consider, and mebbe it ain't true what they say, but it's queer how many folks that have done for her have died.'

"I didn't say anythin', but I considered how she had been Erastus's wife and how he had set his eyes by her, and I made up my mind to go in the next mornin', unless she was better, and see what I could do; but the next mornin' I see her at the window, and pretty soon she came steppin' out as spry as you please, and a little while afterward Mrs Babbit came in and told me that the Doctor had got a girl from out of town, a Sarah Jones, to come there, and she said she was pretty sure that the Doctor was goin' to marry Luella.

"I saw him kiss her in the door that night myself, and I knew it was true. The woman came that afternoon, and the way she flew around was a caution. I don't believe Luella had swept since Maria died. She swept and dusted, and washed and ironed; wet clothes and dusters and carpets were flyin' over there all day, and every time Luella set her foot out when the Doctor wa'n't there there was that Sarah Jones helpin' of her up and down the steps, as if she hadn't learned to walk.

"Well, everybody knew that Luella and the Doctor were goin' to be married, but it wa'n't long before they began to talk about his lookin' so poorly, jest as they had about the others; and they talked about Sarah Jones, too.

"Well, the Doctor did die, and he wanted to be married first, so as to leave what little he had to Luella, but he died before the minister could get there, and Sarah Jones died a week afterward.

"Well, that wound up everything for Luella Miller. Not another soul in the whole town would lift a finger for her. There got to be a sort of panic. Then she began to droop in good earnest. She used to have to go to the store herself, for Mrs Babbit was afraid to let Tommy go for her, and I've seen her goin' past and stoppin' every two or three steps to rest. Well, I stood it as long as I could, but one day I see her comin' with her arms full and stoppin' to lean against the Babbit fence, and I run out and took her bundles and carried them to her house. Then I went home and never spoke one word to her though she called after me dreadful kind of pitiful. Well, that night I was taken sick with a chill, and I was sick as I wanted to be for two weeks. Mrs Babbit had seen me run out to help Luella and she came in and told me I was goin' to die on account of it. I didn't know whether I was or not, but I considered I had done right by Erastus's wife.

"That last two weeks Luella she had a dreadful hard time, I guess. She was pretty sick, and as near as I could make out nobody dared go near her. I don't know as she was really needin' anythin' very much, for there was enough to eat in her house and it was warm weather, and she made out to cook a little flour gruel every day, I know, but I guess she had a hard time, she that had been so petted and done for all her life.

"When I got so I could go out, I went over there one morning. Mrs Babbit had just come in to say she hadn't seen any smoke and she didn't know but it was somebody's duty to go in, but she couldn't help thinkin' of her children, and I got right up, though I hadn't been out of the house for two weeks, and I went in there, and Luella she was layin' on the bed, and she was dyin'.

"She lasted all that day and into the night. But I sat there after the new doctor had gone away. Nobody else dared to go there. It was about midnight that I left her for a minute to run home and get some medicine I had been takin', for I begun to feel rather bad.

"It was a full moon that night, and just as I started out of my door to cross the street back to Luella's, I stopped short, for I saw something."

Lydia Anderson at this juncture always said with a certain defiance that she did not expect to be believed, and then proceeded in a hushed voice:

"I saw what I saw, and I know I saw it, and I will swear on my death bed that I saw it. I saw Luella Miller and Erastus Miller, and Lily, and Aunt Abby, and Maria, and the Doctor, and Sarah, all goin' out of her door, and all but Luella shone white in the moonlight, and they were all helpin' her along till she seemed to fairly fly in the midst of them. Then it all disappeared. I stood a minute with my heart poundin', then I went over there. I thought of goin' for Mrs Babbit, but I thought she'd be afraid. So I went alone, though I knew what had happened. Luella was layin' real peaceful, dead on her bed."

This was the story that the old woman, Lydia Anderson, told, but the sequel was told by the people who survived her, and this is the tale which has become folklore in the village.

Lydia Anderson died when she was eighty-seven. She had continued wonderfully hale and hearty for one of her years until about two weeks before her death.

One bright moonlight evening she was sitting beside a window in her parlour when she made a sudden exclamation, and was out of the house and across the street before the neighbour who was taking care of her could stop her. She followed as fast as possible and found Lydia Anderson stretched on the ground before the door of Luella Miller's deserted house, and she was quite dead.

The next night there was a red gleam of fire athwart the moonlight and the old house of Luella Miller was burned to the ground. Nothing is now left of it except a few old cellar stones and a lilac bush, and in summer a helpless trail of morning glories among the weeds, which might be considered emblematic of Luella herself.

A WATCHER BY THE DEAD

Ambrose Bierce

I

IN AN UPPER ROOM of an unoccupied dwelling in the part of San Francisco known as North Beach lay the body of a man under a sheet. The hour was near nine in the evening; the room was dimly lighted by a single candle. Although the weather was warm, the two windows, contrary to the custom which gives the dead plenty of air, were closed and the blinds drawn down. The furniture of the room consisted of but three pieces—an armchair, a small reading stand, supporting the candle, and a long kitchen table, supporting the body of the man. All these, as also the corpse, seemed to have been recently brought in, for an observer, had there been one, would have seen that all were free from dust, whereas everything else in the room was pretty thickly coated with it, and there were cobwebs in the angles of the walls.

Under the sheet the outlines of the body could be traced, even the features, these having that unnaturally sharp definition which seems to belong to faces of the dead, but is really characteristic of those only that have been wasted by disease. From the silence of the room one would rightly have inferred that it was not in the front of the house, facing a street. It really faced nothing but a high breast of rock, the rear of the building being set into a hill.

As a neighbouring church clock was striking nine with an indolence which seemed to imply such an indifference to the flight of time that one could hardly help wondering why it took the trouble to strike at all, the single door of the room was opened and a man entered, advancing toward the body. As he did so the door closed, apparently of its own volition; there was a grating, as of a key turned with difficulty, and the snap of the lock bolt as it shot into its socket. A sound of retiring footsteps in the passage outside ensued, and the man was to all appearance a prisoner. Advancing to the table, he stood a moment looking down at the body; then with a slight shrug of the shoulders walked over to one of the windows and hoisted the blind. The darkness outside was absolute, the panes were covered with dust, but by wiping this away he could see that the window was fortified with strong iron bars crossing it within a few inches of the glass, and imbedded in the masonry on each side. He examined the other window. It was the same. He manifested no great curiosity in the matter, did not even so much as raise the sash. If he was a prisoner he was apparently a tractable one. Having completed his examination of the room, he seated himself in the armchair, took a book from his pocket, drew the stand with its candle alongside and began to read.

The man was young—not more than thirty—dark in complexion, smooth-shaven, with brown hair. His face was thin and high-nosed, with a broad forehead and a "firmness" of the chin and jaw which is said by those having it to denote resolution. The eyes were grey and steadfast, not moving except with definitive purpose. They were now for the greater part of the time fixed upon his book, but he occasionally withdrew them and turned them to the body on the table, not, apparently, from any dismal fascination which, under such circumstances, it might be supposed to exercise upon even a courageous person, nor with a conscious rebellion against the contrary influence which might dominate a timid one. He looked at it as if in his reading he had come upon something recalling him to a sense of his surroundings. Clearly this watcher by the dead was discharging his trust with intelligence and composure, as became him.

After reading for perhaps a half-hour he seemed to come to the end of a chapter and quietly laid away the book. He then rose, and, taking the reading stand from the floor, carried it into a corner of the room near one of the windows, lifted the candle from it, and returned to the empty fireplace before which he had been sitting.

A moment later he walked over to the body on the table, lifted the sheet and turned it back from the head, exposing a mass of dark hair and a thin face-cloth, beneath which the features showed with even sharper definition than before. Shading his eyes by interposing his free hand between them and the candle, he stood looking at his motionless companion with a serious and tranquil regard. Satisfied with his inspection, he pulled the sheet over the face again and, returning to the chair, took some matches off the candlestick, put them in the side pocket of his sack coat and sat down. He then lifted the candle from its socket and looked at it critically, as if calculating how long it would last. It was barely two inches long; in another hour he would be in darkness! He replaced it in the candlestick and blew it out.

II

In a physician's office in Kearny Street three men sat about a table, drinking punch and smoking. It was late in the evening, almost midnight, indeed, and there had been no lack of punch. The gravest of the three, Dr Helberson, was the host; it was in his rooms they sat. He was about thirty years of age; the others were even younger; all were physicians.

"The superstitious awe with which the living regard the dead," said Dr Helberson, "is hereditary and incurable. One needs no more be ashamed of it than of the fact that he inherits, for example, an incapacity for mathematics, or a tendency to lie."

The others laughed. "Oughtn't a man to be ashamed to be a liar?" asked the youngest of the three, who was in fact a medical student not yet graduated.

"My dear Harper, I said nothing about that. The tendency to lie is one thing; lying is another."

"But do you think," said the third man, "that this superstitious feeling, this fear of the dead, reasonless as we know it to be, is universal? I am myself not conscious of it."

"Oh, but it is 'in your system' for all that," replied Helberson; "it needs only the right conditions—what Shakespeare calls the 'confederate season'—to manifest itself in some very disagreeable way that will open your eyes. Physicians and soldiers are, of course, more nearly free from it than others."

"Physicians and soldiers!—why don't you add hangmen and headsmen? Let us have in all the assassin classes."

"No, my dear Mancher; the juries will not let the public executioners acquire sufficient familiarity with death to be altogether unmoved by it."

Young Harper, who had been helping himself to a fresh cigar at the sideboard, resumed his seat. "What would you consider conditions under which any man of woman born would become insupportably conscious of his share of our common weakness in this regard?" he asked, rather verbosely.

"Well, I should say that if a man were locked up all night with a corpse—alone—in a dark room—of a vacant house—with no bed covers to pull over his head—and lived through it without going altogether mad, he might justly boast himself not of woman born, nor yet, like Macduff, a product of Caesarean section."

"I thought you never would finish piling up conditions," said Harper, "but I know a man who is neither a physician nor a soldier who will accept them all, for any stake you like to name."

"Who is he?"

"His name is Jarette—a stranger in California; comes from my town in New York. I have no money to back him, but he will back himself with dead loads of it."

"How do you know that?"

"He would rather bet than eat. As for fear—I dare say he thinks it some cutaneous disorder, or possibly a particular kind of religious heresy."

"What does he look like?" Helberson was evidently becoming interested.

"Like Mancher, here—might be his twin brother."

"I accept the challenge," said Helberson, promptly.

"Awfully obliged to you for the compliment, I'm sure," drawled Mancher, who was growing sleepy. "Can't I get into this?"

"Not against me," Helberson said. "I don't want *your* money."

"All right," said Mancher; "I'll be the corpse."

The others laughed.

The outcome of this crazy conversation we have seen.

III

In extinguishing his meagre allowance of candle Mr Jarette's object was to preserve it against some unforeseen need. He may have thought, too, or half thought, that the darkness would be no worse at one time than another, and if the situation became insupportable it would be better to have a means of relief, or even release. At any rate, it was wise to have a little reserve of light, even if only to enable him to look at his watch.

No sooner had he blown out the candle and set it on the floor at his side than he settled himself comfortably in the armchair, leaned back and closed his eyes, hoping and expecting to sleep. In this he was disappointed; he had never in his life felt less sleepy, and in a few minutes he gave up the attempt. But what could he do? He could not go groping about in absolute darkness at the risk of bruising himself—at the risk, too, of blundering against the table and rudely disturbing the dead. We all recognize their right to lie at rest, with immunity from all that is harsh and violent. Jarette almost succeeded in making himself believe that considerations of this kind restrained him from risking the collision and fixed him to the chair.

While thinking of this matter he fancied that he heard a faint sound in the direction of the table—what kind of sound he could hardly have explained. He did not turn his head. Why should he—in the darkness? But he listened—why should he not? And listening he grew giddy and grasped the arms of the chair for support. There was a strange ringing in his ears; his head seemed bursting; his chest was oppressed by the constriction of his clothing. He wondered why it was so, and whether these were symptoms of fear. Suddenly, with a long and strong expiration, his chest appeared to collapse, and with the great gasp with which he refilled his exhausted lungs the vertigo left him and he knew that so intently had he listened that he had held his breath almost to suffocation. The revelation was vexatious; he arose, pushed away the chair with his foot and strode to the centre of the room. But one does not stride far in darkness; he began to grope, and finding the wall followed it to an angle, turned, followed it past the two windows and there in another corner came into violent contact with the reading stand, overturning it. It made a clatter that startled him. He was annoyed. "How the devil could I have forgotten where it was!" he muttered, and groped his way along the third wall to the fireplace. "I must put things to rights," said he, feeling the floor for the candle.

Having recovered that, he lighted it and instantly turned his eyes to the table, where, naturally, nothing had undergone any change. The reading stand lay unobserved upon the floor: he had forgotten to "put it to rights." He looked all about the room, dispersing the deeper shadows by movements of the candle in his hand, and, finally, crossing over to the door, tried it by turning and pulling the knob with all his strength. It did not yield, and this seemed to afford him a certain satisfaction; indeed, he secured it more firmly by a bolt which he had not before observed. Returning to his chair, he looked at his watch; it was half-past nine. With a start of surprise he held the watch at his ear. It had not stopped. The candle was now visibly shorter. He again extinguished it, placing it on the floor at his side as before.

Mr Jarette was not at his ease; he was distinctly dissatisfied with his surroundings, and with himself for being so. "What have I to fear?" he thought. "This is ridiculous and disgraceful; I will not be so great a fool." But courage does not come of saying, "I will be courageous," nor of recognizing its appropriateness to the occasion. The more Jarette condemned himself, the more reason he gave himself for condemnation; the greater the number of variations which he played upon the simple theme of the harmlessness of the dead, the more insupportable grew the discord of his emotions. "What!" he cried aloud in the anguish of his spirit, "what! shall I, who have not a shade of superstition in my nature—I, who have no belief in immortality—I, who know (and never more clearly than now) that the after-life is the dream of a desire—shall I lose at once my bet, my honour and my self-respect, perhaps my reason, because certain savage ancestors, dwelling in caves and burrows, conceived the monstrous notion that the dead walk by night; that—" Distinctly, unmistakably, Mr Jarette heard behind him a light, soft sound of footfalls, deliberate, regular, successively nearer!

IV

Just before daybreak the next morning Dr Helberson and his young friend Harper were driving slowly through the streets of North Beach in the doctor's coupé.

"Have you still the confidence of youth in the courage or stolidity of your friend?" said the elder man. "Do you believe that I have lost this wager?"

"I *know* you have," replied the other, with enfeebling emphasis.

"Well, upon my soul, I hope so."

It was spoken earnestly, almost solemnly. There was a silence for a few moments.

"Harper," the doctor resumed, looking very serious in the shifting half-lights that entered the carriage as they passed the street lamps, "I don't feel altogether comfortable about this business. If your friend had not irritated me by the contemptuous manner in which he treated my doubt of his endurance—a purely physical quality—and by the cool incivility of his suggestion that the corpse be that of a physician, I should not have gone on with it. If anything should happen we are ruined, as I fear we deserve to be."

"What can happen? Even if the matter should be taking a serious turn—of which I am not at all afraid—Mancher has only to 'resurrect' himself and explain matters. With a genuine 'subject' from the dissecting room, or one of your late patients, it might be different."

Dr Mancher, then, had been as good as his promise; he was the "corpse."

Dr Helberson was silent for a long time, as the carriage, at a snail's pace, crept along the same street it had travelled two or three times already. Presently he spoke: "Well, let us hope that Mancher, if he has had to rise from the dead, has been discreet about it. A mistake in that might make matters worse instead of better."

"Yes," said Harper, "Jarette would kill him. But, Doctor"—looking at his watch as the carriage passed a gas lamp—"it is nearly four o'clock at last."

A moment later the two had quitted the vehicle and were walking briskly toward the long-unoccupied house belonging to the doctor, in which they had immured Mr Jarette in accordance with the terms of the mad wager. As they neared it they met a man running. "Can you tell me," he cried, suddenly checking his speed, "where I can find a physician?"

"What's the matter?" Helberson asked, non-committal.

"Go and see for yourself," said the man, resuming his running.

They hastened on. Arrived at the house, they saw several persons entering in haste and excitement. In some of the dwellings nearby and across the way the chamber windows were thrown up, showing a protrusion of heads. All heads were asking questions, none heeding the questions of the others. A few of the windows with closed blinds were illuminated; the inmates of those rooms were dressing to come down. Exactly opposite the door of the house that they sought a street lamp threw a yellow, insufficient light upon the scene, seeming to say that it could disclose a good deal more if it wished. Harper paused at the door and laid a hand upon his companion's arm. "It is all up with us, Doctor," he said in extreme agitation, which contrasted strangely with his free-and-easy words; "the game has gone against us all. Let's not go in there; I'm for lying low."

"I'm a physician," said Dr Helberson, calmly; "there may be need of one."

They mounted the doorsteps and were about to enter. The door was open; the street lamp opposite lighted the passage into which it opened. It was full of men. Some had ascended the stairs at the farther end, and, denied admittance above, waited for better fortune. All were talking, none listening. Suddenly, on the upper landing there was a great commotion; a man had sprung out of a door and was breaking away from those endeavouring to detain him. Down through the mass of affrighted idlers he came, pushing them aside, flattening them against the wall on one side, or compelling them to cling to the rail on the other, clutching them by the throat, striking them savagely, thrusting them back down the stairs and walking over the fallen. His clothing was in disorder, he was without a hat. His eyes, wild and restless, had in them something more terrifying than his apparently superhuman strength. His face, smooth-shaven, was bloodless, his hair frost-white.

As the crowd at the foot of the stairs, having more freedom, fell away to let him pass, Harper sprang forward. "Jarette! Jarette!" he cried.

Dr Helberson seized Harper by the collar and dragged him back. The man looked into their faces without seeming to see them and sprang through the door, down the steps, into the street, and away. A stout policeman, who had had inferior success in conquering his way down the stairway, followed a moment later and started in pursuit, all the heads in the windows—those of women and children now—screaming in guidance.

The stairway being now partly cleared, most of the crowd having rushed down to the street to observe the flight and pursuit, Dr Helberson mounted to the landing, followed by Harper. At a door in the upper passage an officer denied them admittance. "We are physicians," said the doctor, and they passed in. The room was full of men, dimly seen, crowded about a table. The newcomers edged their way forward and looked over the shoulders of those in the front rank. Upon the table, the lower limbs covered with a sheet, lay the body of a man, brilliantly illuminated by the beam of a bull's-eye lantern held by a policeman standing at the feet. The others, excepting those near the head—the officer himself—all were in darkness. The face of the body showed yellow, repulsive, horrible! The eyes were partly open and upturned and the jaw fallen; traces of froth defiled the lips, the chin, the cheeks. A tall man, evidently a doctor, bent over the body with his hand thrust under the shirt front. He withdrew it and placed two fingers in the open mouth. "This man has been about two hours dead," said he. "It is a case for the coroner."

He drew a card from his pocket, handed it to the officer and made his way toward the door.

"Clear the room—out, all!" said the officer, sharply, and the body disappeared as if it had been snatched away, as shifting the lantern he flashed its beam of light here and there against the faces of the crowd. The effect was amazing! The men, blinded, confused, almost terrified, made a tumultuous rush for the door, pushing, crowding and tumbling over one another as they fled, like the hosts of Night before the shafts of Apollo. Upon the struggling, trampling mass the officer poured his light without pity and without cessation. Caught in the current, Helberson and Harper were swept out of the room and cascaded down the stairs into the street.

"Good God, Doctor! did I not tell you that Jarette would kill him?" said Harper, as soon as they were clear of the crowd.

"I believe you did," replied the other, without apparent emotion.

They walked on in silence, block after block. Against the greying east the dwellings of the hill tribes showed in silhouette. The familiar milk wagon was already a stir in the streets; the baker's man would soon come upon the scene; the newspaper carrier was abroad in the land.

"It strikes me, youngster," said Helberson, "that you and I have been having too much of the morning air lately. It is unwholesome; we need a change. What do you say to a tour in Europe?"

"When?"

"I'm not particular. I should suppose that four o'clock this afternoon would be early enough."

"I'll meet you at the boat," said Harper.

V

Seven years afterward these two men sat upon a bench in Madison Square, New York, in familiar conversation. Another man, who had been observing them for some time, himself unobserved, approached and, courteously lifting his hat from locks as white as frost, said: "I beg your pardon, gentlemen, but when you have killed a man by coming to life, it is best to change clothes with him, and at the first opportunity make a break for liberty."

Helberson and Harper exchanged significant glances. They were obviously amused. The former then looked the stranger kindly in the eye and replied:

"That has always been my plan. I entirely agree with you as to its advent—"

He stopped suddenly and grew deathly pale. He stared at the man, open-mouthed; he trembled visibly.

"Ah!" said the stranger, "I see that you are indisposed, Doctor. If you cannot treat yourself, Harper can do something for you, I am sure."

"Who the devil are you?" said Harper, bluntly.

The stranger came nearer and, bending toward them, said in a whisper: "I call myself Jarette sometimes, but I don't mind telling you, for old friendship, that I am Dr William Mancher."

The revelation brought Harper to his feet. "Mancher!" he cried; and Helberson added: "It is true, by God!"

"Yes," said the stranger, smiling vaguely, "it is true enough, no doubt."

He hesitated and seemed to be trying to recall something, then began humming a popular air. He had apparently forgotten their presence.

"Look here, Mancher," said the elder of the two, "tell us just what occurred that night—to Jarette, you know."

"Oh, yes, about Jarette," said the other. "It's odd I should have neglected to tell you—I tell it so often. You see I knew, by overhearing him talking to himself, that he was pretty badly frightened. So I couldn't resist the temptation to come to life and have a bit of fun out of him—I couldn't, really. That was all right, though certainly I did not think he would take it so seriously; I did not, truly. And afterward—well, it was a tough job changing places with him, and then—damn you! you didn't let me out!"

Nothing could exceed the ferocity with which these last words were delivered. Both men stepped back in alarm.

"We?—why—why," Helberson stammered, losing his self-possession utterly, "we had nothing to do with it."

"Didn't I say you were Doctors Hellborn and Sharper?" inquired the man, laughing.

"My name is Helberson, yes; and this gentleman is Mr Harper," replied the former, reassured by the laugh. "But we are not physicians now; we are—well, hang it, old man, we are gamblers."

And that was the truth.

"A very good profession—very good, indeed; and, by the way, I hope Sharper here paid over Jarette's money like an honest stakeholder. A very good and honourable profession," he repeated, thoughtfully, moving carelessly away; "but I stick to the old one. I am High Supreme Medical Officer of the Bloomingdale Asylum; it is my duty to cure the superintendent."

THE TWO BOTTLES OF RELISH

Lord Dunsany

SMETHERS IS MY NAME. I'm what you might call a small man, and in a small way of business. I travel for Numnumo, a relish for meats and savouries; the world-famous relish I ought to say. It's really quite good, no deleterious acids in it, and does not affect the heart; so it is quite easy to push. I wouldn't have got the job if it weren't. But I hope some day to get something that's harder to push, as of course the harder they are to push, the better the pay. At present I can just make my way, with nothing at all over; but then I live in a very expensive flat. It happened like this, and that brings me to my story. And it isn't the story you'd expect from a small man like me, yet there's nobody else to tell it. Those that know anything of it besides me are all for hushing it up. Well, I was looking for a room to live in in London when first I got my job; it had to be in London, to be central; and I went to a block of buildings, very gloomy they looked, and saw the man that ran them and asked him for what I wanted; flats they called them; just a bedroom and a sort of a cupboard. Well, he was showing a man round at the time who was a gent, in fact more than that, so he didn't take much notice of me, the man that ran all those flats didn't, I mean. So I just ran behind for a bit, seeing all sorts of rooms, and waiting till I could be shown my class of thing. We came to a very nice flat, a sitting room, bedroom and bathroom, and a sort of little place that they called a hall. And that's how I came to know Linley. He was the bloke that was being shown round.

"Bit expensive," he said.

And the man that ran the flats turned away to the window and picked his teeth. It's funny how much you can show by a simple thing like that. What he meant to say was that he'd hundreds of flats like that, and thousands of people looking for them, and he didn't care who had them or whether they all went on looking. There was no mistaking him, somehow. And yet he never said a word, only looked away out of the window and picked his teeth. And I venture to speak to Mr Linley then; and I said, "How about it, sir, if I paid half, and shared it? I wouldn't be in the way, and I'm out all day, and whatever you said would go, and really I wouldn't be no more in your way than a cat."

You may be surprised at my doing it; and you'll be much more surprised at him accepting it; at least, you would if you knew me, just a small man in a small way of business;

and yet I could see at once that he was taking to me more than he was taking to the man at the window.

“But there’s only one bedroom,” he said.

“I could make up my bed easy in that little room there,” I said.

“The hall,” said the man looking round from the window, without taking his toothpick out.

“And I’d have the bed out of the way and hid in the cupboard by any hour you like,” I said.

He looked thoughtful, and the other man looked out over London; and in the end, do you know, he accepted.

“Friend of yours?” said the flat man.

“Yes,” answered Mr Linley.

It was really very nice of him.

I’ll tell you why I did it. Able to afford it? Of course not. But I heard him tell the flat man that he had just come down from Oxford and wanted to live for a few months in London. It turned out he wanted just to be comfortable and do nothing for a bit while he looked things over and chose a job, or probably just as long as he could afford it. Well, I said to myself, what’s the Oxford manner worth in business, especially a business like mine? Why, simply everything you’ve got. If I picked up only a quarter of it from this Mr Linley I’d be able to double my sales, and that would soon mean I’d be given something a lot harder to push, with perhaps treble the pay. Worth it every time. And you can make a quarter of an education go twice as far again, if you're careful with it. I mean you don't have to quote the whole of the *Inferno* to show that you've read Milton; half a line may do it. Well, about that story I have to tell. And you mightn't think that a little man like me could make you shudder.

I soon forgot about the Oxford manner when we settled down in our flat. I forgot it in the sheer wonder of the man himself. He had a mind like an acrobat's body, like a bird's body. It didn't want education. You didn't notice whether he was educated or not. Ideas were always leaping up in him, things you'd never have thought of. And not only that, but if any ideas were about, he'd sort of catch them. Time and again I've found him knowing just what I was going to say. Not thought-reading, but what they call intuition. I used to try to learn a bit about chess, just to take my thoughts off Numnumo in the evening, when I'd done with it. But problems I never could do. Yet he'd come along and glance at my problem and say, "You probably move that piece first," and I'd say, "But where?" and he'd say, "Oh, one of those three squares." And I'd say, "But it will be taken on all of them." And the piece a queen all the time, mind you. And he'd say, "Yes, it's doing no good there: you're probably meant to lose it." And, do you know, he'd be right. You see, he'd been following out what the other man had been thinking. That's what he'd been doing.

Well, one day there was that ghastly murder at Unge. I don't know if you remember it. But Steeger had gone down to live with a girl in a bungalow on the North Downs, and that was the first we had heard of him. The girl had £200, and he got every penny of it and she utterly disappeared. And Scotland Yard couldn't find her. Well, I'd happened to read that Steeger had bought two bottles of Numnumo; for the Otherthorpe police had found out everything about him, except what he did with the girl; and that of course attracted my attention, or I should have never thought again about the case or said a word of it to Linley. Numnumo was always on my mind, as I always spent every day pushing it, and that kept me from forgetting the other thing. And so one day I said to Linley, "I wonder with all that knack you have for seeing through a chess problem, and thinking of one thing and another, that you don't have a go at that Otherthorpe mystery. It's a problem as much as chess," I said.

"There's not the mystery in ten murders that there is in one game of chess," he answered.

"It's beaten Scotland Yard," I said.

"Has it?" he asked.

"Knocked them endwise," I said.

"It shouldn't have done that," he said. And almost immediately after he said, "What are the facts?"

We were both sitting at supper and I told him the facts, as I had them straight from the papers. She was a pretty blonde, she was small, she was called Nancy Elth, she had £200, they lived at the bungalow for five days. After that he stayed there for another fortnight, but nobody ever saw her alive again. Steeger said she had gone to South America, but later said he had never said South America, but South Africa. None of her money remained in the bank, where she had kept it, and Steeger was shown to have come by at least £150 just at that time. Then Steeger turned out to be a vegetarian. getting all his food from the greengrocer; and that made the constable in the village of Unge suspicious of him, for a vegetarian was something new to the constable. He watched Steeger after that, and it's well he did, for there was nothing that Scotland Yard asked him that he couldn't tell them about him, except of course the one thing. And he told the police at Otherthorpe five or six miles away, and they came and took a hand at it too. They were able to say for one thing that he never went outside the bungalow and its tidy garden ever since she disappeared. You see, the more they watched him the more suspicious they got, as you naturally do if you're watching a man; so that very soon they were watching every move he made, but if it hadn't been for his being a vegetarian they'd never have started to suspect him, and there wouldn't have been enough evidence even for Linley. Not that they found out anything much against him, except that £150 dropping in from nowhere; and it was Scotland Yard that found that, not the police of Otherthorpe. No, what the constable of Unge found out was about the larch trees, and that beat Scotland Yard utterly, and beat Linley up to the very last, and of course it beat me. There were ten larch trees in the bit of a garden, and he'd made some sort of an arrangement with the landlord, Steeger had, before he took the bungalow, by which he could do what he liked with the larch trees. And then, from about the time that little Nancy Elth must have died, he cut every one of them down. Three times a day he went at it for nearly a week, and when they were all down he cut them all up into logs no more than two foot long and laid them all in neat heaps. You never saw such work. And what for? To give an excuse for the axe was one theory. But the excuse was bigger than the axe: it took him a fortnight, hard work every day. And he could have killed a little thing like Nancy Elth without an axe, and cut her up too. Another theory was that he wanted firewood, to make away with the body. But he never used it. He left it all standing there, in those neat stacks. It fairly beat everybody.

Well, those are the facts I told Linley. Oh, yes, and he bought a big butcher's knife. Funny thing, they all do. And yet it isn't so funny after all; if you've got to cut a woman up, you've got to cut her up; and you can't do that without a knife. Then, there were some negative facts. He hadn't burned her. Only had a fire in the small stove now and then, and only used it for cooking. They got on to that pretty smartly, the Unge constable did, and the men that were lending him a hand from Otherthorpe. There were some little woody places lying round, shaws they call them in that part of the country, the country people do, and they could climb a tree handy and unobserved and get a sniff at the smoke in almost any direction it might be blowing. They did that now and then and there was no smell of flesh burning, just ordinary cooking. Pretty smart of the Otherthorpe police that was, though of course it didn't help to hang Steeger. Then later on the Scotland Yard men went down and got another fact, negative but narrowing things down all the while. And that was that the chalk under the bungalow and under the little garden had none of it been disturbed. And he'd never been outside it since Nancy disappeared. Oh, yes, and he had a big file besides the knife. But there was no sign of any ground bones found on the file, or any blood on the knife. He'd washed them of course. I told all that to Linley.

Now I ought to warn you before I go any further; I am a small man myself and you probably don't expect anything horrible from me. But I ought to warn you this man was a murderer, or at any rate somebody was; the woman had been made away with, a nice pretty little girl too, and the man that had done that wasn't necessarily going to stop at things you might think he'd stop at. With the mind to do a thing like that, and with the long thin shadow of the rope to drive him further, you can't say what he'd stop at. Murder tales seem nice things sometimes for a lady to sit and read all by herself by the fire. But murder isn't a nice thing, and when a murderer's desperate and trying to hide his tracks he isn't even as nice as he was before. I'll ask you to bear that in mind. Well, I've warned you.

So I says to Linley, “And what do you make of it?”

“Drains?” said Linley.

“No,” I says, “you’re wrong there. Scotland Yard has been into that. And the Otherthorpe people before them. They’ve had a look in the drains, such as they are, a little thing running into a cesspool beyond the garden; and nothing has gone down it, nothing that oughtn’t to have, I mean.”

He made one or two other suggestions, but Scotland Yard had been before him in every case. That’s really the crab of my story, if you’ll excuse the expression. You want a man who sets out to be a detective to take his magnifying glass and go down to the spot; to go to the spot before everything; and then to measure the footmarks and pick up the clues and find the knife that the police have overlooked. But Linley never even went near the place and he hadn’t got a magnifying glass, not as I ever saw, and Scotland Yard were before him every time.

In fact they had more clues than anybody could make head or tail of. Every kind of clue to show that he’d murdered the poor little girl;. every kind of clue to show that he hadn’t disposed of the body; and yet the body wasn’t there. It wasn’t in South America either, and not much more likely in South Africa. And all the time, mind you, that enormous bunch of chopped larch wood, a clue that was staring everyone in the face and leading nowhere. No, we didn’t seem to want any more clues, and Linley never went near the place. The trouble was to deal with the clues we’d got. I was completely mystified; so was Scotland Yard; and Linley seemed to be getting no forwarder; and all the while the mystery was hanging on me. I mean, if it were not for the trifle I'd chanced to remember, and if it were not for one chance word I said to Linley, that mystery would have gone the way of all the other mysteries that men have made nothing of, a darkness, a little patch of night in history.

Well, the fact was Linley didn't take much interest in it at first, but I was so absolutely sure that he could do it, that I kept him to the idea. "You can do chess problems," I said. "That's ten times harder," he said sticking to his point. "Then why don't you do this?" I said.

"Then go and take a look at the board for me," said Linley.

That was his way of talking. We'd been a fortnight together, and I knew it by now. He meant go down to the bungalow at Unge. I know you'll say why didn't he go himself, but the plain truth of it is that if he'd been tearing about the countryside he'd never have been thinking, whereas sitting there in his chair by the fire in our flat there was no limit to the ground he could cover, if you follow my meaning. So down I went by train next day, and got out at Unge station. And there were the North Downs rising up before me, somehow like music.

"It's up there, isn't it?" I said to the porter.

"That's right," he said. "Up there by the lane; and mind to turn to your right when you get to the old yew tree, a very big tree, you can't mistake it, and then…" and he told me the way so that I couldn't go wrong. I found them all like that, very nice and helpful. You see it was Unge's day at last; everyone had heard of Unge now; you could have got a letter there any time just then without putting the county or post-town; and this was what Unge had to show. I dare say if you tried to find Unge now…; well, anyway, they were making hay while the sun shone.

Well, there the hill was, going up into sunlight, going up like a song. You don't want to hear about the spring, and all the may rioting, and the colour that came down over everything later on in the day, and all those birds; but I thought, `What a nice place to bring a girl to.' And then when I thought that he'd killed her there, well, I'm only a small man, as I said, but when I thought of her on that hill with all the birds singing, I said to myself, 'Wouldn't it be odd if it turned out to be me after all that got that man killed, if he did murder her.' So I soon found my way up to the bungalow and began prying about, looking over the hedge into the garden. And I didn't find much, and I found nothing at all that the police hadn't found already, but there were those heaps of larch logs staring me in the face and looking very queer.

I did a lot of thinking, leaning against the hedge, breathing the smell of the may, and looking over the top of it at the larch logs, and the neat little bungalow the other side of the garden. Lots of theories I thought of; till

I came to the best thought of all; and that was that if I left the thinking to Linley, with his Oxford-and-Cambridge education, and only brought him the facts, as he had told me, I should be doing more good in my way than if I tried to do any big thinking. I forgot to tell you that I had gone to Scotland Yard in the morning. Well, there wasn't really much to tell. What they asked me was, what I wanted. And, not having an answer exactly ready, I didn't find out very much from them. But it was quite different at Unge; everyone was most obliging; it was their day there, as I said. The constable let me go indoors, so long as I didn't touch anything, and he gave me a look at the garden from the inside. And I saw the stumps of the ten larch trees, and I noticed one thing that Linley said was very observant of me, not that it turned out to be any use, but anyway I was doing my best; I noticed that the stumps had been all chopped anyhow. And from that I thought that the man that did it didn't know much about chopping. The constable said that was a deduction. So then I said that the axe was blunt when he used it; and that certainly made the constable think, though he didn't actually say I was right this time. Did I tell you that Steeger never went outdoors, except to the little garden to chop wood, ever since Nancy disappeared? I think I did. Well, it was perfectly true. They'd watched him night and day, one or another of them, and the Unge constable told me that himself. That limited things a good deal. The only thing

I didn't like about it was that I felt Linley ought to have found all that out instead of ordinary policemen, and I felt that he could have too. There'd have been romance in a story like that. And they'd never have done it if the news hadn't gone round that the man was a vegetarian and only dealt at the greengrocers. Likely as not even that was only started out of pique by the butcher. It's queer what little things may trip a man up. Best to keep straight is my motto. But perhaps I'm straying a bit away from my story. I should like to do that for ever; forget that it ever was; but I can't.

Well, I picked up all sorts of information; clues I suppose I should call it in a story like this; though they none of them seemed to lead anywhere. For instance, I found out everything he ever bought at the village, I could even tell you the kind of salt he bought, quite plain with no phosphates in it, that they sometimes put in to make it tidy. And then he got ice from the fishmongers, and plenty of vegetables, as I said, from the greengrocer, Mergin & Sons. And I had a bit of a talk over it all with the constable. Slugger he said his name was. I wondered why he hadn't come in and searched the place as soon as the girl was missing. "Well, you can't do that," he said. "And besides, we didn't suspect at once, not about the girl that is. We only suspected there was something wrong about him on account of him being a vegetarian. He stayed a good fortnight after the last that was seen of her. And then we slipped in like a knife. But, you see, no one had been enquiring about her, there was no warrant out."

"And what did you find," I asked Slugger, "when you went in?"

"Just a big file," he said, "and the knife and the axe that he must have got to chop her up with."

"But he got the axe to chop trees with," I said.

"Well, yes," he said, but rather grudgingly.

"And what did he chop them for?" I asked.

"Well of course, my superiors has theories about that," he said, "that they mightn't tell to everybody."

You see, it was those logs that were beating them.

"But did he cut her up at all?" I asked.

"Well, he said that she was going to South America," he answered. Which was really very fair-minded of him. I don't remember now much else that he told me. Steeger left the plates and dishes all washed up and very neat, he said.

Well, I brought all this back to Linley, going up by the train that started just about sunset. I'd like to tell you about the late spring evening, so calm over that grim bungalow, closing in with a glory all round it, as though it were blessing it; but you'll want to hear of the murder. Well, I told Linley everything, though much of it didn't seem to me to be worth the telling. The trouble was that the moment I began to leave anything out, he'd know it, and make me drag it in.

"You can't tell what may be vital," he'd say. "A tin-tack swept away by a housemaid might hang a man."

All very well, but be consistent even if you are educated at Eton and Harrow, and whenever I mentioned Numnumo, which after all was the beginning of the whole story, because he wouldn't have heard of it if it hadn't been for me, and my noticing that Steeger had bought two bottles of it, why then he said that things like that were trivial and we should keep to the main issues. I naturally talked a bit about Numnumo, because only that day I had pushed close on fifty bottles of it in Unge. A murder certainly stimulates people's minds, and Steeger's two bottles gave me an opportunity that only a fool could have failed to make something of. But of course all that was nothing at all to Linley.

You can't see a man's thoughts and you can't look into his mind, so that all the most exciting things in the world can never be told of. But what I think happened all that evening with Linley, while I talked to him before supper, and all through supper, and sitting smoking afterwards in front of our fire, was that his thoughts were stuck at a barrier there was no getting over. And the barrier wasn't the difficulty of finding ways and means by which Steeger might have made away with the body, but the impossibility of finding why he chopped those masses of wood every day for a fortnight, and paid, as I'd just found out, £25 to his landlord to be allowed to do it. That's what was beating Linley. As for the ways by which Steeger might have hidden the body, it seemed to me that every way was blocked by the police. If you said he buried it they said the chalk was undisturbed, if you said he carried it away they said he never left the place, if you said he burned it they said no smell of burning was ever noticed when the smoke blew low, and when it didn't they climbed trees after it. I'd taken to Linley wonderfully, and I didn't have to be educated to see there was something big in a mind like his, and I thought that he could have done it. When I saw the police getting in before him like that, and no way that I could see of getting past them, I felt really sorry.

Did anyone come to the house? he asked me once or twice. Did anyone take anything away from it? But we couldn't account for it that way. Then perhaps I made some suggestion that was no good, or perhaps I started talking of Numnumo again, and he interrupted me rather sharply.

"But what would you do, Smethers?" he said. "What would you do yourself?"

"If I'd murdered poor Nancy Elth?" I asked.

"Yes," he said.

"I can't ever imagine doing of such a thing," I told him.

He sighed at that, as though it were something against me.

"I suppose I should never be a detective," I said. And he just shook his head. Then he looked broodingly into the fire for what seemed an hour. And then he shook his head again. We both went to bed after that.

I shall remember the next day all my life. I was out till evening, as usual, pushing Numnumo. And we sat down to supper about nine. You couldn't get things cooked at those flats, so of course we had it cold. And Linley began with a salad. I can see it now, every bit of it. Well, I was still a bit full of what I'd done in Unge, pushing Numnumo. Only a fool, I know, would have been unable to push it there; but still, I had pushed it; and about fifty bottles, forty-eight to be exact, are something in a small village, whatever the circumstances. So I was talking about it a bit; and then all of a sudden I realized that Numnumo was nothing to Linley, and I pulled myself up with a jerk. It was really very kind of him; do you know what he did? He must have known at once why I stopped and he just stretched out a hand and said: "Would you give me a little of your Numnumo for my salad?"

I was so touched I nearly gave it him. But of course you don't take Numnumo with salad. Only for meats and savouries. That's on the bottle.

So I just said to him, "Only for meats and savouries." Though I don't know what savouries are. Never had any.

I never saw a man's face go like that before.

He seemed still for a whole minute. And nothing speaking about him but that expression. Like a man that's seen a ghost, one is tempted to write. But it wasn't really at all. I'll tell you what he looked like. Like a man that's seen something that no one has ever looked at before, something he thought couldn't be.

And then he said in a voice that was all quite changed,

more low and gentle and quiet it seemed, “No good for vegetables, eh?”

“Not a bit,” I said.

And at that he gave a kind of sob in his throat. I hadn’t thought he could feel things like that. Of course I didn’t know what it was all about; but, whatever it was, I thought all that sort of thing would have been knocked out of him at Eton and Harrow, an educated man like that. There were no tears in his eyes but he was feeling something horribly.

And then he began to speak with big spaces between his words, saying, “A man might make a mistake perhaps, and use Numnumo with vegetables.”

“Not twice,” I said. What else could I say?

And he repeated that after me as though I had told of the end of the world, and adding an awful emphasis to my words, till they seemed all clammy with some frightful significance, and shaking his head as he said it.

Then he was quite silent.

“What is it?” I asked.

“Smethers,” he said.

“Yes,” I said.

“Smethers,” said he.

“Look here, Smethers,” he said, “you must phone down to the grocer at Unge and find out from him this.”

“Yes?” I said.

"Whether Steeger bought those two bottles, as I expect he did, on the same day, and not a few days apart. He couldn't have done that."

I waited to see if any more was coming, and then I ran out and did what I was told. It took me some time, being after nine o'clock, and only then with the help of the police. About six days apart they said; and so I came back and told Linley. He looked up at me so hopefully when I came in, but I saw that it was the wrong answer by his eyes.

You can't take things to heart like that without being ill, and when he didn't speak I said: "What you want is a good brandy, and go to bed early."

And he said: "No. I must see someone from Scotland Yard. Phone round to them. Say here at once."

"But," I said, "I can't get an inspector from Scotland Yard to call on us at this hour."

His eyes were all lit up. He was all there all right.

"Then tell them," he said, "they'll never find Nancy Elth. Tell one of them to come here and I'll tell him why." And he added, I think only for me, "They must watch Steeger, till one day they get him over something else."

And, do you know, he came. Inspector Ulton; he came himself.

While we were waiting I tried to talk to Linley. Partly curiosity, I admit. But I didn't want to leave him to those thoughts of his, brooding away by the fire. I tried to ask him what it was all about. But he wouldn't tell me. "Murder is horrible" is all he would say. "And as a man covers his tracks up it only gets worse."

He wouldn't tell me. "There are tales," he said, "that one never wants to hear."

That's true enough. I wish I'd never heard this one. I never did actually. But I guessed it from Linley's last words to Inspector Ulton, the only ones that I overheard. And perhaps this is the point at which to stop reading my story, so that you don't guess it too; even if you think you want murder stories. For don't you rather want a murder story with a bit of a romantic twist, and not a story about real foul murder? Well, just as you like.

In came Inspector Ulton, and Linley shook hands in silence, and pointed the way to his bedroom; and they went in there and talked in low voices, and I never heard a word. A fairly hearty-looking man was the inspector when they went into that room. They walked through our sitting room in silence when they came out, and together they went into the hall, and there I heard the only words they said to each other. It was the inspector that first broke that silence.

"But why," he said, "did he cut down the trees?"

"Solely," said Linley, "in order to get an appetite."

LOST HEARTS

M.R. James

IT WAS, as far as I can ascertain, in September of the year 1811 that a post-chaise drew up before the door of Aswarby Hall, in the heart of Lincolnshire. The little boy who was the only passenger in the chaise, and who jumped out as soon as it had stopped, looked about him with the keenest curiosity during the short interval that elapsed between the ringing of the bell and the opening of the hall door. He saw a tall, square, red-brick house, built in the reign of Anne; a stone-pillared porch had been added in the purer classical style of 1790; the windows of the house were many, tall and narrow, with small panes and thick white woodwork. A pediment, pierced with a round window, crowned the front. There were wings to right and left, connected by curious glazed galleries, supported by colonnades, with the central block. These wings plainly contained the stables and offices of the house. Each was surmounted by an ornamental cupola with a gilded vane.

An evening light shone on the building, making the windowpanes glow like so many fires. Away from the Hall in front stretched a flat park studded with oaks and fringed with firs, which stood out against the sky. The clock in the church tower, buried in trees on the edge of the park, only its golden weathercock catching the light, was striking six, and the sound came gently beating down the wind. It was altogether a pleasant impression, though tinged with the sort of melancholy appropriate to an evening in early autumn, that was conveyed to the mind of the boy who was standing in the porch waiting for the door to open to him.

He had just come from Warwickshire, and some six months ago had been left an orphan. Now, owing to the generous and unexpected offer of his elderly cousin, Mr Abney, he had come to live at Aswarby. The offer was unexpected, because all who knew anything of Mr Abney looked upon him as a somewhat austere recluse, into whose steady-going household the advent of a small boy would import a new and, it seemed, incongruous element. The truth is that very little was known of Mr Abney's pursuits or temper. The Professor of Greek at Cambridge had been heard to say that no one knew more of the religious beliefs of the later pagans than did the owner of Aswarby. Certainly his library contained all the then available books bearing on the Mysteries, the Orphic poems, the worship of Mithras and the Neo-Platonists. In the marble-paved hall stood a fine group of Mithras slaying a bull, which had been imported from the Levant at great expense by the owner. He had contributed a description of it to the *Gentleman's Magazine*, and he had written a remarkable series of articles in the *Critical Museum* on the superstitions of the Romans of the Lower Empire. He was looked upon, in fine, as a man wrapped up in his books, and it was a matter of great surprise among his neighbours that he should ever have heard of his orphan cousin, Stephen Elliott, much more that he should have volunteered to make him an inmate of Aswarby Hall.

Whatever may have been expected by his neighbours, it is certain that Mr Abney—the tall, the thin, the austere—seemed inclined to give his young cousin a kindly reception. The moment the front door was opened he darted out of his study, rubbing his hands with delight.

'How are you, my boy?—how are you? How old are you?" said he—"that is, you are not too much tired, I hope, by your journey to eat your supper?"

"No, thank you, sir," said Master Elliott; "I am pretty well."

"That's a good lad," said Mr Abney. "And how old are you, my boy?"

It seemed a little odd that he should have asked the question twice in the first two minutes of their acquaintance.

"I'm twelve years old next birthday, sir," said Stephen.

"And when is your birthday, my dear boy? Eleventh of September, eh? That's well—that's very well. Nearly a year hence, isn't it? I like—ha, ha!—I like to get these things down in my book. Sure it's twelve? Certain?"

"Yes, quite sure, sir."

"Well, well! Take him to Mrs Bunch's room, Parkes, and let him have his tea—supper—whatever it is."

"Yes, sir," answered the staid Mr Parkes; and conducted Stephen to the lower regions.

Mrs Bunch was the most comfortable and human person whom Stephen had as yet met at Aswarby. She made him completely at home; they were great friends in a quarter of an hour: and great friends they remained. Mrs Bunch had been born in the neighbourhood some fifty-five years before the date of Stephen's arrival, and her residence at the Hall was of twenty years' standing. Consequently, if anyone knew the ins and outs of the house and the district, Mrs Bunch knew them; and she was by no means disinclined to communicate her information.

Certainly there were plenty of things about the Hall and the Hall gardens which Stephen, who was of an adventurous and inquiring turn, was anxious to have explained to him. "Who built the temple at the end of the laurel walk? Who was the old man whose picture hung on the staircase, sitting at a table, with a skull under his hand?" These and many similar points were cleared up by the resources of Mrs Bunch's powerful intellect. There were others, however, of which the explanations furnished were less satisfactory.

One November evening Stephen was sitting by the fire in the housekeeper's room reflecting on his surroundings.

"Is Mr Abney a good man, and will he go to heaven?" he suddenly asked, with the peculiar confidence which children possess in the ability of their elders to settle these questions, the decision of which is believed to be reserved for other tribunals.

"Good?—bless the child!" said Mrs Bunch. "Master's as kind a soul as ever I see! Didn't I never tell you of the little boy as he took in out of the street, as you may say, this seven years back? and the little girl, two years after I first come here?"

"No. Do tell me all about them, Mrs Bunch—now, this minute!"

"Well," said Mrs Bunch, "the little girl I don't seem to recollect so much about. I know master brought her back with him from his walk one day, and give orders to Mrs Ellis, as was housekeeper then, as she should be took every care with. And the pore child hadn't no one belonging to her—she telled me so her own self—and here she lived with us a matter of three weeks it might be; and then, whether she were somethink of a gipsy in her blood or what not, but one morning she out of her bed afore any of us had opened a eye, and neither track nor yet trace of her have I set eyes on since. Master was wonderful put about, and had all the ponds dragged; but it's my belief she was had away by them gipsies, for there was singing round the house for as much as an hour the night she went, and Parkes, he declare as he heard them a-calling in the woods all that afternoon. Dear, dear! a hodd child she was, so silent in her ways and all, but I was wonderful taken up with her, so domesticated she was—surprising."

"And what about the little boy?" said Stephen.

"Ah, that pore boy!" sighed Mrs Bunch. "He were a foreigner—Jevanny he called hisself—and he come a-tweaking his 'urdy-gurdy round and about the drive one winter day, and master 'ad him in that minute, and ast all about where he came from, and how old he was, and how he made his way, and where was his relatives, and all as kind as heart could wish. But it went the same way with him. They're a hunruly lot, them foreign nations, I do suppose, and he was off one fine morning just the same as the girl. Why he went and what he done was our question for as much as a year after; for he never took his 'urdy-gurdy, and there it lays on the shelf."

The remainder of the evening was spent by Stephen in miscellaneous cross-examination of Mrs Bunch and in efforts to extract a tune from the hurdy-gurdy.

That night he had a curious dream. At the end of the passage at the top of the house, in which his bedroom was situated, there was an old disused bathroom. It was kept locked, but the upper half of the door was glazed, and, since the muslin curtains which used to hang there had long been gone, you could look in and see the lead-lined bath affixed to the wall on the right hand, with its head towards the window.

On the night of which I am speaking, Stephen Elliott found himself, as he thought, looking through the glazed door. The moon was shining through the window, and he was gazing at a figure which lay in the bath.

His description of what he saw reminds me of what I once beheld myself in the famous vaults of St Michan's Church in Dublin, which possesses the horrid property of preserving corpses from decay for centuries. A figure inexpressibly thin and pathetic, of a dusty leaden colour, enveloped in a shroud-like garment, the thin lips crooked into a faint and dreadful smile, the hands pressed tightly over the region of the heart.

As he looked upon it, a distant, almost inaudible moan seemed to issue from its lips, and the arms began to stir. The terror of the sight forced Stephen backwards and he awoke to the fact that he was indeed standing on the cold boarded floor of the passage in the full light of the moon. With a courage which I do not think can be common among boys of his age, he went to the door of the bathroom to ascertain if the figure of his dreams were really there. It was not, and he went back to bed.

Mrs Bunch was much impressed next morning by his story, and went so far as to replace the muslin curtain over the glazed door of the bathroom. Mr Abney, moreover, to whom he confided his experiences at breakfast, was greatly interested and made notes of the matter in what he called "his book."

The spring equinox was approaching, as Mr Abney frequently reminded his cousin, adding that this had been always considered by the ancients to be a critical time for the young: that Stephen would do well to take care of himself, and to shut his bedroom window at night; and that Censorinus had some valuable remarks on the subject. Two incidents that occurred about this time made an impression upon Stephen's mind.

The first was after an unusually uneasy and oppressed night that he had passed—though he could not recall any particular dream that he had had. The following evening Mrs Bunch was occupying herself in mending his nightgown.

"Gracious me, Master Stephen!" she broke forth rather irritably, "how do you manage to tear your nightdress all to flinders this way? Look here, sir, what trouble you do give to poor servants that have to darn and mend after you!"

There was indeed a most destructive and apparently wanton series of slits or scorings in the garment, which would undoubtedly require a skilful needle to make good. They were confined to the left side of the chest—long, parallel slits about six inches in length, some of them not quite piercing the texture of the linen. Stephen could only express his entire ignorance of their origin: he was sure they were not there the night before.

"But," he said, "Mrs Bunch, they are just the same as the scratches on the outside of my bedroom door: and I'm sure I never had anything to do with making *them*."

Mrs Bunch gazed at him open-mouthed, then snatched up a candle, departed hastily from the room, and was heard making her way upstairs. In a few minutes she came down.

"Well," she said, "Master Stephen, it's a funny thing to me how them marks and scratches can 'a' come there—too high up for any cat or dog to 'ave made 'em, much less a rat: for all the world like a Chinaman's finger-nails, as my uncle in the tea-trade used to tell us of when we was girls together. I wouldn't say nothing to master, not if I was you, Master Stephen, my dear; and just turn the key of the door when you go to your bed."

"I always do, Mrs Bunch, as soon as I've said my prayers."

"Ah, that's a good child: always say your prayers, and then no one can't hurt you."

Herewith Mrs Bunch addressed herself to mending the injured nightgown, with intervals of meditation, until bedtime. This was on a Friday night in March, 1812.

On the following evening the usual duet of Stephen and Mrs Bunch was augmented by the sudden arrival of Mr Parkes, the butler, who as a rule kept himself rather *to* himself in his own pantry. He did not see that Stephen was there: he was, moreover, flustered and less slow of speech than was his wont.

"Master may get up his own wine, if he likes, of an evening," was his first remark. "Either I do it in the daytime or not at all, Mrs Bunch. I don't know what it may be: very like it's the rats, or the wind got into the cellars; but I'm not so young as I was, and I can't go through with it as I have done."

"Well, Mr Parkes, you know it is a surprising place for the rats, is the Hall."

"I'm not denying that, Mrs Bunch; and, to be sure, many a time I've heard the tale from the men in the shipyards about the rat that could speak. I never laid no confidence in that before; but tonight, if I'd demeaned myself to lay my ear to the door of the further bin, I could pretty much have heard what they was saying."

"Oh, there, Mr Parkes, I've no patience with your fancies! Rats talking in the wine cellar indeed!"

"Well, Mrs Bunch, I've no wish to argue with you: all I say is, if you choose to go to the far bin, and lay your ear to the door, you may prove my words this minute."

"What nonsense you do talk, Mr Parkes—not fit for children to listen to! Why, you'll be frightening Master Stephen there out of his wits."

"What! Master Stephen?" said Parkes, awaking to the consciousness of the boy's presence. "Master Stephen knows well enough when I'm a-playing a joke with you, Mrs Bunch."

In fact, Master Stephen knew much too well to suppose that Mr Parkes had in the first instance intended a joke. He was interested, not altogether pleasantly, in the situation; but all his questions were unsuccessful in inducing the butler to give any more detailed account of his experiences in the wine cellar.

❦

We have now arrived at March 24, 1812. It was a day of curious experiences for Stephen: a windy, noisy day, which filled the house and the gardens with a restless impression. As Stephen stood by the fence of the grounds, and looked out into the park, he felt as if an endless procession of unseen people were sweeping past him on the wind, borne on resistlessly and aimlessly, vainly striving to stop themselves, to catch at something that might arrest their flight and bring them once again into contact with the living world of which they had formed a part. After luncheon that day Mr Abney said:

"Stephen, my boy, do you think you could manage to come to me tonight as late as eleven o'clock in my study? I shall be busy until that time, and I wish to show you something connected with your future life which it is most important that you should know. You are not to mention this matter to Mrs Bunch nor to anyone else in the house; and you had better go to your room at the usual time."

Here was a new excitement added to life: Stephen eagerly grasped at the opportunity of sitting up till eleven o'clock. He looked in at the library door on his way upstairs that evening, and saw a brazier, which he had often noticed in the corner of the room, moved out before the fire; an old silver-gilt cup stood on the table, filled with red wine, and some written sheets of paper lay near it. Mr Abney was sprinkling some incense on the brazier from a round silver box as Stephen passed, but did not seem to notice his step.

The wind had fallen, and there was a still night and a full moon. At about ten o'clock Stephen was standing at the open window of his bedroom, looking out over the country. Still as the night was, the mysterious population of the distant moonlit woods was not yet lulled to rest. From time to time strange cries as of lost and despairing wanderers sounded from across the mere. They might be the notes of owls or waterbirds, yet they did not quite resemble either sound. Were not they coming nearer? Now they sounded from the nearer side of the water, and in a few moments they seemed to be floating about among the shrubberies. Then they ceased; but just as Stephen was thinking of shutting the window and resuming his reading of *Robinson Crusoe*, he caught sight of two figures standing on the gravelled terrace that ran along the garden side of the Hall—the figures of a boy and girl, as it seemed; they stood side by side, looking up at the windows. Something in the form of the girl recalled irresistibly his dream of the figure in the bath. The boy inspired him with more acute fear.

Whilst the girl stood still, half smiling, with her hands clasped over her heart, the boy, a thin shape, with black hair and ragged clothing, raised his arms in the air with an appearance of menace and of unappeasable hunger and longing. The moon shone upon his almost transparent hands, and Stephen saw that the nails were fearfully long and that the light shone through them. As he stood with his arms thus raised, he disclosed a terrifying spectacle. On the left side of his chest there opened a black and gaping rent; and there fell upon Stephen's brain, rather than upon his ear, the impression of one of those hungry and desolate cries that he had heard resounding over the woods of Aswarby all that evening. In another moment this dreadful pair had moved swiftly and noiselessly over the dry gravel, and he saw them no more.

Inexpressibly frightened as he was, he determined to take his candle and go down to Mr Abney's study, for the hour appointed for their meeting was near at hand. The study or library opened out of the front hall on one side, and Stephen, urged on by his terrors, did not take long in getting there. To effect an entrance was not so easy. It was not locked, he felt sure, for the key was on the outside of the door as usual. His repeated knocks produced no answer. Mr Abney was engaged: he was speaking. What! why did he try to cry out? and why was the cry choked in his throat? Had he, too, seen the mysterious children? But now everything was quiet, and the door yielded to Stephen's terrified and frantic pushing.

❦

On the table in Mr Abney's study certain papers were found which explained the situation to Stephen Elliott when he was of an age to understand them. The most important sentences were as follows:

"It was a belief very strongly and generally held by the ancients—of whose wisdom in these matters I have had such experience as induces me to place confidence in their assertions—that by enacting certain processes, which to us moderns have something of a barbaric complexion, a very remarkable enlightenment of the spiritual faculties in man may be attained: that, for example, by absorbing the personalities of a certain number of his fellow-creatures, an individual may gain a complete ascendancy over those orders of spiritual beings which control the elemental forces of our universe.

"It is recorded of Simon Magus that he was able to fly in the air, to become invisible, or to assume any form he pleased, by the agency of the soul of a boy whom, to use the libellous phrase employed by the author of the *Clementine Recognitions*, he had 'murdered'. I find it set down, moreover, with considerable detail in the writings of Hermes Trismegistus, that similar happy results may be produced by the absorption of the hearts of not less than three human beings below the age of twenty-one years. To the testing of the truth of this receipt I have devoted the greater part of the last twenty years, selecting as the *corpora vilia* of my experiment such persons as could conveniently be removed without occasioning a sensible gap in society. The first step I effected by the removal of one Phoebe Stanley, a girl of gipsy extraction, on March 24, 1792. The second, by the removal of a wandering Italian lad, named Giovanni Paoli, on the night of March 23, 1805. The final 'victim'—to employ a word repugnant in the highest degree to my feelings—must be my cousin, Stephen Elliott. His day must be this March 24, 1812.

"The best means of effecting the required absorption is to remove the heart from the *living* subject, to reduce it to ashes, and to mingle them with about a pint of some red wine, preferably port. The remains of the first two subjects, at least, it will be well to conceal: a disused bathroom or wine cellar will be found convenient for such a purpose. Some annoyance may be experienced from the psychic portion of the subjects, which popular language dignifies with the name of ghosts. But the man of philosophic temperament—to whom alone the experiment is appropriate—will be little prone to attach importance to the feeble efforts of these beings to wreak their vengeance on him. I contemplate with the liveliest satisfaction the enlarged and emancipated existence which the experiment, if successful, will confer on me; not only placing me beyond the reach of human justice (so-called), but eliminating to a great extent the prospect of death itself."

Mr Abney was found in his chair, his head thrown back, his face stamped with an expression of rage, fright and mortal pain. In his left side was a terrible lacerated wound, exposing the heart. There was no blood on his hands, and a long knife that lay on the table was perfectly clean. A savage wildcat might have inflicted the injuries. The window of the study was open, and it was the opinion of the coroner that Mr Abney had met his death by the agency of some wild creature. But Stephen Elliott's study of the papers I have quoted led him to a very different conclusion.

CATERPILLARS

E.F. Benson

I SAW a month or two ago in an Italian paper that the Villa Cascana, in which I once stayed, had been pulled down, and that a manufactory of some sort was in process of erection on its site. There is therefore no longer any reason for refraining from writing of those things which I myself saw (or imagined I saw) in a certain room and on a certain landing of the villa in question, nor from mentioning the circumstances which followed, which may or may not (according to the opinion of the reader) throw some light on or be somehow connected with this experience.

The Villa Cascana was in all ways but one a perfectly delightful house, yet, if it were standing now, nothing in the world—I use the phrase in its literal sense—would induce me to set foot in it again, for I believe it to have been haunted in a very terrible and practical manner. Most ghosts, when all is said and done, do not do much harm; they may perhaps terrify, but the person whom they visit usually gets over their visitation. They may on the other hand be entirely friendly and beneficent. But the appearances in the Villa Cascana were not beneficent, and had they made their "visit" in a very slightly different manner, I do not suppose I should have got over it any more than Arthur Inglis did.

❦

The house stood on an ilex-clad hill not far from Sestri di Levante on the Italian Riviera, looking out over the iridescent blues of that enchanted sea, while behind it rose the pale green chestnut woods that climb up the hillsides till they give place to the pines that, black in contrast with them, crown the slopes. All round it the garden in the luxuriance of mid-spring bloomed and was fragrant, and the scent of magnolia and rose, borne on the salt freshness of the winds from the sea, flowed like a stream through the cool vaulted rooms.

On the ground floor a broad pillared *loggia* ran round three sides of the house, the top of which formed a balcony for certain rooms of the first floor. The main staircase, broad and of grey marble steps, led up from the hall to the landing outside these rooms, which were three in number, namely two big sitting rooms and a bedroom arranged en suite. The latter was unoccupied, the sitting rooms were in use. From these the main staircase was continued to the second floor, where were situated certain bedrooms, one of which I occupied, while from the other side of the first-floor landing some half-dozen steps led to another suite of rooms, where, at the time I am speaking of, Arthur Inglis, the artist, had his bedroom and studio. Thus the landing outside my bedroom at the top of the house commanded both the landing of the first floor, and also the steps that led to Inglis' rooms. Jim Stanley and his wife, finally (whose guest I was), occupied rooms in another wing of the house, where also were the servants' quarters.

I arrived just in time for lunch on a brilliant noon of mid-May. The garden was shouting with colour and fragrance, and not less delightful after my broiling walk up from the *marina* should have been the coming from the reverberating heat and blaze of the day into the marble coolness of the villa. Only (the reader has my bare word for this, and nothing more), the moment I set foot in the house I felt that something was wrong. This feeling, I may say, was quite vague, though very strong, and I remember that when I saw letters waiting for me on the table in the hall I felt certain that the explanation was here: I was convinced that there was bad news of some sort for me. Yet when I opened them I found no such explanation of my premonition: my correspondents all reeked of prosperity. Yet this clear miscarriage of a presentiment did not dissipate my uneasiness. In that cool fragrant house there was something wrong.

I am at pains to mention this because to the general view it may explain that though I am as a rule so excellent a sleeper that the extinction of my light on getting into bed is apparently contemporaneous with being called on the following morning, I slept very badly on my first night in the Villa Cascana. It may also explain the fact that when I did sleep (if it was indeed in sleep that I saw what I thought I saw) I dreamed in a very vivid and original manner, original, that is to say, in the sense that something that, as far as I knew, had never previously entered into my consciousness usurped it then. But since, in addition to this evil premonition, certain words and events occurring during the rest of the day might have suggested something of what I thought happened that night, it will be well to relate them.

After lunch, then, I went round the house with Mrs Stanley, and during our tour she referred, it is true, to the unoccupied bedroom on the first floor, which opened out of the room where we had lunched.

"We left that unoccupied," she said, "because Jim and I have a charming bedroom and dressing room, as you saw, in the wing, and if we used it ourselves we should have to turn the dining room into a dressing room and have our meals downstairs. As it is, however, we have our little flat there, Arthur Inglis has his little flat in the other passage; and I remembered (aren't I extraordinary?) that you once said that the higher up you were in a house the better you were pleased. So I put you at the top of the house, instead of giving you that room."

It is true that a doubt, vague as my uneasy premonition, crossed my mind at this. I did not see why Mrs Stanley should have explained all this, if there had not been more to explain. I allow, therefore, that the thought that there was something to explain about the unoccupied bedroom was momentarily present to my mind.

The second thing that may have borne on my dream was this.

At dinner the conversation turned for a moment on ghosts. Inglis, with the certainty of conviction, expressed his belief that anybody who could possibly believe in the existence of supernatural phenomena was unworthy of the name of an ass. The subject instantly dropped. As far as I can recollect, nothing else occurred or was said that could bear on what follows.

We all went to bed rather early, and personally I yawned my way upstairs, feeling hideously sleepy. My room was rather hot, and I threw all the windows wide, and from without poured in the white light of the moon, and the love song of many nightingales. I undressed quickly, and got into bed, but though I had felt so sleepy before, I now felt extremely wide awake. But I was quite content to be awake: I did not toss or turn, I felt perfectly happy listening to the song and seeing the light. Then, it is possible, I may have gone to sleep, and what follows may have been a dream. I thought anyhow that after a time the nightingales ceased singing and the moon sank. I thought also that if, for some unexplained reason, I was going to lie awake all night, I might as well read, and I remembered that I had left a book in which I was interested in the dining room on the first floor. So I got out of bed, lit a candle, and went downstairs. I went into the room, saw on a side table the book I had come to look for, and then, simultaneously, saw that the door into the unoccupied bedroom was open. A curious grey light, not of dawn nor of moonshine, came out of it, and I looked in.

The bed stood just opposite the door, a big four-poster, hung with tapestry at the head. Then I saw that the greyish light of the bedroom came from the bed, or rather from what was on the bed. For it was covered with great caterpillars, a foot or more in length, which crawled over it. They were faintly luminous, and it was the light from them that showed me the room. Instead of the sucker-feet of ordinary caterpillars they had rows of pincers like crabs, and they moved by grasping what they lay on with their pincers, and then sliding their bodies forward.

In colour these dreadful insects were yellowish-grey, and they were covered with irregular lumps and swellings. There must have been hundreds of them, for they formed a sort of writhing, crawling pyramid on the bed. Occasionally one fell off on to the floor, with a soft fleshy thud, and though the floor was of hard concrete, it yielded to the pincer-feet as if it had been putty, and, crawling back, the caterpillar would mount on to the bed again, to rejoin its fearful companions. They appeared to have no faces, so to speak, but at one end of them there was a mouth that opened sideways in respiration.

Then, as I looked, it seemed to me as if they all suddenly became conscious of my presence. All the mouths at any rate were turned in my direction, and next moment they began dropping off the bed with those soft fleshy thuds on to the floor, and wriggling towards me. For one second a paralysis as of a dream was on me, but the next I was running upstairs again to my room, and I remember feeling the cold of the marble steps on my bare feet. I rushed into my bedroom, and slammed the door behind me, and then—I was certainly wide awake now—I found myself standing by my bed with the sweat of terror pouring from me. The noise of the banged door still rang in my ears. But, as would have been more usual, if this had been mere nightmare, the terror that had been mine when I saw those foul beasts crawling about the bed or dropping softly on to the floor did not cease then. Awake now, if dreaming before, I did not at all recover from the horror of dream: it did not seem to me that I had dreamed. And until dawn, I sat or stood, not daring to lie down, thinking that every rustle or movement that I heard was the approach of the caterpillars. To them and the claws that bit into the cement the wood of the door was child's play: steel would not keep them out.

But with the sweet and noble return of day the horror vanished: the whisper of wind became benignant again;

the nameless fear, whatever it was, was smoothed out and terrified me no longer. Dawn broke, hueless at first; then it grew dove-coloured, then the flaming pageant of light spread over the sky.

The admirable rule of the house was that everybody had breakfast where and when he pleased, and in consequence it was not till lunchtime that I met any of the other members of our party, since I had breakfast on my balcony, and wrote letters and other things till lunch. In fact, I got down to that meal rather late, after the other three had begun. Between my knife and fork there was a small pill-box of cardboard, and as I sat down Inglis spoke.

"Do look at that," he said, "since you are interested in natural history. I found it crawling on my counterpane last night, and I don't know what it is."

I think that before I opened the pill-box I expected something of the sort which I found in it. Inside it, anyhow, was a small caterpillar, greyish-yellow in colour, with curious bumps and excrescences on its rings. It was extremely active, and hurried round the box, this way and that. Its feet were unlike the feet of any caterpillar I ever saw: they were like the pincers of a crab. I looked, and shut the lid down again.

"No, I don't know it," I said, "but it looks rather unwholesome. What are you going to do with it?"

“Oh, I shall keep it,” said Inglis. “It has begun to spin: I want to see what sort of a moth it turns into.”

I opened the box again, and saw that these hurrying movements were indeed the beginning of the spinning of the web of its cocoon. Then Inglis spoke again.

“It has got funny feet, too,” he said. “They are like crabs’ pincers.

“What’s the Latin for crab? Oh, yes, Cancer. So in case it is unique, let’s christen it: ‘Cancer Inglisensis’.”

Then something happened in my brain, some momentary piecing together of all that I had seen or dreamed. Something in his words seemed to me to throw light on it all, and my own intense horror at the experience of the night before linked itself on to what he had just said. In effect, I took the box and threw it, caterpillar and all, out of the window. There was a gravel path just outside, and beyond it a fountain playing into a basin. The box fell on to the middle of this.

Inglis laughed.

“So the students of the occult don’t like solid facts,” he said. “My poor caterpillar!”

The talk went off again at once on to other subjects, and I have only given in detail, as they happened, these trivialities in order to be sure myself that I have recorded everything that could have borne on occult subjects or on the subject of caterpillars. But at the moment when I threw the pill-box into the fountain, I lost my head: my only excuse is that, as is probably plain, the tenant of it was, in miniature, exactly what I had seen crowded on to the bed in the unoccupied room. And though this translation of those phantoms into flesh and blood—or whatever it is that caterpillars are made of—ought perhaps to have relieved the horror of the night, as a matter of fact it did nothing of the kind. It only made the crawling pyramid that covered the bed in the unoccupied room more hideously real.

After lunch we spent a lazy hour or two strolling about the garden or sitting in the loggia, and it must have been about four o'clock when Stanley and I started off to bathe, down the path that led by the fountain into which I had thrown the pill-box. The water was shallow and clear, and at the bottom of it I saw its white remains. The water had disintegrated the cardboard, and it had become no more than a few strips and shreds of sodden paper. The centre of the fountain was a marble Italian Cupid which squirted the water out of a wineskin held under its arm. And crawling up its leg was the caterpillar. Strange and scarcely credible as it seemed, it must have survived the falling-to-bits of its prison, and made its way to shore, and there it was, out of arm's reach, weaving and waving this way and that as it evolved its cocoon.

Then, as I looked at it, it seemed to me again that, like the caterpillar I had seen last night, it saw me, and, breaking out of the threads that surrounded it, it crawled down the marble leg of the Cupid and began swimming like a snake across the water of the fountain towards me. It came with extraordinary speed (the fact of a caterpillar being able to swim was new to me), and in another moment was crawling up the marble lip of the basin. Just then Inglis joined us.

"Why, if it isn't old 'Cancer Inglisensis' again," he said, catching sight of the beast. "What a tearing hurry it is in."

We were standing side by side on the path, and when the caterpillar had advanced to within about a yard of us, it stopped, and began waving again, as if in doubt as to the direction in which it should go. Then it appeared to make up its mind, and crawled onto Inglis' shoe.

"It likes me best," he said, "but I don't really know that I like it. And as it won't drown I think perhaps—"

He shook it off his shoe on to the gravel path and trod on it.

❦

All afternoon the air got heavier and heavier with the Sirocco that was without doubt coming up from the south, and that night again I went up to bed feeling very sleepy; but below my drowsiness, so to speak, there was the consciousness, stronger than before, that there was something wrong in the house, that something dangerous was close at hand. But I fell asleep at once, and—how long after I do not know—either woke or dreamed I awoke, feeling that I must get up at once, *or I should be too late.* Then (dreaming or awake) I lay and fought this fear, telling myself that I was but the prey of my own nerves disordered by Sirocco or whatnot, and at the same time quite clearly knowing in another part of my mind, so to speak, that every moment's delay added to the danger. At last this second feeling became irresistible, and I put on coat and trousers and went out of my room onto the landing. And then I saw that I had already delayed too long, and that I was now too late.

The whole of the landing of the first floor below was invisible under the swarm of caterpillars that crawled there. The folding doors into the sitting room, from which opened the bedroom where I had seen them last night, were shut, but they were squeezing through the cracks of it, and dropping one by one through the keyhole, elongating themselves into mere string as they passed, and growing fat and lumpy again on emerging.

Some, as if exploring, were nosing about the steps into the passage at the end of which were Inglis' rooms, others were crawling on the lowest steps of the staircase that led up to where I stood. The landing, however, was completely covered with them: I was cut off. And of the frozen horror that seized me when I saw that, I can give no idea in words.

Then at last a general movement began to take place, and they grew thicker on the steps that led to Inglis' room.

Gradually, like some hideous tide of flesh, they advanced along the passage, and I saw the foremost, visible by the pale grey luminousness that came from them, reach his door. Again and again I tried to shout and warn him, in terror all the time that they would turn at the sound of my voice and mount my stair instead, but for all my efforts I felt that no sound came from my throat. They crawled along the hinge-crack of his door, passing through as they had done before, and still I stood there making impotent efforts to shout to him, to bid him escape while there was time.

At last the passage was completely empty: they had all gone, and at that moment I was conscious for the first time of the cold of the marble landing on which I stood barefooted. The dawn was just beginning to break in the Eastern sky.

Six months later I met Mrs Stanley in a country house in England. We talked on many subjects and at last she said: "I don't think I have seen you since I got that dreadful news about Arthur Inglis a month ago."

"I haven't heard," said I.

"No? He has got cancer. They don't even advise an operation, for there is no hope of a cure: he is riddled with it, the doctors say."

Now during all these six months I do not think a day had passed on which I had not had in my mind the dreams (or whatever you like to call them) which I had seen in the Villa Cascana.

"It is awful, is it not?" she continued, "and I feel, I can't help feeling, that he may have—"

"Caught it at the villa?" I asked.

She looked at me in blank surprise.

"Why did you say that?" she asked. "How did you know?"

Then she told me. In the unoccupied bedroom a year before there had been a fatal case of cancer. She had, of course, taken the best advice and had been told that the utmost dictates of prudence would be obeyed so long as she did not put anybody to sleep in the room, which had also been thoroughly disinfected and newly whitewashed and painted. But—

SOURCES

Benson, E.F., 'Caterpillars', from *The Room in the Tower, and Other Stories*, Mills & Boon, London, 1912.

Bierce, Ambrose, 'A Watcher by the Dead', collected in *In the Midst of Life: Tales of Soldiers and Civilians*, Chatto, London, 1892.

Blackwood, Algernon, 'The Second Generation', collected in *Ten Minute Stories*, John Murray, London, 1914.

Burke, Thomas, 'The Black Courtyard', collected in *Night Pieces*, Constable, London, 1935.

Lord Dunsany, 'The Two Bottles of Relish', from *The Little Tales of Smethers and Other Stories*, Jarrolds, London, 1952.

Jacobs, W.W., 'The Interruption', collected in *Sea Whisperers*, Charles Scribner's Sons, New York, 1927.

James, M.R., 'Lost Hearts', collected in *Ghost Stories of an Antiquary*, Penguin, London, 1938.

Lovecraft, H.P., 'The Haunter of the Dark', collected in *The Haunter of the Dark and Other Tales of Horror*, Gollancz, London, 1951.

Machen, Arthur, 'Change', from *The Children of the Pool and Other Stories*, Hutchinson, London, 1936.

Nesbit, E., 'The Portent of the Shadow', collected in *Fear*, Stanley Paul, London, 1910.

Stoker, Bram, 'The Judge's House', collected in *Dracula's Guest and Other Weird Stories*, George Routledge & Sons, 1914.

Wharton, Edith, 'Afterward', collected in *Tales of Men and Ghosts*, Macmillan, London, 1910.

Wilkins Freeman, Mary, 'Luella Miller', from *The Wind in the Rosebush,* Doubleday, New York, 1903.

Williams, Herbert (ed.), *Terror at Night*, Avon Book Company, New York, 1947.

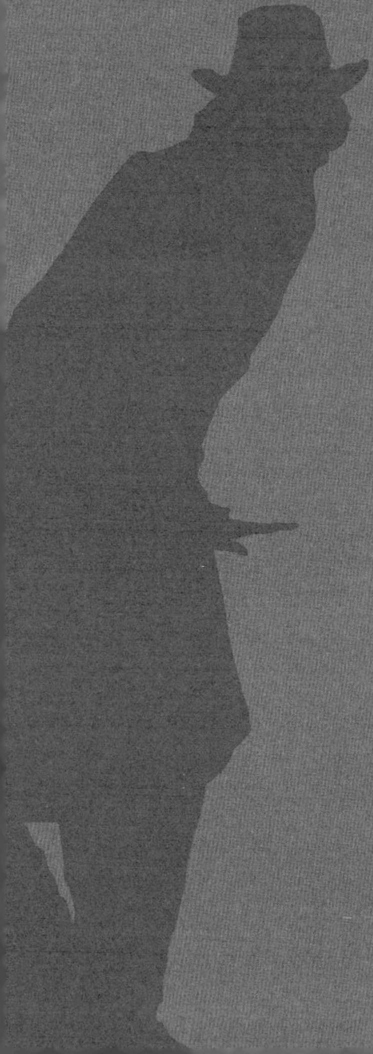

POCKET
BAYEUX
TAPESTRY

POCKET BAYEUX TAPESTRY

Emily A. Winkler

BODLEIAN
LIBRARY
PUBLISHING

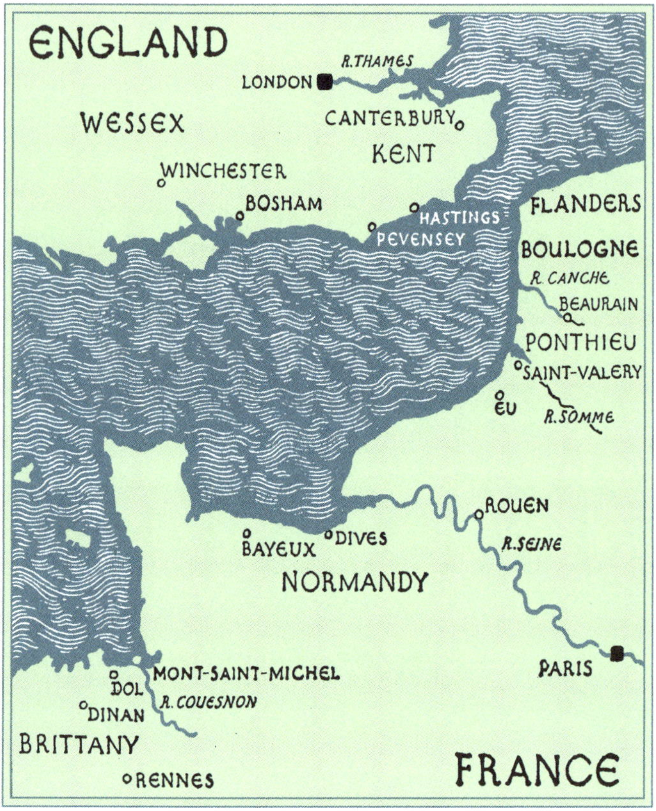

ENGLAND
R.THAMES
LONDON
WESSEX
CANTERBURY
KENT
WINCHESTER
BOSHAM
HASTINGS
PEVENSEY
FLANDERS
BOULOGNE
R. CANCHE
BEAURAIN
PONTHIEU
SAINT-VALERY
EU
R.SOMME
ROUEN
R.SEINE
BAYEUX
DIVES
NORMANDY
PARIS
MONT-SAINT-MICHEL
DOL
R. COUESNON
DINAN
BRITTANY
RENNES
FRANCE

CONTENTS

PEOPLE

Conan II, count of Brittany (d. 1066)
Conan, the son of William of Normandy's former ally Alan III of Brittany, surrendered to William during William's progress through Normandy, according to the Bayeux Tapestry.

Edith Godwineson (d. 1075)
Harold's sister, King Edward's wife and England's queen, Edith remained a respected political figure in England after the Norman Conquest.

Edward the Confessor (d. 1066)
King of England from 1042 to 1066.

Emma of Normandy (d. 1052)
Wife and queen consort successively to two kings of England, Æthelred II and Cnut, and mother of King Edward through her marriage to Æthelred.

Godwine, earl of Wessex (d. 1053)
Father of Harold and head of the wealthiest family in England, he rose to prominence during the reign of King Cnut.

Guy I, count of Ponthieu (d. 1100)
A former prisoner of William of Normandy, Guy took Harold into custody during Harold's journey to the Continent in 1065, and delivered him into William's custody later that year.

Gyrth Godwineson (d. 1066)
Harold's younger brother and earl of East Anglia, Gyrth was killed in the Battle of Hastings.

Harold Godwineson (d. 1066)
As earl of Wessex and King Edward's second-in-command, he was elected king in 1066 and killed later that year at the Battle of Hastings.

Leofwine Godwineson (d. 1066)
Harold's younger brother and earl of Kent, Leofwine was killed in the Battle of Hastings.

Matilda of Flanders (d. 1083)
Duchess of Normandy, and later queen and regent of England, through her marriage to William of Normandy.

Odo, bishop of Bayeux (d. 1097)
Through his mother, Herleva, half-brother of William of Normandy; Odo's father was Herluin of Conteville.

Robert, count of Mortain (d. c.1095)
Through his mother, Herleva, half-brother of William of Normandy; Robert's father was Herluin of Conteville.

Stigand, archbishop of Canterbury (d. 1072)
Stigand, formerly a senior advisor of England's Danish kings, was archbishop of Canterbury from 1052 to 1070.

William, duke of Normandy (d. 1087)
As duke of Normandy, William conquered England and became its king in 1066.

TIMELINE

Late summer 1065

Harold Godwineson, earl of Wessex, goes on a mission to the Continent. After spending time in the court of Guy I, count of Ponthieu, he is handed over to Duke William of Normandy. William and Harold campaign together in Brittany. William honours Harold for his service. Before Harold departs for England he swears an oath to William.

5 January 1066

King Edward the Confessor dies.

6 January 1066

The governing council of nobles of the English kingdom meet to choose their new king. They elect Harold and give him the crown. From this moment he is the king of England.

Late February 1066

An assembly convenes at Lillebonne in Normandy. On Duke William's orders it is agreed to assemble a fleet of ships for an invasion of England.

24 April 1066

Halley's Comet, called the long-tailed star, is observed over England and Normandy.

August 1066

William spends the month collecting his fleet at the port of Dives and in nearby harbours.

8 September 1066
Harold's fleet at the Isle of Wight sails for London.

12 September 1066
William's fleet sails from Dives and later lands at Saint-Valery-sur-Somme.

20 September 1066
In the north, King Harald Hardrada of Norway defeats the Mercian earl Edwin and his brother Morcar at the Battle of Fulford.

25 September 1066
King Harold attacks Hardrada, defeating and killing him at the Battle of Stamford Bridge.

27 September 1066, evening
As night falls and the tide goes out, William's fleet sails from Saint-Valery, bound for Pevensey.

28 September 1066, morning
William lands at Pevensey.

14 October 1066
After a full day of battle, William defeats Harold at the Battle of Hastings.

25 December 1066
William is crowned king of England at Westminster Abbey.

INTRODUCTION

The Bayeux Tapestry tells the story of the Norman Conquest of England, culminating in the Battle of Hastings on 14 October 1066. The conquest, unusually decisive even for the eleventh century, remains the last successful invasion of England. The Tapestry offers both an intimate glimpse and a public display of the long battle, first of wits and then of weapons, between William of Normandy and Harold Godwineson as they struggled for England's throne.

It is an adventure story, a tale of desperate measures and last resorts. Throughout, it shows how people under pressure faced a crisis. Unlike a still life or a portrait, no scene is frozen in time. There is always something, or someone, beckoning you to find out what happens next. It is suspenseful even if you know how it ends.

Eleventh-century people immediately realized the enormity of the conquest as an historical event. They knew it had been a high-risk venture, bringing immense rewards for the Normans and losses for the English. The colossal efforts of all involved were worthy of record. Artists depicted news brought by eager messengers on horses; Normans stocking ships with food; the English closing ranks to defend their king. This was an event to remember.

The Tapestry is a work of commemorative art. It reflects an urge to create a memorial, a desire that was strong among past peoples who knew how easily lives and deeds might pass into oblivion. These events possessed intrinsic value that made them worth keeping – to learn from, to celebrate, to lament or simply to know. To animate a work of embroidered art with the lives of those who lived through the conquest was a way to preserve them, and to contend against the loss of forgetting.

The Story the Tapestry Tells

The Tapestry tells the story of three kings of England: Edward, Harold and William. King Edward the Confessor, raised in Normandy in exile, had an English father, King Æthelred II of the House of Wessex, a direct descendant of Alfred the Great. Edward's Norman mother, Emma, married first to Æthelred and then to England's Danish conqueror, Cnut, established the Norman presence in England that offered a pretext for the conquest. She embodied the connected world of the North Sea that forms the Tapestry's backdrop. Edward led England through civil discord and foreign threat. But because he and his wife Edith Godwineson had no children, the succession remained an open question and a temptation for ambitious leaders.

Harold Godwineson, earl of Wessex, belonged to the wealthiest, most powerful family in England, the Anglo-Danish Godwines, who by the 1060s controlled more assets than the king. He was Edward's star general. Harold had won many campaigns on the king's behalf. As Edward's brother-in-law and second-in-command, Harold was a powerful and reliable leader, well placed to steer the kingdom through troubled times.

William, duke of Normandy, inherited the duchy at a young age. He spent his youth learning to defend himself against threats from the French king and neighbouring lords. Alert to the politics of the coastal world in which he lived, friendly with King Edward and possessing strategic intelligence gathered from Norman-held abbeys on England's south coast, William plotted a daring enterprise: seizing the English crown for himself. After he was crowned king of England in 1066, William would cast himself as Edward's successor and erase Harold's name from royal records.

This is a tale of a rivalry between two great lords, loyal to their men and unafraid of risk. Although concerned with true events, the Tapestry does not tell a complete history. It simplifies the story into an epic contest between two comrades who became adversaries. Harold and William, however, were not the only men vying to take Edward's place as king of England. The Tapestry leaves out two major contenders for the throne: Edgar Ætheling and Harald Hardrada. King Edward, trying desperately to find a successor of royal blood – a prince of the House of Wessex, worthy of the throne – had summoned his cousin's family from Hungary, and adopted the young Edgar Ætheling as his heir apparent in the early 1060s. Another contender emerged in 1066. Three weeks before the Battle of Hastings, the king of Norway, Harald Hardrada, had invaded England in the north, hoping to seize the crown.

But William and Harold were formidable competitors. Harold defeated and killed Hardrada at Stamford Bridge near York. Edgar, an inconvenient reminder to both Harold and William of rightful royal succession, was kept under surveillance after 1066, and probably omitted from parts of the Anglo-Saxon Chronicle. Harold and William commanded assets, men and courage. They defeated rivals with weapons and words. Neither had a secure claim to be England's ruler. They were the two who faced each other in the last battle for the crown.

The Normans tried to justify conquest. Their chroniclers declared that Edward formally promised the throne to William in 1051, and that in the 1060s Harold swore to support William's claim. English chronicles, by contrast, claimed that a dying Edward bequeathed the throne to Harold. In eleventh-century England, kingship was not strictly hereditary. Although royal blood mattered, the governing council of nobles chose an experienced leader who could command men and govern well. They elected Harold king of England in January 1066.

The Tapestry's tale of two rivals, therefore, forms but one part of a larger story of history that happened offstage. An epic, it is unstinting in showing the staggering labour required for victory, the role of chance in war and the grim cost in homes and lives.

The drama unfolds in three acts. In the first, Harold, with Edward's approval, travels to the Continent on a mission. Swept up in the rivalries and ambitions of continental lords, he joins William on a military campaign in Brittany. In the second, their friendship falls apart: England's governing council names Harold king of England, and as Harold reigns, William prepares for a massive invasion. In the third, English and Norman forces join battle to decide the kingdom's fate.

For each act the backdrop is the sea. The Tapestry follows events that happened almost exclusively on or by the sea, on the banks of rivers and along the coastal corridor between England and Normandy. Medieval lords were itinerant, seldom holding still, always inspecting their own realm, quelling rebellions and seeking allies in lands farther afield. The Tapestry is one of the best sources from medieval Europe for this world of perpetual motion. Horses, winds and ships carry men and messages all about this coastal realm at great speed. Trees and buildings offer only brief pauses in the swift activities of bearing news, digging ditches and leading armies to battle. Only Edward, England's ageing king, slows the action to confer quietly with his commander, Harold, and to hold our gaze as he dies and is borne in a dignified procession to his resting place at Westminster. These doings, preserved on a textile, are imbued with a tangible sense of life and breath.

William intended to conquer, as the Tapestry makes explicit. Harold, given the crown by England's governing council, is given the title of king by the designers. William invaded. He seized English lands. At the same time, the Tapestry is remarkable because it offers flexibility in perspective instead of a dogmatic tale of right and wrong. The Tapestry tells the 'how' story of the conquest.

It shows how people managed crises, sailed ships, faced dangers, carted wine, attacked, showed affection, realized ambitions.

As a piece of storytelling and a work of art, the Tapestry is highly sophisticated. It animates a brilliantly wrought gathering of people and events – and deliberately invites viewers to take on the task of interpreting and understanding it. In the years after 1066, rebellions drove William to malign Harold's memory, and to present him not as a fallen comrade but a vicious enemy. Yet the Tapestry fits perfectly with both English and Norman versions of events. Where chroniclers traded accusations about broken promises, stolen crowns and war crimes, the Tapestry stands mute. It is ingeniously diplomatic and studiously discreet. Viewers can return repeatedly to notice things for the first time, and to see different stories revealed in the same pictures. Still, it is not tentative. It is vivid and blunt in depicting history, from the pith of human endeavour to the brutality of war. Its artistry worked, and works, at the highest level. The Tapestry's creators passed away long ago. Their creation survives.

The Tapestry's Own Story

The Bayeux Tapestry is a truly Anglo-Norman work. Its content and design illustrate the intermingled relationship between Normandy and England that had existed long before 1066. The Tapestry is an embroidery of dyed woollen yarn sewn onto linen panels. Measuring one and a half metres in height and about seventy metres long, it remains a treasure of world heritage and a startling, vivid moment of historical drama and art from nearly a thousand years ago. Tapestries telling stories were common at the time, adorning walls of bedchambers, corridors, dining halls and churches. It is now the only one of its kind.

The Tapestry was made in the eleventh century, almost certainly within five or ten years of the Norman Conquest, and very likely in southern England. English artists embroidered the Tapestry. These women, trained since childhood in the arts of weaving, colour, texture and design, were famous throughout Europe for their exquisite needlework. Artists may have included churchwomen trained in workshops at Wilton Abbey and laywomen of Canterbury, skilled and virtuosic in embroidery and other textile arts. English women worked wonders in woollen yarn.

The design of the Tapestry was inspired by artwork from Canterbury, a centre of learning in south-eastern England. Monastic communities in Canterbury were known for making high-quality books and art. The Tapestry's designers and makers would have had access to a wealth of inspiration. They had a treasury of visual art: decorative patterns in textiles, illustrations in Canterbury manuscripts and Anglo-Scandinavian designs in stone sculpture. They had a library of literature, including Virgil's ancient epic the *Aeneid*, biblical stories of invasion and new narratives about the Norman Conquest written by monks. They had stories from life, perhaps gained from conversations with shipwrights and soldiers. With these ideas artists created a new story.

A decorated textile, unlike a sculpture or a stone-carven frieze, was designed to be portable and displayed in different settings. The Tapestry could have hung in the great hall of a secular lord or the refectory of a monastic house, to be marvelled over while lords and ladies, clerics or visitors were dining. It might have been set around the centre keep of a coastal castle, to remind nobles of their loyalty to their lords and the deeds of their comrades.

We do not know whose idea it was to make the Tapestry. Odo, bishop of Bayeux, has long been considered a likely patron; before that, William's wife, Matilda of Flanders, was a popular choice; more recently, Edward the Confessor's widow Edith or the monks of Canterbury have been proposed. What we do know is that it must have been a collaborative enterprise, a creation imagined and made by many people of different rank in what was probably a surprisingly short time. If the Tapestry had one or more patrons, they might have proposed, approved, paid for or accepted the Tapestry. It might have been a commission, in which labourers were employed to complete it to specification. Or, it might have been made collectively and dedicated or offered as a gift. Whether the Tapestry emerged from discussions or directives, the idea was powerful enough to engage the efforts of many and the eyes of more.

Looking at the Tapestry

For the first five hundred years of its existence, records of the Tapestry are few. The early twelfth-century poet Baudri of Bourgueil almost certainly saw it. Anglo-Norman chroniclers, working soon after, may have seen it too. The first explicit reference to the Tapestry appears in an inventory of Bayeux Cathedral from 1476. There are earlier tantalizing possibilities. It may be the textile depicting Duke William listed among the tapestries of King Charles VI of France in 1422, or the one portraying the conquest of England in the collection of Philip of Burgundy, around 1430.

The Tapestry you see today is not how it would have originally looked. The bright and brilliant colours, from blues and greens to russets and yellows, have faded. Restorers fixed damage and imposed new images. The myth of Harold and the arrow is the best example. The soldier holding the arrow is not Harold and the Tapestry did not originally show this man holding an arrow. The earliest surviving drawings of the Tapestry, from the eighteenth century, reveal that this soldier, like his comrades in the shield-wall, was holding a spear shaft. Nineteenth-century artists lowered the angle of the spear in their drawings and added fletching to make the spear look like an arrow. Restorers altered the Tapestry to match. The notion that Harold died by arrow, most likely inspired by the fateful arrows of Virgil's *Aeneid* that changed heroes' destinies, emerged many years after the Battle of Hastings. Later chroniclers developed the idea until it achieved the legendary status it holds today.

The drawings of Victor Sansonetti, which feature in this book, offer a snapshot of the Tapestry earlier in time, two hundred years closer to its making. In 1838 Sansonetti, a French artist and former pupil of the noted French neoclassical painter Jean-Auguste-Dominique Ingres, was commissioned to draw the Tapestry for a book of great historical French textiles. This book by Achille Jubinal, a French antiquarian, followed a British printing of the Tapestry twenty years prior. Charles Stothard, a British historical draughtsman, had been commissioned by the Society of Antiquaries in 1816 to copy the Bayeux Tapestry for publication. The Society wanted Britain to have its own version for research and for wider promotion of historical knowledge. Based on Stothard's engravings of 1819, Sansonetti's drawings include original material as well as Stothard's speculative reconstructions: Stothard had drawn in nearly twenty arrows and added guesses about the names of people and buildings.

Sansonetti's fine line drawings have their own unique character. Notably, Sansonetti employed a greater range of shapes for eyes, noses and facial expressions. In this respect his designs are more similar to the original Tapestry, compared with Stothard's more uniform use of geometric forms for facial features. The Sansonetti drawings of 1838 give insight into what the Tapestry looked like before the major interventions later that century. They capture rips and tears, and preserve words missing letters before they were reconstructed. These drawings are a reminder of the Tapestry's robustness and fragility, and of the ongoing impulse to preserve it. There is much we can tell from what remains, so we will move in for a closer look at the Tapestry.

The decorative border of the Tapestry is one of its distinctive features, fascinating in its display of artistic skill and its interplay with the story's main events. Images from Aesop's Fables appear in the borders, commenting wryly on the behaviour of medieval lords. The fables reveal parallels and contrasts in lords' deeds. They offer bawdy comedy and dry wit. They make shrewd observations that probe the very idea of conquest.

The fables show that power works among humans as it does in the wild. Rival lords look for the advantage, cleverly or foolishly seeking the spoils of war. One fable depicts a fox and a crow competing for stolen cheese that does not belong to either of them, just as lords vie for the lands of others. Another fable shows that although conquest meant a change of kings, it changed little for the poor. A donkey, as a labouring creature already bearing a load, refuses to run away from the conquerors. For one already oppressed, one master is much like the next.

Embroidered Latin text runs throughout the Tapestry, describing the main scenes. The varied spellings and syntax show that native English and French speakers contributed to the text. Certain figures are labelled with their names and, sometimes, office. The text uses pithy prose for events.

The Tapestry's visual narrative generally proceeds from left to right, but sometimes the action moves from right to left. Westminster Abbey is portrayed after Harold's return to England. Farther to the right, Edward's deathbed scene appears and his funeral procession leads leftwards, back to the abbey. Likewise, the Norman envoys ride from William's imposing stone castle at Rouen leftwards to Guy's palace, a centre of action and discussion, located farther back along the Tapestry. Time is not running backwards. Rather, the designers sometimes used the Tapestry's physical space to stand in for real space, more like a map or a theatre set than a linear narrative. A vital building occupies one place while human beings converge on it. In the Battle of Hastings, key events are located centrally, such as the English shield-wall's defence and Harold's death, with Normans closing in from both sides.

Artists designed the Tapestry to be experienced in the round. It creates the effect of an arena or stadium – one in which you, the viewer, stand centrally and the spectacle occurs around you. The Tapestry is a two-dimensional representation, yet the embroidery's texture and the staging of the figures create a remarkable drama. Asking for your regard, the Tapestry positions you as an eyewitness to the events of the conquest. You are invited to peek in on hushed private conferences, to inspect the building of ships and the loading of cargo, and to search the blood-soaked field of battle for familiar figures among the fallen.

The original audience is unknown. The Tapestry's story would have had wide appeal for noblemen and kings, rural women and children, monks and nuns, craftspeople and labourers. In its fables and depictions of working lives, it offered familiarity. For those curious to discover happenings beyond their own experience, it gave a chance to explore. An ambitious creation of this scale sought an audience as wide as its vast scope. It was for anyone who wanted to know.

The Tapestry belonged to a long medieval tradition of commemorative creative works driven by war. Before the Norman Conquest, when England faced frequent Danish invasions, the English leader Byrhtnoth was defeated and killed in the Battle of Maldon in 991. The battle inspired epic poetry and chronicles, as well as art: Byrhtnoth's widow Ælfflaed gave as a gift to the abbey of Ely a tapestry that told the story of her husband's deeds. It would be kept in a place where it would be cared for and have a chance of lasting. It was offered in his honour as a memorial.

As a war memorial does, the Bayeux Tapestry remembers the lives of those who were there for the conquest. It neither celebrated victory nor condemned defeat. It celebrated the memory of the event and those involved. What it condemned was forgetting.

Above all, medieval artists and writers crafted it for posterity: future readers, listeners and viewers. Oblivion was among a creator's greatest fears. Aware of the fragility of memory, the expense of recording and threats of destruction, they lived daily with the knowledge that they must do something, or make something, lest their times be forgotten. From an eleventh-century perspective, you are a future viewer. When you look, a story of the Norman Conquest is remembered again. The Tapestry is for you.

THE TAPESTRY

1 EDWARD REX [U]BI HAROLD DUX ANGLORUM ET SUI MILITES ...

THE FIRST SCENE of the Bayeux Tapestry, like the opening line of many stories, signals a key theme of the narrative to come. The Tapestry begins the tale of the Norman Conquest of England with an enthroned Edward the Confessor, king of England, presiding over his court in 1065. Edward mattered in this story because it was through him that William the Conqueror claimed to be, not an invader or usurper, but the rightful heir to the English throne. Edward had been raised in exile in Normandy and his mother, Queen Emma, was Norman.

King Edward. Where Harold, earl of the English, and his soldiers ...

Edward, flanked by the towers of his royal palace, is seated in a hall, wearing his crown and holding the royal sceptre. This backdrop affirms Edward's royal authority as he discusses a mission to the Continent. One of the men addressing him is Harold Godwineson, earl of Wessex, the leading general of Edward's army. Harold appears again on horseback on the right, holding aloft a bird of prey and preceded by a pack of hunting dogs. With a party of five mounted soldiers pictured behind him, Harold is already cast as a man of action and a leader.

2 ... EQUITANT AD BOSHAM. ECCLESIA.

HAROLD JOURNEYS TO Holy Trinity Church in Bosham on England's south coast. The Tapestry gives a stylized impression of an Anglo-Saxon church, tall and narrow with small, high windows. Harold and a companion enter the church with bent knees ready to pray, perhaps for safe passage and a successful mission. For a medieval audience, Harold was displaying a good lord's priorities by showing humility before God.

Adjacent to the church lay a splendid manor house, home of Edward's Norman kinsman Osbern FitzOsbern, near the strategic Chichester Harbour. Harold and his

... ride to Bosham. The church.

men drink and dine well: Harold, the Tapestry shows us, lived like a king. Harold's father and predecessor as earl of Wessex, Godwine, had substantial lands in the county of Sussex. Some were rewards for his service to England's Danish King Cnut and King Edward the Confessor. The Godwines were the wealthiest family in Sussex, and their wealth rivalled that of the royal family.

Interrupting the lively feast, a messenger bounds up the stairs, pointing towards a ship. One man stands ready with an oar; another gives the urgent message to Harold that it is time to sail.

3 **HIC HAROLD MARE NAVIGAVIT ET VELIS VENTO PLENIS VENIT IN T[ERR]A WIDONIS COMITIS.**

CARRYING A HUNTING dog and his hawk, Harold boards a ship. The Tapestry does not tell us why Harold was on a mission to cross the Channel. Harold's younger brother Wulfnoth and nephew Hakon were hostages of Duke William of Normandy. Harold may have requested permission from King Edward to negotiate for their release, to find continental allies to help him or to rescue them in a daring raid.

These are realistic depictions of medieval sailing ships. The ships in Harold's fleet were powered by oars and sails: in the left-hand ship, skilled oarsmen work the waves as

Here Harold sailed across the sea and, with sails filled with wind, came to the land of Count Guy.

they row out of Chichester Harbour. Now in open waters, the right-hand ship flies a square-rig sail, the classic style of a Viking ship. Finely wrought curves show folds in the sail's fabric, catching the wind. Forestays and backstays, the ropes that tension the mast against the bow and stern, are visible. One sailor adjusts the sidestays that support the mast. Meanwhile, Harold's soldiers, with their shields arrayed, await their mission on the Continent.

4 HAROLD. HIC APPREHENDIT WIDO HAROLDUM …

WITH SMOOTH SAILING and a vigorous wind, Harold has reached Ponthieu, a small coastal county between the greater powers of Normand (to the west) and Flanders (to the north-east). Men scramble to beach the ships. One nimble sailor climbs the mast, three steady the halyards, or ropes to adjust the sails, and a team hauls in the sails. Another leans overboard to drop anchor. Harold is instantly taken by the local lord, Count Guy I of Ponthieu. Harold's men reach for their swords. Guy restrains Harold with one hand, pointing inland with the other.

Harold. Here Guy seized Harold ...

Norman and English chronicles diverge sharply on their interpretation of Harold's encounter with Guy. One Norman story casts Guy as a dangerous aggressor attacking Harold, and William of Normandy as Harold's valiant rescuer. An English source portrays Harold secretly gathering information and allies on the Continent. The Tapestry, silent on the nature of their conversation, fits both versions. Guy might have ordered Harold, his prisoner, to follow. Or, he might have urged Harold to come somewhere safe where the two lords could talk in private.

5 … ET DUXIT EUM AD BELREM [ET] IBI EUM TENUIT.

GUY OF PONTHIEU seized Harold and an opportunity. Guy owed service to William of Normandy, but had cause to stay alert to opportunities to resist William. After William had defeated Guy in 1054 after a long conflict, William kept Guy a prisoner in Bayeux for two years. On his release, Guy had to swear permanent faith to William. He had even agreed to send a hundred men for William's military service whenever William commanded.

Nevertheless, long-term tensions between the powerful realms of Flanders and Normandy meant that the counties of Boulogne and Ponthieu, sandwiched between, found

... and led him to Beaurain and held him there.

chances to bargain for more security and influence. Count Guy would have known that his high-ranking English captive was worth much, whether as a formidable opponent or prospective ally, to Guy's more powerful neighbours. Harold might prove a valuable comrade for Guy in a bid to press back against Norman power.

Beaurain Castle was a strategic location in the county of Saint-Pol, near the realm of Count Eustace II of Boulogne, with whom Guy shared an interest in restraining Norman power. Safely inland, Beaurain was a good distance from Normandy.

6 UBI HAROLD ET WIDO PARABOLANT.

IN GUY'S CUSTODY, Harold could expect to be treated well. High-ranking prisoners were valuable assets. Captors could earn considerable sums through ransom or gain personal advantages through compromise and negotiation. Because of Harold's high status, he was permitted to carry his sheathed sword when speaking with Guy. Even powerful lords required trust and mutual respect to do business.

This was not their first meeting. Guy and Harold had met in Flanders in 1056. At that time, Harold may have been acting on King Edward's behalf to summon the

Where Harold and Guy parley.

English royal family back to England from Hungary. The royal family's return to England in 1057, however, did not remove the spectre of Normandy's potential interest in the succession. Harold and Guy might have discussed power balances along the Channel, the future of the English throne and potential alliances with other coastal lords.

The Tapestry offers a scene of palace intrigue and hushed, huddled waiting outside the audience chamber. The figure on the far right leans in to listen, unobserved. He may be one of William of Normandy's spies.

7 UBI NUNTII WIL[L]ELMI DUCIS VENERUNT AD WIDONE. TUROLD.

IF THE EAVESDROPPER in the previous scene was a spy for William of Normandy, he did quick work. William's messengers, visible centrally, have just dismounted. An elegantly dressed Count Guy, hand on hip in a posture of noble ease, holds a long axe as a symbol of status. He receives William's envoy with a formal, but not submissive, welcome. While they confer, peasants follow the routine of farming in the lower margin.

The identity of Turold is one of two great puzzles of identity in the Tapestry. All other name-markers in the Tapestry appear above the figure's head. Turold may be

Where the envoys of Duke William have come to Guy. Turold.

the bearded man, depicted in the background, who steadies the rearing horse. Or, he may be the armed knight in red. Turold of Rochester, steward of William's half-brother Odo of Bayeux, is one popular contender. Turold was a common name, so his identity remains a mystery.

Medieval artists devised ways to convey three-dimensional space. Human figures and ships (as in Plate 25) were sometimes portrayed relatively smaller to imply distance. Embroiderers used different colours for a horse's far legs to evoke shadow and depth.

8 NUNTII WILLELMI. HIC VENIT NUNTIUS AD WILGELMUM DUCEM.

DUKE WILLIAM OF NORMANDY first appears in the Tapestry here, on the right. His grand seat, sword and cloak signal his authority as he receives news of Harold's presence in Ponthieu. Behind him is the stone castle of Rouen, manned by guards.

The central tree with the lookout marks a scene break. William's envoys on the left, riding swiftly to Beaurain, belong to the scene on the previous plate. There we witnessed the encounter: William's envoys rode to Guy to demand that Guy surrender Harold to William. English and Norman chroniclers agree that William's message

William's envoys. Here a messenger came to Duke William.

contained a threat. If Guy did not comply, William would bring an army to Ponthieu to collect Harold. William was reminding Guy of his promise of perpetual loyalty.

The Tapestry's artists were interested in the ambiguous nature of custody among medieval lords. The fable of the stag and lion plays out in the lower border. The stag is chased by five hunting dogs and a hunter, only to be captured by a lion. When Harold is turned over to William, he will trade one captivity for another.

9 HIC WIDO ADDUXIT HAROLDUM AD WILGELMUM NORMANNORUM DUCEM ...

GUY COMPLIED PROMPTLY. The Tapestry portrays him riding in front of a stately procession, holding a bird of prey. He points back at Harold, who carries his hawk and rides just behind Guy. Even the horses are in step, which shows the amount of control and care Guy has put into the ceremony of the handover. The encounter was a critical moment and it was important not to show aggression, even by accident. Another potential claimant to the English throne, Walter of Mantes – count of Maine and King Edward's nephew – had already died in William's prison, so Guy had reason to

Here Guy has led Harold to William, duke of the Normans.

worry about William's threats. The head of Duke William's horse, and William's pointing hand, are just visible on the right.

Medieval kings and lords frequently met on their mutual borders to conduct diplomacy and make treaties. The handover of the prisoner Harold occurred in Eu, on the Bresle River. Eu belonged to William and was a logical choice for him. It was near the coast, far from Guy's potential allies in Boulogne, and on the border between Ponthieu and Normandy.

DUKE WILLIAM IS on his steed, on the left, accepting Guy's surrender of the prisoner Harold. A new scene begins to the right of the entwined trees. William appears again, now holding Harold's hawk. Harold rides in front as they travel to William's stronghold at Rouen.

The Bayeux Tapestry depicts about two hundred horses, mules and donkeys. Medieval Normandy was renowned for its horses, especially Arabian types. Norman lords who went on raids in Spain often returned with fine horses among their plunder. Neighbouring lords and kings

Here Duke William, with Harold ...

would attempt to win Duke William's favour by sending him gifts of steeds. The Norman dukes' famous mounts helped attract allies and followers from neighbouring realms. The stallion William rode to battle at Hastings was probably the one given to him by King Alfonso of Aragon.

Monasteries in Normandy, as well as nobles' estates, were critical places for breeding, raising, buying and selling horses. As skilled equine breeders and business managers, monks provided secular lords with impressive high-quality steeds.

11 ... VENIT AD PALATIUM SUUM. UBI UNUS CLERICUS ET ÆLFGYVA.

ENGLISH AND Norman chronicles report that, at this meeting, William and Harold discussed two marriage alliances to ensure good faith and prevent war: William's daughter to Harold and Harold's kinswoman to a Norman noble. Neither marriage took place.

Ælfgyva, standing in a gateway, is probably a subject of the marriage alliance discussion in the palace. Two towers, on each side of the plate, frame these episodes as one scene. Harold had a cousin named Ælfgyva and possibly a sister of the same name. Noblewomen were frequently educated at abbeys alongside nuns. Some took vows. If

... has come to his palace. Where [are] one cleric and Ælfgyva.

Ælfgyva had committed her life to her faith, she would not be free to marry.

Ælfgyva's identity is the Tapestry's greatest mystery. Centuries of debate have yielded many theories but no consensus. She may be receiving last rites. Or, the cleric may be revealing the miraculous restoration of her eyesight from a well-known story about an abbess Ælfgyva. The nude figure, relegated to the margin, mirrors the cleric's stance. The figure may comment on the contrast illustrated in these two connected episodes: the men trading women's futures, and the man acknowledging a woman of the faith.

12 HIC WILLEM DUX ET EXCERCITUS EIUS VENERUNT AD MONTE MICHAELIS ...

A NEW DRAMA begins in the Tapestry's narrative: William's military campaign in the county of Brittany. The Breton lord of Dol had requested William's assistance in a dispute with Count Conan II of Brittany. As a medieval lord, William not only expected loyalty from his followers: he was bound, in turn, to aid his less powerful supporters.

The campaign gave William an opportunity to demonstrate Norman superiority to the lords of lands to the west of the duchy. Progressing steadily through Brittany, William sought to win supporters for his plan to

Here Duke William and his army came to Mont-Saint-Michel ...

take the English throne. By compelling or persuading Breton lords to accept his authority, and by displaying his array of wealth, power and followers, William could demonstrate his ability to reward the loyal.

As though emerging from the tide, the coastal abbey of Mont-Saint-Michel rises into the upper border, perched atop its lone hill. This is a stylized picture of the building based on representations of architecture in eleventh-century art. Built on the order of William's grandfather, Richard II of Normandy, Mont-Saint-Michel lay on the frontier between Brittany and Normandy.

13 **... ET HIC TRANSIERUNT FLUMEN COSNONIS. HIC HAROLD DUX TRAHEBAT EOS DE ARENA. ET VENERUNT AD DOL ET CONAN FUGA VERTIT.**

THIS PLATE features Harold's most heroic moment in the Tapestry. During the crossing of the tidal river Couesnon, he rescues two of William's men from the treacherous muddy sands. He carries one on his back and has the other firmly by the wrist. The imagery may have been inspired by Virgil's ancient epic poem, the *Aeneid*. According to Virgil, Aeneas escaped from the burning city of Troy, bearing his father Anchises on his back and leading his son Ascanius by the hand. Medieval readers loved the *Aeneid*. Reading the poem was a favourite way to study Latin. This portrayal of Harold's Aeneas-like

... and here they crossed the river Couesnon. Here Earl Harold pulled them out of the sand. And they came to Dol, and Conan fled.

bravery showed him taking risks and doing his duty as an honourable man.

A tightly packed Norman force, ready for combat, approaches the castle of Dol. In a daring escape or a dis-honourable desertion, Count Conan climbs down a rope on the far side. The Tapestry never depicts the lord of Dol thanking William's army for their support. Instead, with a lively sense of urgency, it follows William's pursuit of Conan. The hunt in the lower margin, led by a mythical centaur, drives the story ahead.

14 [REDNES.] HIC MILITES WILLELMI DUCIS PUGNANT CONTRA DINANTES ...

THE WORD 'Rednes' does not appear in two of the earliest surviving drawings of the Tapestry. If this city is not Rennes, William's progress through Brittany, according to the Tapestry, was in a straight line of thirty miles: approximately fifteen miles from Mont-Saint-Michel to Dol, and another fifteen from Dol to the city of Dinan. This tower may serve, as others do in the Tapestry, to divide sequential episodes. The Normans' attack and Dinan's defence begins to appear on the right. The chase is on.

According to William's chaplain and chronicler, William of Poitiers, Norman dukes had been Brittany's rightful lords

[Rennes.] Here Duke William's soldiers fight against the men of Dinan ...

for over a hundred years, ever since the king of France gave land to Normandy's Viking founder, Rollo. By chasing Conan, William sought to bring a subordinate lord into line, not to vanquish him. Brittany had long been Normandy's ally. Conan's father, Alan of Brittany, had died twenty years prior, fighting for a teenage Duke William. William wanted a commanding win, but it was in his interests to preserve peace among competing factions in Brittany, not to make an enemy.

15 ... ET CUNAN CLAVES PORREXIT. HIC WILLELM DEDIT ARMA HAROLDO.

AT THE CITY of Dinan, where Conan has retreated, we witness a siege of a medieval castle. Torches are lit and flags planted. Conan surrenders: the keys to the castle dangle from his spear and William extends his own spear to collect them. Conan's submission and William's acceptance of it were important public events. Performing a symbolic act before witnesses, such as the giving of gate keys, allowed medieval lords to make new agreements. Later in 1066, rivals Conan and the lord of Dol reached an accord. William's campaign in Brittany, for which the Tapestry

... and Conan held out the keys. Here William gave arms to Harold.

is the only detailed source, ended in success for William.

Harold and William had now spent several months together. They knew each other well. In a famous scene, the Tapestry depicts the two, looking more alike than different, as William gives arms to Harold. In this way William thanked Harold for his distinguished role in the Brittany campaign. This military honour established a formal bond of friendship between the two lords. William's gratitude, however, reinforced the key point that Harold was still in William's custody.

16 HIC WILLELM VENIT BAGIAS. UBI HAROLD SACRAMENTUM FECIT WILLELMO DUCI.

ON THE RETURN from Dinan, William's party paused in Bayeux before continuing north-east to the coast. The Tapestry places the supposed oath shortly before Harold sailed back to England. The portable boxes framing Harold are reliquaries. Relics of Christian saints, carefully kept in these finely wrought boxes, were thought to enhance the sacred act of giving one's word. One figure points to the word for 'oath': 'sacramentum'.

The Tapestry shows the witnessing of an oath, but does not explain its nature. According to Norman chroniclers, Harold swore fealty to William. William's chronicler

Here William came to Bayeux. Where Harold made an oath to Duke William.

reported that Harold promised to uphold William's claim to the English throne and swore to act as William's deputy in England until William was crowned. This chronicler took care to argue that Harold took the oath willingly. Had Harold done so under duress, a medieval audience would have seen the oath as invalid. Other chroniclers argued that Harold was coerced into making the oath, or tricked into taking it over holy relics without his knowledge. If Harold did swear an oath, it was most likely to affirm his betrothal to William's daughter.

17 HIC HAROLD DUX REVERSUS EST AD ANGLICAM TERRAM ...

HAROLD OFTEN returned victorious to England, serving his king well and earning his trust. In summer 1064, Harold led a military campaign in Wales, during which Welsh conqueror Gruffudd ap Llywelyn was killed. Harold, acting on behalf of his king, arranged new leadership in Wales among Gruffudd's brothers. By intervening, Harold sought to quell threats to England and to strengthen King Edward's sway across Britain's kingdoms. Harold would later marry Gruffudd's widow, Ealdgyth of Mercia, the sister of Mercia's powerful Earl Edwin. Had Harold lived longer, this political marriage

Here Earl Harold returned to the English land ...

stood to affirm England's power over Wales and to align Harold's Wessex with the rival earldom of Mercia for a stronger England.

Harold's return is eagerly awaited by the men in the watchtower, but he is not bringing good news. The marriage alliance mooted with William's daughter would jeopardize the possibility of his marriage to Ealdgyth. His eventual marriage to Ealdgyth was bound to strain his newly forged bond with William. Whatever Harold and Edward agreed, Harold's mission did not go according to plan because William of Normandy had intervened.

18 ... E[T] VENIT AD EDWARDUM REGEM. HIC PORTATUR CORPUS EADWARDI REGIS ...

A CLOAKED HAROLD addresses King Edward. Harold, his head bowed unusually low, had successes and failures to report. He had secured the release of his nephew Hakon, but not his brother Wulfnoth, the king's brother-in-law. It may be Hakon holding a long axe who stands behind Harold. Wulfnoth would remain in William's custody until William's death in 1087. Throughout his reign as king of England, William judged the Godwine family, scattered though it was, to be a threat.

Westminster Abbey is the most famous architectural

... and came to King Edward. Here the body of King Edward is borne ...

moment in the Tapestry. Of all the buildings depicted, it is the sole portrayal of a specific building, not a stylized impression of one. Westminster featured Romanesque architecture, known for its distinctive rounded arches. This style, popular in Normandy, embraced the function and fashion of ancient Roman architectural design. King Edward, who had grown up in exile in Normandy, had the abbey built. According to the chronicle of Edward's life, commissioned by his wife, this house of God was the proudest achievement of his reign. The approving hand of God emerges from the sky, pointing to Westminster Abbey.

19 **... AD ECCLESIAM SANCTI PETRI APLI. HIC EADWARDUS REX IN [L]ECTO ALLOQUIT FIDELES ET HIC DEFUNCTUS EST. HIC DEDERUNT HAROLDO CORONA[M] REGIS.**

KING EDWARD, on his deathbed in the upper storey, speaks with his most trusted followers. Queen Edith, Edward's wife and Harold's sister, sits mourning at the foot of Edward's bed. In the foreground, kneeling at the king's side, is Harold. He and the king prepare to clasp hands. Edward entrusts Harold with the safety of the queen and the care of the kingdom. The deathbed scene is almost identical to, and may have been inspired by, the account in the chronicle of Edward's life, completed soon after the conquest. Its author, possibly Goscelin of Saint-Bertin, may have provided material for

... to the Church of Saint Peter the Apostle. Here King Edward, in bed, addresses his loyal subjects and here he has died. Here they gave the king's crown to Harold.

the Tapestry. After the king's body is prepared for burial below, with Archbishop Stigand in attendance, it is borne to Westminster Abbey in a stately procession leftwards. Two men ring handbells.

On the right, Harold stands with a long axe, addressed by England's governing council of nobles. They elect Harold as their king. One leader gives Harold the crown and points towards the prior king, Edward. In the eleventh century, this council's decision was what made a king of England.

20 HIC RESIDET HAROLD REX ANGLORUM. STIGANT ARCHIEPS. ISTI MIRANT STELLA. HAROLD.

HAROLD AND STIGAND, archbishop of Canterbury, are two of the three figures in the Tapestry who face the viewer directly. Stigand, a senior advisor of England's Danish kings, led a reconciliation between the Godwine family and King Edward in 1052, prevented a siege of London and averted civil war in England. Stigand's presence in the Tapestry affirmed the strength of the ongoing relationship between the families of Edward and Harold, and the continuity of Anglo-Danish England. This scene asserts Harold's authority as king of England.

The striking tableau of King Harold in residence depicts

Here resides Harold, king of the English. Archbishop Stigand. These people marvel at the star. Harold.

royal ceremony, at his consecration or on a formal occasion afterwards. On 24 April, Halley's Comet appeared over Europe and was visible in England and Normandy. The crowd points at the long-tailed star. Some thought it a good omen; others believed it a portent of disaster for the English kingdom.

On the right, Harold listens to an advisor, who may be warning him about William. The fleet in the margin may depict beached ships. It may foreshadow William's invasion, or Harold's immediate reaction: to marshal his own fleet near the Isle of Wight.

21 HIC NAVIS ANGLICA VENIT IN TERRAM WILLELMI DUCIS.

THIS SHIP likely brings the news of Harold's coronation to William. The sailor with the anchor has removed his trousers and hitched up his tunic to keep his clothes dry as he wades to shore.

Striking trees frame scenes throughout the Tapestry. Their distinctive interlocking design derived from the fusion of Anglo-Saxon and Scandinavian styles, in which artists transformed trees into patterns of lace and lattice. The trees' design was unique to English art. Similar trees are carven into the sculpture of Ely Cathedral and Canterbury Cathedral. The Tapestry's smaller trees

Here an English ship came to the land of Duke William.

resemble the ornamented letters of the eleventh-century Winchcombe Psalter, a beautiful bound book with spectacular decoration and artwork.

These trees' design reflects England's history as an integral part of a North Sea world. In the ninth century, years of Viking invasions brought encampments, colonies and finally settlements. In 1016, the Danish King Cnut conquered England. He already had supporters in eastern England, which faced the North Sea: local communities kept their shared heritage and, sometimes, shared loyalties. The realm William conquered, in essence, was Anglo-Danish England.

22 HIC WILLELM DUX IUSSIT NAVES EDIFICARE.

ASSEMBLING A FLEET to conquer England was a major logistical operation. Fourteen of Duke William's Norman lords supplied most of his ships, including longships for war and cargo ships, totalling nearly a thousand. The support of these fourteen men was critical to William because they had rights over coastal and river ports. William's men were obliged to equip him with soldiers and ships based on their means, but for this unusually large-scale invasion, most gave far more than the minimum. Spurred on by the prospect of great rewards if the conquest were successful, they supported William's

Here Duke William commanded that ships be built.

endeavour. Remarkably, the fleet was gathered and built in less than six months.

The Tapestry captures the immediate, physical impact of William's command. William appears enthroned, with flowing cape and broad pose, issuing the order to build ships. Odo of Bayeux, who organized the supply of many ships, confers with William, and a shipbuilder holding a side-axe points to the felling of trees and building of ships, as if these are happening just outside. Notably, the Tapestry portrays shipbuilding tools and techniques realistically.

23 HIC TRAHUNT NAVES AD MARE[M].

WILLIAM COULD NOT have built his entire fleet from scratch. Doing so would have deforested much of the Seine valley. He had the wealth to hire ships and crews from Normandy and beyond, including paid navies from Flanders. William's fleet included warships and transport ships of different sizes.

Because building ships was costly in materials, labour and time, ships were built to endure. Shipbuilders normally used seasoned wood. This process involved allowing timber to dry out or soaking it in brine. Seasoned planks

Here they haul the ships to the sea.

were stored in ports, ready for assembly, but not enough for an invasion of this scale. William could not afford a half-hearted invasion. He needed lots of ships. Although ships made of freshly cut wood were prone to rot, William expanded his fleet with new ones. Even if these short-lived ships lasted only for one expedition, the conquest of England would be worth their loss.

In a graceful blend of field and frame, the firm trunk of the growing tree seems to strengthen the sterns of four ships. It was an elegant reminder that, not long ago, some of William's ships had been trees.

24 ISTI PORTANT ARMAS AD NAVES ET HIC TRAHUNT CARRUM CUM VINO ET ARMIS.

THE BARRELS, casks and wineskins being loaded here probably held spiced wine, produced in Normandy's many vineyards. Flavouring wine with spices, herbs, honey and aromatic plants was common, a popular way to add variety to this everyday drink. On William's way to England, according to his chronicler, he hosted a shipboard meal and served spiced wine. The story of the feast was probably inspired by Virgil's *Aeneid*, but the description of the wine is accurate. The spiced wine William offered would have been a light wine. Tasty and enjoyable, it would have quenched the men's thirst.

These men carry arms to the ships and here they pull a wagon with wine and weapons.

William was preparing thoroughly, but he would find wine in England too. Vineyards had been kept in south-eastern Britain since the eighth century. After the conquest, monasteries and estates under Norman control would produce wine in south-eastern England on a much larger scale.

The Tapestry's long supply sequence demonstrates William's effective leadership, from planning to improvising. He engaged and employed the skills and labour of men and women throughout Normandy to give their lord the best prospect of success in England.

25 HIC WILLELM DUX IN MAGNO NAVIGIO MARE TRANSIVIT …

A FOREST MADE a fleet. It took over seventy oak trees to build a typical North Sea transport ship for men, arms and horses. The tree to make the keel had to be more than eighteen metres tall. William's ships were clinker-built cargo ships, a style of construction in which overlapping planks were assembled securely. Deep on the draught, they were stable seafaring ships guided with rudders, with sides low enough for horses to board and disembark easily. Classic Viking longships, by contrast, tended to be long and narrow, well suited to rivers and coastal waters.

Here Duke William crossed the sea in a great ship ...

It was a night crossing. The fleet sailed quietly by the lantern light of a single ship. Duke William's chronicler recorded that, during the crossing, William's ship got far ahead and lost sight of the fleet, so it held position and waited for daylight. A lookout climbed the mast three times. First, he reported nothing but open sea and sky. Later, he glimpsed four ships. On his third check, he called excitedly to the duke that he had seen so many that it was like a dense, sail-bearing woodland.

26 ... ET VENIT AD PEVENESÆ.

MATILDA OF Flanders, William's wife, outfitted the fleet with its flagship, the Mora. The Mora is visible in the Tapestry directly under the words for its destination on the English coast: 'to Pevensey'. An inventory of William's fleet describes in detail the special figurehead for the prow that Matilda commissioned: a golden child pointing to England while sounding an ivory horn, perhaps meant to herald the prospect of a new Norman dynasty across the Channel. A similar figurehead appears here on the Mora's stern. The Mora is the only ship on the Tapestry flying a standard with a cross atop the

... and came to Pevensey.

mast. The standard represents the papal banner given to William by Pope Alexander II. By displaying it prominently as he sailed aboard the Mora, William affirmed the pope's support for his enterprise.

William rewarded those who served him. On its voyage to England, the Mora was captained by a man named Stephen, son of Airard. After the conquest, William gave Stephen lands in England. Stephen's daughter would become a nun in the distinguished English abbey of Romsey, and Stephen's son would serve as a captain in the royal fleet.

27 HIC EXEUNT CABALLI DE NAVIBUS, ET HIC MILITES ...

WILLIAM HAD gathered valuable intelligence about the English coast before his invasion. Pevensey may not have been his preferred landing site, but it had strategic advantages. The port was already partly fortified with a stone wall that once protected an ancient Roman fort. The area has silted up in the last thousand years, so today the coast is a mile away. In 1066, William's rapidly built wooden fortification occupied a high point directly overlooking the sea. In this scene, horses, which made the crossing in separate ships from William's army, are led ashore.

Here the horses disembark from the ships, and here the soldiers …

Harold's fleet had been stationed at the Isle of Wight that summer, ready to intercept an invading fleet from Normandy. However, on 8 September Harold's fleet sailed for London because supplies were running low. Norman agents brought this news to William at Dives. William immediately gathered his fleet from nearby harbours. He sailed on 12 September, likely bound for England. Facing adverse conditions, he regrouped at a new launch point: Saint-Valery. Only sixty miles from England, Saint-Valery offered another opportunity to catch favourable tides and a southerly wind.

28 ... FESTINAVERUNT HA[E]STINGA UT CIBUM RAPERENTUR.

THE TAPESTRY features the procurement of food as well as conquest and kings. Whereas some chroniclers deemed it unworthy of record, the Tapestry's artists illustrated the logistics of invasion. The Normans plunder the countryside for food. Homes of English coastal inhabitants are visible in the background. In a style typical of eleventh-century rural dwellings, the main door is on the long side of each house.

'To seize' was not a phrase used for honourable deeds. The Tapestry's designers relayed with candour a reality of conquest: for the conquerors to eat, they had to steal

... hurry to Hastings to seize food.

food from the local inhabitants, thus depriving them of the means to survive. One figure holds an axe as another leads away a sheep. A cow is herded away and a pig is carried off with other spoils.

Harold's army and fleet were away defending England against invasion in the north, but English coastal forces fought back against the Normans. Some of William's ships, separated from the fleet, had landed farther east along the coast at Romney. They were defeated in battle by an English force. Many died on both sides.

29 HIC EST WADARD. HIC COQUITUR CAR[O] ET HIC MINISTRAVERUNT MINISTRI.

WADARD, THE MOUNTED LORD in armour, watches as a Norman soldier steals an English pony. As a supervisor of procurement, his service was as critical to the invasion's success as were the fighting of a commander and the prayers of a bishop. After the conquest, when he served as a tenant of Bishop Odo, earl of Kent, Wadard acquired significant English property. His acquisitions are well documented in Domesday Book, King William's monumental survey and census of English lands and lords in 1086. Wadard's assets included houses in Dover, lordships of many lands in Kent and still more

Here is Wadard. Here meat is cooked and here servants served it.

property in counties across the kingdom, from Dorset in the south-west to Lincolnshire in the north-east. Wadard was one of many who benefitted from the conquest at the expense of the English people.

As soon as camp is set up, meal preparation is underway. On the right, one man hands skewered meat and roast local farmyard and woodland fowl directly to his comrades on the next plate. They stand close by, eating near the cooks, ready to be handed seconds.

30 HIC FECERUNT PRANDIUM ET HIC EPISCOPUS CIBUM ET POTU[M] BENEDICIT. ODO EP[ISCOPU S. WILLELM. ROTBERT.

WILLIAM KNEW that his men needed nourishing meals for his invasion to succeed. On the left, lower-status Norman men eat a scattered meal, standing at a table improvised from shields. One sounds a horn to call his comrades to the feast. Music also boosted morale before a battle. According to one story, William's minstrel would launch the first arrow at Hastings. A servant bears hot food in a lidded serving bowl to the nobles sitting a civilized distance from the cooking fires.

As Bishop Odo blesses the meal, his companions ignore him. Their attention is consumed by the food.

Here they took a meal and here the bishop blesses the food and drink. Bishop Odo. William. Robert.

Two, conversing, are already eating hungrily; one is already drinking. All were warriors savouring the flavours of stolen food, some perhaps eagerly confident of victory, others wondering if this meal would count among their last.

To the right, William convenes a war council. He meets with his half-brothers, Odo and Robert, with whom he shared a mother, Herleva. Odo, bishop of Bayeux, supported his brother's mission with ships, prayers and counsel. Robert, count of Mortain, was a knight and a key advisor throughout William's career.

31 **ISTE IUSSIT UT FODERETUR CASTELLUM AT HESTINGA CEASTRA. HIC NUNTIATUM EST WILLELMO DE HAROLD.**

ROBERT OF MORTAIN ordered Hastings Castle built. The Tapestry's word choice 'fodere', to make by digging, calls attention to the colossal effort of moving earth to construct a motte-and-bailey castle. At least 20,000 tonnes of earth were required to build a mound, or motte, on which to erect a wooden keep. A bailey, or walled yard, encircled it, and palisades protected the fortress. Nearby, diggers play at battle with iron-edged wooden shovels.

Harold's arrival was major news. The king of Norway, Harald Hardrada, had invaded England in the north-east,

He ordered that a castle be made by digging at Hastings. The fort. Here William is informed about Harold.

hoping to conquer. At the Battle of Fulford near York, Hardrada defeated the Mercians on 20 September. Five days later, Harold, in a daring surprise attack, defeated Hardrada at the Battle of Stamford Bridge. Although the victory was resounding, the English had suffered many casualties in both battles. They had little time to regroup. Still, Harold had reached Hastings swiftly, bringing many men.

William holds the papal banner from Pope Alexander II. Even so, the first reactions to the Norman Conquest across Europe almost universally judged it not a God-sanctioned achievement, but a sin and an atrocity.

32 HIC DOMUS INCENDITUR. HIC MILITES EXIERUNT DE HESTENGA ...

THE TAPESTRY'S ARTISTS confronted wartime experiences of fear and violence among non-combatants. The artists are explicit that this is an act of arson. The text does not just comment that a house is burning. It names the act: it is being set on fire deliberately. An English woman and child are at home as Norman men set their house alight. The woman holds the child's hand, showing love and a desire to protect – the only such gesture i the Tapestry.

Devastating food supplies, homes and land, and terrorizi people, were brutal realities of eleventh-century warfare.

Here a home is being set on fire. Here the soldiers went forth from Hastings ...

At the same time, William, thinking not only as a conqueror but as a future king, expected his men to conduct themselves abroad on campaign as they would at home. William's orders protected unarmed English people and churchmen later demanded penance from those who indulged in excessive violence.

After the invasion, women sought asylum in English abbeys: fleeing the aggression of Norman soldiers, escaping arranged marriages with conquerors or seeking a new home if widowed by the Battle of Hastings. Refuge, however, was realistically available only to a few of the wealthiest English and Norman women.

33 ... ET VENERUNT AD PRELIUM CONTRA HAROLDUM REGE[M].

THIS IS A SOMBRE moment in the Tapestry: the word 'battle' appears for the first time. Pitched battle was extremely rare in the earlier Middle Ages. To fight in battle was a last resort. Outcomes were unpredictable and depended largely on luck and chance. The prospect of enormous losses of armour, weapons and above all highly-trained soldiers – not easily replaced as fighters and irreplaceable as men – meant that leaders avoided battles.

To resolve serious disputes, kings and commanders far preferred diplomacy and compromise. Where necessary,

... and come to battle against King Harold.

siege warfare involved attacking a castle until it surrendered. One common approach was to surround a castle and wait until its inhabitants ran out of food. These events did not make for very exciting stories. Battles did.

The rarity of battles made them a popular subject in medieval songs and stories. Audiences were fascinated by human experience at points of great danger inaccessible to them in daily life. Commanders knew that their forces needed to be prepared for worst-case scenarios. Imagining epic battles, fought by ordinary men or ancient heroes, was a way to ready oneself to face peril.

34 HIC WILLELM DUX INTERROGAT VITAL SI VIDISSET HAROLDI EXERCITUM.

VITALIS, A FOLLOWER of Odo, was the scout charged to bring reconnaissance. By career, he was a wealthy merchant. After 1066, as an Anglo-Norman noble, he would aid Canterbury's abbey of St Augustine in procuring not information, but construction materials. He shipped stone from Caen in Normandy for building the new church. In return, he was granted an honorary association with the abbey. It was an act both of generosity and of reinforcing, literally and figuratively, the architecture of Norman power in England.

Here Duke William asks Vital if he has seen Harold's army.

The object of William's pillage and plundering of homes and farms along the south coast was to draw Harold into battle as soon as possible. In this scene, Vitalis's job is to find out if Norman raiding has generated a response from England's defender. Vitalis was an ambiguous figure. Reliable in war, he attracted attention as both benefactor and foe of the people of Canterbury in peacetime.

35 **ISTE NUNTIAT HAROLDUM REGEM DE EXERCITU WILLELMI DUCIS.**

BOTH ARMIES depended on good information and communication. A messenger on horseback could travel fifty miles in a day, so commanders could get current reports on the status of the enemy. In addition to sending scouts on reconnaissance missions, each leader reportedly sent an envoy to his enemy to discuss terms. William offered to settle the matter in single combat with Harold. A duel was realistically unlikely, but the choreography of making and refusing the offer allowed both commanders to retain their moral standing in the eyes of their men and their enemy. Both argued that God

This man informs Harold about Duke William's army.

was on their side, which the outcome of the battle would prove.

William may have offered Harold a deal. If Harold surrendered now, he would be allowed to retain his lands in south-eastern England peacefully if he accepted William as king. Harold, however, was not at Hastings to barter for a personal position as earl or regent. To defend his kingdom he had to refuse William's deal, or he would have consented to be conquered. On the right, a messenger announces that William's army is near. Harold gives the order to engage the enemy.

36 HIC WILLELM DUX ALLOQUITUR SUIS MILITIBUS ...

THIS IS the last time we will see a tree until the final fragments of surviving Tapestry. It marks the end of firm frames and distinct episodes. The ensuing battle sequence is framed as a series of dramatic set pieces only by the orientation and arrangement of the horses and men in the fight. The whole battle unrolls in one movement, impelling the eyes forward.

Medieval chroniclers, inspired by ancient Roman writers, liked to compose eloquent pre-battle speeches. They were not attempting to take down the exact words of their leader's speech, but they were trying to capture

Here Duke William exhorts his soldiers ...

something of the truth of the experience of a battle. The event itself would be bewildering, bloody and grim. A soldier would struggle to see and to hear. Yet by capturing the nature of how a leader might have inspired his men, a writer could help others remember why men fought and died together. The Tapestry here alludes to this critical moment in preparing for a battle. Material preparations had been made: now it was time to prepare the mind.

37 ... UT PREPARAREN[T] SE VIRILITER ET SAPIENTER AD PRELIU[M] ...

WILLIAM'S pre-battle speech was not recorded, but his chronicler reported its core. William did more than declaim the Normans' fame, invoke the name of God as supporter of his just cause and stir his men to prove their courage by doing great deeds. He relayed key tactical and strategic information. This day, said William, would not decide England's ruler, but who would escape with his life. They could not expect to be spared, as they might in other encounters.

He reminded them of a sober reality: the terrain. Retreat was not an option. There was nowhere to go.

... to ready themselves bravely and wisely for battle ...

Ahead lay an unfriendly undiscovered land, behind lay the sea, and English forces guarded both. He told them not to fear if their numbers were fewer, for skill could well win the day. This advice was rooted in the ancient handbook by the Roman military analyst Vegetius, an enormously popular book among medieval commanders and battle chroniclers. Lastly, William charged his men, they must trust in their vigour and valour. Here, in its first use of adverbs, the Tapestry captures the essence of this final command from William to his men.

38 ... CONTRA ANGLORUM EXERCITU[M].

THE BATTLE OF HASTINGS pitted two of the most formidable armies in western Europe against one another. Between ten and fifteen thousand men fought at Hastings. These warriors were evenly matched in number and skill. William's army attacked in three divisions: Normans, French and Flemish, and Breton. The Norman army was structured in companies for recruitment, training and fighting. Many Norman soldiers were mounted, and William also fought with many well-armed infantry. The archers depicted here show the versatility of William's fighting force. At the centre of its drama, the Tapestry

... against the army of the English.

places William's cavalry and its uphill charge against Harold's infantry: the human fortress of the English shield-wall.

Although their tactics differed, the English and Norman armies' armour, helmets and weapons often featured similar designs. Their societies and armies were akin. For hundreds of years, they had all inhabited a northern Anglo-Scandinavian-French world around the sea, meeting, intermarrying and fighting.

The horses' strides lengthen, and the almost audible drum of their hooves on the ground builds the momentum of the Normans' approach to the battlefield of Hastings.

39

THE TAPESTRY offers a moment of silence. This is the first extended section of artwork without words, at once impressive and moving. The tightly packed English shield-wall, visible here left and centre, forms the middle of a wider scene that stretches across the previous plate. The Norman cavalry advances from left and right, charging against this single, impregnable obstacle.

When battles did occur, they were normally over within an hour or two. The Battle of Hastings lasted all day. This shows that the opponents were evenly matched. Harold, however, began with the advantage. The English infantry

were well trained and Harold had arranged the shield-wall on a ridge. He commanded the high ground. His infantry's dense formation posed a formidable challenge for William's expert cavalry, which had to make the ascent from the marshy ground below.

In the battle's first encounter, bodies begin to litter the lower borders, cut off from the violent land of the living above. Throughout the battle sequence, the great drama of the conflict will be continuously shown together with its great tragedy.

40 HIC CECIDERUNT LEWINE ET GYRÐ FRATRES HAROLDI REGIS.

THE TAPESTRY commemorated the loyalty of brothers. William planned for battle with his two half-brothers Odo and Robert; now, in the battle sequence, Harold's two brothers Leofwine and Gyrth die fighting for him. A small band of English soldiers defend themselves valiantly, but they have been surrounded by Norman riders. The two sprawling figures at the centre of this tableau are Leofwine and Gyrth. Three Norman cavalry riding from the left, and three from the right (see next plate), frame the tableau.

Leofwine, as earl of Kent, and Gyrth, as earl of

Here Leofwine and Gyrth, brothers of King Harold, fell.

East Anglia, shared with Harold absolute control over south-eastern England. They were the lords directly responsible for deflecting William's invasion. English and Norman chronicles recorded that Leofwine and Gyrth died at Hastings, but only the Tapestry offered clues as to when or how. The idea of brotherhood in battle remained compelling, and medieval people wanted to know more about Harold's loyal, tragic brothers. Stories grew to satisfy this insistent curiosity around the Battle of Hastings. A legend emerged depicting Gyrth as Harold's trusted advisor, wisest counsellor and second conscience.

41 HIC CECIDERUNT SIMUL ANGLI ET FRANCI IN PRELIO.

THE MALFOSSE incident was an episode late in the battle in which many Norman and English combatants fell together to their deaths. Norman horses, amid the crush of bodies, were among the casualties. The name 'Malfosse' means, literally, 'evil valley'. It was a ditch, a hidden marshy hollow or a concealed rampart. The next plate reveals the steep ravine that English and Norman fighters discovered too late.

This event became the iconic moment that illustrated the horrors of war. A horse turns his head, terrified by the catastrophe behind him. In graphic detail, the Tapestry

Here English and Normans fell together in battle.

depicted surprise, terror, powerlessness and the suffocating crush of bodies. It embodied the fear of dying in battle by accident, not by fighting nobly for a cause. Later medieval writers, perhaps inspired by the Tapestry, viewed the Malfosse incident with sorrow. To them it was not God's punishment for sin. It was simply a tragedy.

Above all, the Tapestry was commemorative art. This grim scene conveys the essence of the Tapestry's purpose: to honour all the fallen. English and Normans fought and died together.

42 HIC ODO EPS BACULU[M] TENENS CONFORTAT PUEROS.

THE ENGLISH INFANTRY still controls the higher ground, keeping away from the battlefield's treacherous pit. To the left, the gruesome Malfosse incident, with horses falling and limbs flying, remains visible. By this point in the battle, both armies were scattered. They needed clever strategies, and some inspiration, to win.

Odo, as a bishop, would have carried a staff as a symbol of his ecclesiastical office and his duty to comfort, to console and to show mercy. Odo is dressed in different attire from his secular comrades, but he sensibly wears a

Here Bishop Odo, holding a staff, encourages the younger men.

helmet and mail armour underneath, peeking out around his neck and forearms. Chroniclers report that he did not fight, but he rides like a warrior to inspire Norman fighters.

Churchmen were not supposed to fight in battle. Some did. After the conquest they had to do penance, according to the Penitential Ordinance, a decree issued by Norman bishops to punish excessive violence among the conquerors. These fighting churchmen may have taken up arms out of loyalty to their leader, driven more by the gravity of the dispute than by the duties of their office.

43 HIC EST WILLELMUS DUX [... IUS]. HIC FRANCI PUGNANT ...

ACROSS ACCOUNTS of the battle, the crisis for the Normans was the period in which the army believed their duke had been killed. This image captures the famous story in which William lifted his helmet, revealing his face, to show his men that he was alive and well. The sight of their leader heartened and inspired the army afresh, filling them with renewed vigour to pursue victory. The Normans once again took up the fight. This event marked a turning point in the battle.

Before Charles Stothard added the letters 'E' and 'T', the only surviving letters of the name-marker in the upper

Here is Duke William. [... ius]. Here the Normans fight ...

border were 'IUS'. The named figure next to William, who is pointing out that the duke is still alive and holding aloft the banner, is likely William's half-brother Robert, count of Mortain. Robert bore the standard of Saint Michael into battle. Robert fought at Hastings, staying near his brother throughout the battle as supporter and defender.

Alternatively, the figure could be Eustace, count of Boulogne, who reportedly came to William's rescue when he lost his horse. Or, he could be Turstin, William's standard-bearer.

44 ... ET CECIDERUNT QUI ERANT CUM [H]AROLDO.

ACCORDING TO some accounts of the battle, the Normans achieved an advantage when they executed a complex tactical manoeuvre. They pretended to retreat, which encouraged the English to break ranks and pursue them in a counter-attack. Once the English were out of formation, they were vulnerable, and the Normans swiftly entrapped them. The English could have fought on, but they had little recourse because they had lost several of their leaders.

In his pre-battle speech, William had spoken of the battle as making survivors rather than winners. He was

... and those who were with Harold fell.

not exaggerating. Even in the rare occurrence of a medieval battle, the taking of captives, for ransom and bargaining, was common. There is no evidence that prisoners of war were taken at the Battle of Hastings. This grim reality is a reminder that both sides fought relentlessly and desperately because they had everything to lose, and their enemy would give no quarter.

45 HIC HAROLD REX INTERFECTUS EST.

IN A SOMBRE set piece, perfectly captured by the framing of this plate, Harold is depicted falling beneath the words 'interfectus est', slain by the sword of a mounted Norman soldier who has broken through the shield-wall. His axe flies from his hand. Framing the death scene, on both sides, are the last men standing of the English shield-wall. Three standing on the left, and three on the right, ready weapons and shields to meet the mounted Normans closing in from both sides. The earliest narratives of the battle claim that Harold was killed during the battle, probably late in the day.

Here King Harold was killed.

The word 'Harold' functions only as a word in a sentence, not as a name-marker, but it is often misconstrued as a label for the soldier beneath. This nameless man, made famous by myth and misconception, nevertheless played a role in the battle worth remembering. Whoever he was, he stood his ground as his king's last loyal defender.

46 ET FUGA VERTERUNT ANGLI.

HAROLD'S DEATH precipitates the English retreat. Corpses are already being stripped of their armour and left naked on the ground, as in the previous plate. Although this part of the Tapestry is badly damaged and is mostly conjectural restoration, this practice reflects the reality of medieval battles. It is why archaeological finds of weapons and armour in battlefields are so rare.

One legend about Harold from Waltham Abbey, where he was likely buried, reports that after the battle, his comrades took with them Harold's long-term partner, Edith Swanneck, because only someone who knew the

And the English fled.

king's body intimately would be able to identify him among the slaughtered. In another story, Harold's mother Gytha pleaded with William the Conqueror to return her son's body for a proper burial, as the Trojan father Priam did with Achilles for his son Hector.

The Battle of Hastings was decisive. It was exceptionally bloody by medieval standards: battle was a last resort for good reason. More than half of the English army was killed. William would later replace much of England's aristocracy with his followers, giving them English lands as rewards for service.

THE MISSING ENDING

The end of the Bayeux Tapestry has been lost.

Most historians think the Tapestry would have included William's capture of London later that autumn and the coronation of William the Conqueror at Westminster as king of England on Christmas Day in 1066. That event would have completed the story of the conquest and the dispute for the English throne. Although forced to live under William's rule, not all of the English accepted it. Rebellions continued to occur. Visually, the coronation would have brought balance to the story of three kings, crowned and enthroned: Edward, Harold and now William.

We may have one early eyewitness to the Tapestry's ending. Around the turn of the twelfth century, the Norman poet Baudri of Bourgueil wrote a poem for William's daughter Adela, countess of Blois. In it, he described her wall-hanging that told the story of the Norman Conquest. Although inspired more by Virgil's eloquence than by eleventh-century embroidery, his account is strikingly similar to the Tapestry's. The last scene of Adela's tapestry, according to Baudri, was her father's coronation.

Baudri's poem is our first record of what it felt like to see the Tapestry in person. What struck Baudri most was the animation of the Tapestry's figures. As he wrote, 'If these likenesses had flesh and feeling, I would think they were real and alive.'

FURTHER READING

Bates, David, *William the Conqueror*, Yale University Press, New Haven and London, 2016

Bouet, Pierre, François Neveux and Brian Levy (eds), *The Bayeux Tapestry: Embroidering the Facts of History*, Presses Universitaires de Caen, Caen, 2004

Brunning, Sue, Lloyd de Beer, Michael Lewis and Naomi Speakman, with Millie Horton-Insch (eds), *The Bayeux Tapestry*, British Museum Press, London, 2026

Foys, Martin K., Karen Eileen Overbey and Dan Terkla, *The Bayeux Tapestry: New Interpretations*, Boydell Press, Woodbridge, 2009

Gameson, Richard (ed.), *The Study of the Bayeux Tapestry*, Boydell Press, Woodbridge, 1997

Hicks, Carola, *The Bayeux Tapestry: The Life Story of a Masterpiece*, Chatto & Windus, London, 2006

Lewis, Michael John, *The Archaeological Authority of the Bayeux Tapestry*, BAR British Series, Oxford, 2005

Lewis, Michael John, Gale R. Owen-Crocker and Dan Terkla (eds), *The Bayeux Tapestry: New Approaches: Proceedings of a Conference at the British Museum*, Oxbow Books, Oxford, 2010

Licence, Tom, *Edward the Confessor: Last of the Royal Blood*, Yale University Press, New Haven and London, 2020

Licence, Tom, *Harold: Warrior King*, Yale University Press, New Haven and London, 2026

Musset, Lucien, *The Bayeux Tapestry* (new ed.), Boydell Press, Woodbridge, 2005

Owen-Crocker, Gale R., *The Bayeux Tapestry: Collected Papers*, Ashgate Variorum, Farnham, 2012

Owen-Crocker, Gale R. (ed.), *King Harold II and the Bayeux Tapestry*, Boydell Press, Woodbridge, 2005

Pastan, Elizabeth Carson, and Stephen D. White, with Kate Gilbert, *The Bayeux Tapestry and Its Contexts: A Reassessment*, Boydell Press, Woodbridge, 2014

Rowley, Trevor, *An Archaeological Study of the Bayeux Tapestry: The Landscapes, Buildings & Places*, Pen & Sword Archaeology, Barnsley, 2016

Stafford, Pauline, *Queen Emma & Queen Edith: Queenship and Women's Power in Eleventh-Century England*, Wiley-Blackwell, Oxford, 2001

Wilson, David M. (ed.), *The Bayeux Tapestry: The Complete Tapestry in Colour*, Thames & Hudson, London, 1985

INDEX

First published in 2026 by Bodleian Library Publishing
Broad Street, Oxford OX1 3BG
www.bodleianshop.co.uk

ISBN: 978 1 85124 693 9

Illustrations by Victor Sansonetti from *Les anciennes tapisseries historiées*, Vol. 1, 1838. The Miriam and Ira D. Wallach Division of Art, Prints and Photographs: Art & Architecture Collection, The New York Public Library.

Publisher: Samuel Fanous
Managing Editor: Susie Foster
Editor: Janet Phillips
Picture Editor: Leanda Shrimpton
Designed and typeset by Dot Little at the Bodleian Library in 9.8/13 Freight Text
Printed and bound in Slovenia by DZS Grafik on 115gsm Munken Premium Cream paper

MIX
Paper | Supporting responsible forestry
FSC® C106600
FSC www.fsc.org

EU GPSR Authorised Representative LOGOS EUROPE,
9 rue Nicolas Poussin, 17000, LA ROCHELLE, France Contact@logoseurope.eu

British Library Catalogue in Publishing Data
A CIP record of this publication is available from the British Library